WATERLOGGED

Carol Ann Ross

0.5

DEDICATION

This book is dedicated to
the people of Topsail Island.

ACKNOWLEDGEMENTS

Thank you to the many people who helped me gather information; Chief Mike Halstead and Officer Chris Houser, SCPD, Randy Batts, Eris Jones, Doug Thomas and James Brown.

Special thanks to Officer Lee McKnight who helped me sound like I knew what I was talking about.

For technical support I offer my sincere thanks to Mary Ellen Rochelle, Gigi Oberlin, Patti Blacknight, and Claire Braxton. Thank you all for your hard work and insights.

Special thanks to Shari Bruce. A very knowledgeable lady. My hat is off to anyone who exhibits more patience than me.

INTRODUCTION

It was one of those days–one of those mornings–the kind when there is barely any breeze at all. The sun was bold and growing bolder as it slowly climbed into the eastern sky. It was glaring, but not too glaring, and warm, but not too warm.

It was typical springtime on Topsail Island, the weekend before Memorial Day, so it was relatively quiet. This time of year was referred to by most locals as *the calm before the storm.*

Shop owners sat on the stoops of their stores and waved at passersby and local folks walked along the roadside waving back to the store owners.

One could still make a right turn at the light without waiting for several cars to go through–and one didn't have to stand in line at a local restaurant until a table became available.

The fishing piers were not crowded either–not yet.

Fishermen smiled and nodded to one another as they cast their lines into the Atlantic. It was a friendly, wordless exchange–*quiet* is the mantra for the serious fisherman, even if that means never catching a fish.

Everyone knows that fishing isn't all about catching anyway; it's about respite from the rush of life–the connection between one's self and Mother Nature.

Lines whirred through the stilled air; the clicks of bales being set could be heard among the calm spring day.

The island was at the threshold of summer's door. Memorial Day would bring a deluge of tourists from all over the country to descend like a multitude of seagulls scrambling for bread crumbs.

Flipping the bale of *his* reel, Phil, a novice fisherman, shortened what would have been a good long cast out into the coastal waters. The pole jerked a bit; immediately he worried about a snarl of line, but luckily that didn't happen. Nodding his head, he allowed the weighted line to sink; for a second it floated with the movement of the waves, then settled into the spot Phil felt was an appropriate place.

Moving backwards a few inches, his legs bumped into one of the wooden benches of the fishing pier; he seated himself slowly, keeping a keen eye on the monofilament fishing line until it faded into the blue of the sky.

His eyes searched the blue-green water and found the pin prick sign of where it had entered. Grinning, he settled his young frame more comfortably onto the wooden bench, and the fishing pole into a carved groove in the railing.

As he sighed lightly, Phil looked around to see if anyone had noticed his clumsy cast–the other fishermen were all busy with their own rods and reels, engaged in their own fishing experience on Surf City Fishing Pier.

He sighed more heavily now and folded his arms across his chest, and turned his head left to scan the shore where beachgoers were slowly beginning to accumulate.

Phil sat, ignoring the rod and reel beside him—now lost in the study of individuals making their entrance on to the beach.

He was oblivious, as was everyone else on the fishing pier, that twenty or so feet below him the baited hook of his line was skimming the body of a woman. With each push and pull of the waves, the floating tackle danced some sort of ethereal ballet.

Clasped by shards of pilings and spiky barnacles, it seemed that the pier itself had snagged its own catch. And it relentlessly held on to it by the clothing it wore.

Still, with each tidal movement the razor-like sharpness of the barnacles tore at the skin.

Already crabs had eaten the left eye; the right one was still mostly intact, but not for long. Three blue crabs scuttled against one another for the gel—their fighting seemed choreographed as they too fought the tidal movement. And, probably from pounding against the barnacles and splintered shards of wood from the pilings, the woman's lower lip had become jagged and torn, along with the right side of her face and neck, just where an ear was located.

Each brush against the pilings produced wisps of feathered skin; pin fish were having a feast.

3

Above, still seated on the wooden bench, sat Phil. He noticed the slackness of his line and reeled it in a bit, then rested the fishing pole again into the groove of the railing. He jiggled the pole and shrugged. He wasn't sure if he liked fishing or not.

The two ounce weight he'd attached earlier to his rig skimmed the bloated female body again; the tackle still danced around her head and neck area along with the crabs and pin fish.

Bored, Phil toyed with the shrimp he'd cut earlier for bait, two pieces lie on the railing; it would be only minutes before the sun would dry them to it. Phil chuckled; his father had told him time and again to never leave the shrimp there.

Put the pieces you're not using back into the bag so they won't dry out. Phil could hear his father's admonishing words as he eyed the two pieces; he touched them with his fingers, they felt rubbery; already the sun was baking them. The corners of his mouth curved upward in defiant glee.

Leaning back against the fishing pier bench the young teenager propped his feet against the wooden slats. He reached into a small cooler and fished out a Sun Drop;-it tingled his throat as he gulped it nearly to half empty, then from his shirt pocket he grasped the pack of Pall Mall he had bought earlier that morning at Grocery World.

He thought of the girl there, the one with the wispy blond hair; her name tag said *Mindy*. She never asked for his I.D. He grinned; she was cute, though a little thick through the middle.

Phil always flirted with her, knowing he could tap that anytime he wanted. But today, he wanted to go fishing or at least he'd been compelled to do so by the urging of his father.

As he lit a cigarette with his father's lighter, the one with the brass Marine Corps insignia, Phil tilted his head back and gently pulled the nicotine deep into his lungs. His father would really be mad if he knew he was smoking.

What a joke on him, Phil thought, *I've been smoking for nearly a year and the old man's got no clue.*

He filled his lungs again and exhaled, squinted his eyes against the sun and watched the plume of smoke until it became part of the atmosphere around him.

Looking toward the shore again, the rising sun glared as the boy shaded his eyes; he pulled down the visor of his cap, refocusing as he scanned the beach. Surfers were already in the water and sun-bathers were settling their paraphernalia in the sand.

A fat lady in a black bathing suit sat sprawled at the water's edge scooping sand over her large legs; Phil rolled his eyes.

A mother and her three children had just come down the steps from the Surf City Welcome Center; he could hear the woman yelling at her brood: *you better get your sunscreen on!* He watched as they raced for their mother to slather lotion on their bodies and then race back toward the ocean.

"Humph." He shook his head and scanned the still sparsely populated beach. Only a few blankets and umbrellas dotted the area; *families with snot nose kids, old ladies with one piece bathing suit*

-women with rolls of fat hanging over the bottoms of their bikinis. Yuck. Phil shook his head as he eyed the few beachgoers.

Suddenly his eyes settled on a girl in a tie-dyed tee-shirt standing at the top of the stairs; her tanned legs seemed to go on forever. He followed the line of her body all the way to the bright pink cap she wore atop her head where tendrils of brown hair streamed about her oval face.

He watched as she descended the stairway, her hips swaying from side to side, her right arm gliding along the banister.

Reaching the bottom of the stairs, the girl stepped onto the warm sand.

Captivated by her fluid movements, Phil ogled her, his eyes following her as she made her way north.

Trudging through the sand she walked fifty feet or so, and then dropped the two totes she held bundled in her arms.

Moving closer to the railing, Phil leaned forward and cupped his chin in his hands. He watched as the girl kicked her flip flops off.

He could feel his stomach tighten as she removed her faded cut off jeans and exposed the bottom part of her bikini.

Wow! Butt floss! He scooted to the very edge of the bench and leaned forward even more, ignoring his fishing pole.

The girl's buttocks were tanned deeply and her small belly flaunted a dangling teardrop shaped gem that caught the sun's light.

Reaching to grasp the corners of her tee-shirt, she tugged upward.

Mesmerized, Phil anticipated her next move as she began raising the shirt over her abdomen and the bra of her bikini. He leaned forward even more, *Why didn't I take the old man's binoculars?* he thought; as he strained to see the girl go through the motions of taking off her clothes—it was if a strip tease were being performed solely for him.

Mere patches of cloth covered the young girl's breasts;-attached strings tied around her neck held them in place.

Phil watched the girl struggle as she pulled the shirt to her shoulders. Tendrils of her long brown hair already tumbled from beneath the snug cap as she began to pull the shirt over her head.

Stupid girl, forgot to take your cap off. Phil scrutinized her wriggling body as she tussled with the neck opening of her shirt.

The girl's exposed flat and tan belly gyrated as her hands pulled at the shirt. Raising her arms higher, she tugged more and more, pulling the small patches of cloth from her breasts, exposing them. Quickly she pulled the cloth back to cover herself. Then, with a final jerk, she removed the shirt and cap at once.

Shaking her head, she released her mane in a cloud of brown, then pulled it tightly, gathering it to stuff back into the pink cap.

Phil sniggered, and continued to watch as the girl reached into a large straw tote to remove a blanket; she flapped it in the air and waited for the light breeze to help settle it to the sand.

Rising, bending, stooping—she placed a shoe on a corner and one of the totes on another. *Thank goodness for the wind,* Phil thought, watching her hips spread as she bent and stooped.

Beside him, leaning against the railings of the pier, the fishing pole arched deeply, quivering as it strained against the taut line. It then tipped to the side, brushing against Phil's leg.

Startled, his concentration broken, Phil grabbed the pole. "Damn," he said loudly, annoyed at the interruption. "What in the freaking hell ..."

"Young man, could you watch your language over there?" the fisherman across from him called politely.

"Sorry," The word slid snidely from his sneering lips. "And screw you, you old fart," Phil mumbled as he shrugged at the man and turned, searching for the girl in the pink hat.

The fishing pole in his hand quivered once more. Excited, Phil drew his attention from thoughts of finding the girl in the pink hat to what might be on the end of his hook.

"This better be something good," he shook his head, still holding the pole as it dipped and shook.

"It has got to be a monster—bet it's that sheepshead I saw yesterday." Phil tugged, first gently on the pole, bending it a bit more, and then wound some line onto the reel.

He pictured the huge sheepshead fish, its large broad striped body straining against the line and hook hung deep in its mouth. He grinned wide, his teeth showing, "Ha! Man oh man, Dad can't say I don't know how to fish, now."

He reeled in a few more inches of line and felt it tighten. "There ain't no give." He tugged lightly and tried winding the line again; it moved barely an inch, bending the pole even farther.

"Hell, it's just snagged on something," Phil sulked. He jerked quickly on the line, another thing his father had always told him not to do. *You might lose your tackle if you jerk hard enough*, his father's voice echoed in his head.

Phil jerked again, this time harder; the pole straightened and the line slacked. "Son of a bitch, whatever it was hooked to, ain't there no more." Phil stomped his foot and released a string of curse words; the image of the big fish swimming away filled his head as he pictured his father's *I told you so* grin.

"Freaking crap," he blurted loudly.

The man directly across from him released an angry *ahem*; disapproving eyes glared at Phil. "Son, I've told you to watch your mouth over there and all I've heard this morning out of you is one cuss word after another. If I have to remind you one more time, I'm reporting you to the office and they'll make you leave."

"Sorry," Phil feigned an apologetic glance and nodded, then turned his head, rolled his eyes, and began to search for the pink cap and thong bikini as he slowly wound the handle of the reel.

The girl was gone. "Damn," Phil muttered under his breath, his eyes searching the shore as he turned the reel handle.

Still scanning the beach and farther out into the breakers, where she might have been frolicking,

9

he envisioned her breasts bouncing up and down as she splashed among the waves.

Again his concentration was broken as he continued winding the reel; the tackle meeting the top eye of the fishing pole sent a twanging vibration down to his wrist—there was no more line to reel in.

Phil annoyingly eyed the tip of his pole and the tackle that hung loosely from it. "What the—what in the hell is that?" His fingers grasped the shrimp-less top hook of the tackle; a gold bauble caught in the barb of the hook glistened back at him. He touched it, moving it from side to side. "What's this?" he questioned, as he touched the fleshy mass attached between the faux gem and earring backing.

"Ugh! Freaking shit!" The pole slid from his hands and onto the pier decking. Phil stared at the earring for a few seconds then looked around him to see if anyone else had noticed.

"Doggone tourists come here and act like they own the place . . . rude, arrogant, no respect." The man across from Phil settled his pole on the railing and glared at the boy. "Young man, I've just about had—"

"Man! It's some lady's ear!" Phil pointed toward the pole and tackle that lay sprawled on the deck. The man rolled his eyes and walked slowly toward Phil's fishing pole.

"Freaking shit," Phil whispered again as he bent to look more closely at the earring; he poked at it with his flip flop clad foot, nausea rose in his throat and he turned his head.

Reaching the railing of the pier just in time, he bent deeply over the side, retching; his breakfast and Sun Drop poured from his throat. He watched as it spattered into the waves below.

"What the hell," he spoke louder and leaned even farther over the side. A light breeze, coming from the north, brushed against his sweaty face; he watched the swell of waves move rhythmically to the south as they glided past the pilings.

He closed his eyes; the picture of the ear would not go away. *Was it really **that**?* Phil thought. Peering deeply into the water, Phil rubbed his eyes, his stomach tightened, "Holy shit!" he called out loudly.

Phil turned toward the few people that had begun to gather near his bench. "There's a lady down there–down there!" He pointed as he leaned again over the edge of the pier. "See, she's wedged in between the pilings."

Chapter One

"Hi, how are you doing today? Welcome to Grocery World." Carrie made it a point to smile when she said the words; after all, people had told her she had a nice smile and she even thought she could make her blue eyes twinkle a bit as she parted her lips and showed her nearly perfect white teeth. But none of it seemed to work on the tourists–the "terrorists," as they were referred to by the locals.

It didn't matter if she smiled or not, they treated her like a fixture–like one of the self checkout machines.

Sighing, Carrie, found her eyes meeting those of the man standing before her. The look on his face confirmed her thoughts.

Oh, how I hate this job. She feigned a weak smile and continued scanning his grocery order.

"That'll be thirty-four, sixteen." Turning her head as she spoke the words, Carrie watched as the man pulled a credit card from his wallet and swiped it through the scanner.

Bright green letters announced *declined* on her screen. "I'm sorry sir, would you like to swipe your card again?"

Carrie watched as the man's mouth tightened into a straight line. Angrily he swiped his card again and again the letters read *declined*.

"I'm sorry sir, would you like to try another card?"

Feeling the man's humiliation, Carrie tried to be kind as she searched his face.

"Hell no, you people down here don't know what in the hell you're doing. There's nothing wrong with my Visa." Angrily he reached into his wallet, opened it wide and fingered through several bills. Grasping them, he threw them on the counter in front of Carrie.

She felt the anger well inside of her and fought the impulse to pick the money up and throw it back in his face. Instead she said, "I'm so sorry for the problem with the credit card."

Placing the man's change in his outstretched hand, Carrie fought the impulse to throw the coins on the counter and have him pick them up himself. Instead she smiled and began bagging his groceries.

As she slid the loaf of bread into a paper bag; she didn't fight her impulses as before. This time as her fingers wrapped around the loaf she squeezed hard. "Thank you for shopping Grocery World." The phrase fell a jumbled mess from her lips as she avoided the man's eyes.

Immediately she felt guilty for squeezing the customer's bread, but she shook her head, *no, he deserved it for being such an ass.*

Exhaling a long sigh, Carrie pulled the cell phone from her pant's pocket and checked the time; *three minutes till break.* Tapping her fingers on the counter, she scanned the space before her station and saw no one approaching. Quickly she reached to turn off the open sign above her register.

As she turned to leave, a couple pulled their cart to the counter. Carrie shrugged and lifted her head to the sign overhead.

"Sorry," she mouthed, "I'm closed now."

Walking through the busy aisles toward the back door leading to the break area, Carrie thought how, after nearly two years, she was still not used to the push and rush of the summer tourist season.

Last summer had been tough; it was her first year, her first time dealing with nonstop customers that more times than not were rude and who were always in a hurry.

"Why do they have to be so nasty?" Carrie whispered to herself as she rolled her eyes and pushed the swinging door open; bright sunshine flooded in to blind her briefly.

Pulling a pack of off-brand cigarettes from her pocket, she picked one from the pack and placed it between her lips; a flash of heat from her lighter lit it as she sucked in the nicotine.

"I've got to quit smoking," she mumbled as the calming effect of the nicotine soothed her. "But not this summer, not yet."

Leaning against the picnic table, Carrie lowered herself to a sitting position and raised her feet off the ground. She rotated her ankles from the left and then to the right until she heard the familiar *pop*. "My feet are killing me," she sighed, as she took another long drag from the cigarette.

"My back is killing me too." She stretched her arms and reached for the sky, then bent from the waist to touch the ground; she held the pose for a moment and inhaled deeply, then slowly exhaled, releasing the built up tension in her lower back.

"Aah, that's better." Relaxing, she took another drag from the cigarette.

What in the world is wrong with these people? she thought as she closed her eyes and pressed her face into the sunlight. Releasing a spiral of smoke, she answered herself aloud, "They're on vacation and think they can do whatever they want, that's what."

Shaking her head, Carrie smirked, *oh, but they're not all bad. I must remind myself of that.*

Continuing to lean against the table, Carrie's eyes perused the clouds, observing the shapes among the blueness; closing them, she let the frustration and tension peel away. Then she thought of the last customer and the loaf of bread she had squeezed; the corners of her mouth drew slightly upward as she opened her eyes.

"What a job," she sighed, "humph."

Forcing herself to think of good things, Carrie concentrated on the laid-back rhythm of the off-season months when locals strolled in to purchase groceries. There was always a few minutes then to chat a bit and get to know the people of the community.

The weather was great then too—even winter months, when it might get cold enough to freeze for a few days or so—they were good. It was the community that made Topsail so inviting. There was a relaxing, extended family, sense of the place that made it feel like home.

In just the short time she had been here, the local folks in the Topsail Island area had become her friends. They were easy going, trusting and she gossiped with them as if she'd known them forever.

Carrie felt as if she was in the *loop* and it all made her feel very much welcomed.

Chuckling to herself, Carrie felt the tension melt away as she recalled how often most of the local people helped her bag their groceries and how once an elderly man, who had come to call her "sweetie pie," helped her clean a spill next to the register.

"Yep, I got it good," Carrie said, nodding; she liked all the terms of endearment exchanged between the locals and herself—everyone was either *sweetie*, *dear*, *sugar* or *honey*.

But the tourists were another matter. She could imagine the terms they used and they weren't those of endearment, she'd heard a few of them: *stupid, bitch, idiot, slow*—just to name a few.

Smiling for them, being polite and patient was a chore. But to keep her job it was a necessity.

And here it is Memorial Day, the beginning. She grimaced at the thought and snuffed out her cigarette in the sand-filled bucket next to the picnic table.

She sighed again, this time more heavily, *It's tourist season, it will pass. It's tourist season, it will pass.*

Rising from the bench, Carrie stuffed the pack of cigarettes in her pocket and caught a glimpse of Paula's red Camaro as it pulled into the parking lot at the side of the building.

Paula was probably the best friend she'd made since coming to Surf City. They were close in age and looked at many things from the same point of view. Plus, Paula knew just about everything about everybody in the Topsail Island neighborhood.

Unlike Carrie, Paula was very self-confident and patient. Even during the hectic summer months she exuded calmness. Paula never seemed to lose her cool and was always polite.

What she does to relieve stress, beats me, thought Carrie. *Doesn't smoke, doesn't drink, and hardly ever cusses.*

Giggling as she recalled their last conversation, Carrie leaned back against the table.

"Some northern tourists–*terrorists*, are okay, but for the most part they're *Yankees* and they fall into one of two categories, one–regular Yankees. Those are the ones that are rather aloof, don't make eye contact, don't say please, thank you or excuse me. They want everyone to get out of *their* way so they can get to where *they* want to go, as if no one else matters. *They* assume we're all stupid and treat us as such. They complain about everything, then leave. Good riddance to them.

The second category is the *damn* Yankees . . . they're the ones that stay."

To Carrie it wasn't so much a north/south thing as it was a city/country thing. She'd met a few with accents just as southern as her own, who were condescending and arrogant. Still, she had to admit that the majority of rude people came from places north of the Mason Dixon line.

As Paula exited the Camaro, Carrie smiled and chuckled to herself. She admired Paula's coolness and was glad she'd made friends with her. "But I wouldn't want her as an enemy," she spoke softly, "there's something beneath those *still* waters."

Carrie wondered how Paula coped with it all, the tourists and all the loss her family had withstood:

Last summer, Carrie's first tourist season, Paula had explained during one of their breaks, how the hurricanes had destroyed just about everything her family had worked for and how nearly everyone on the island lost homes and businesses.

"One time we had over fifty acres. We had a nice little tackle shop and dock where Daddy kept his shrimp boat. But when hurricanes Bertha and Fran came through here in 1996 they blew it all away."

Gone was the Weldon family homestead, the tackle shop and docks, and even more devastating, Paul Weldon's fifty-six foot shrimp boat.

The family was forced to sell what land they had to pay taxes and purchase another trawler, leaving them living in one of the local trailer parks.

"Momma calls them carpetbaggers, just like after the Civil War when northerners came down and took advantage of all the ruin.

"The land we used to own was bulldozed and developed. It's now-tennis courts, swimming pools, condos-and they call it Dunes Landing. Why in the world it's called that is beyond me. There aren't even any dunes there anymore.

"But I guess it's just the way things go, besides, Daddy gets to dock the trawler at the fancy docks, it's written in the contract."

Paula was the first of all her cousins to go to college, though she left after two years to pursue a degree in cosmetology.

When asked why she had not completed either quest, Paula answered, "You know, there is nothing like being up before dawn and heading out through the inlet, seeing the sunrise when you're on the ocean, no degree is going to buy me that."

She worked summers only at the grocery store and commercial fished the rest of the year.

Emptiness settled in the pit of Carrie's stomach; she felt sorry for the Weldon family and understood some of the bitterness felt among locals and newcomers. Their whole way of life had disappeared overnight and their livelihoods had been compromised. It was enough to make anyone angry.

Carrie waved as Paula approached the table. "Gotta get back on the clock," she stood, slipping a hand into her pants pocket to retrieve a breath mint.

Paula nodded and jogged to catch up with her.

"Having a fun day?" She pushed against Carrie's shoulder with her own.

"Hardy har har, you trying to be funny. It's a damn madhouse in there."

"Don't let the small stuff bother you, just think, by September we'll have our little town back and we can return to our simple way of living."

"You're weird," Carrie slid an annoyed glance Paula's way. "You're supposed to sympathize with me and my irritability."

"Okay, I hope everyone who is nasty today steps on a jellyfish."

"That's better," Carrie laughed.

"Hmm," Paula nodded, her smile disappeared, "you go on in, I've got a few minutes more."

"Hey, I didn't mean to put you in a bad mood."

"No, I'm not. I just need some alone time before I face the masses."

Chapter Two

"Today I'm going to try really hard," Carrie spoke to herself as she walked to work. "It's not worth it to let their crappy attitudes ruin my whole day. I'm just not going to let them get to me." She took a deep breath and raised her head as she stepped through the sliding doors of Grocery World.

The lines at each register were long, people bustled about. She could hear the mandatory *thank you for shopping Grocery World* and she heard the *ding ding* of the items as they crossed the scanner. The occasional *put my cold items all together* could be heard, as well as *don't break my eggs* and *don't squash my bread.* It was full tilt summer, Memorial Day opened the flood gates and all the sharks were swimming around.

The population of the coastal town more than quadrupled during the summer months, with those vacationing at their own summer houses, those renting for the summer and the regular weekenders.

Sighing as she mustered a smile, Carrie flipped the ON light to her register and made immediate eye contact with a scowling middle-aged man. His paunchy stomach strained against the light blue cotton of his taut tee-shirt.

He grunted as he placed a jar of green olives in front of her.

The corners of Carrie's lips rose to smile as she began, "Welcome to–"

"Save it," the man grumbled. Reaching into his pants pocket he retrieved a few crumpled dollar bills and several coins. "Here," he growled, flicking two of the bills toward her as he glanced at the lighted numbers on the screen.

"Two and a nickel." He picked through the change and left the remainder, then picked up his jar of olives and left.

I'm not going to get upset this early in the day. Just let it roll off my back, Carrie reminded herself. Releasing a heavy sigh, she lifted her face to meet that of Mrs. Lloyd, sweet Mrs. Lloyd.

"Thank you for shopping Grocery World." She smiled at the elderly lady.

Mrs. Lloyd was another local person and Carrie liked her very much. She must have been in her late seventies, and every time Carrie saw her she always had a smile on her face.

"Sugar, you have such a hard job here." Mrs. Lloyd winked then shook her head, "Oh, for a man to be that grouchy this early in the day, imagine what the rest of his day is going to be like." The elderly woman tittered. Carrie laughed too. It was nice having someone sympathize and recognize that some customers were a pain in the butt.

Exchanging pleasantries as she scanned the groceries, Carrie felt the tension leave her body. "Mrs. Lloyd, you have a nice day now," Carrie touched the woman's hand and grinned. "I made sure not to make the bags too heavy for you."

"Thank you so much, Sugar. I'm not as strong as I used to be and Harold is fishing with the grandkids today, so it's just me."

From her peripheral vision, Carrie noticed the next customer in line; she heard his sigh as he continued taking items from his cart to place them on the conveyor belt. Carrie pressed the button to move the items forward as she continued talking to Mrs. Lloyd.

She could feel the man's cold stare.

"Your little puppy doing better?" Mrs. Lloyd asked as she fumbled with her change purse.

"Yes. He just swallowed an aspirin I dropped on the floor. The vet said he'd be okay, just not to let him get hold of anything medicinal. His poor little tummy can't take human stuff." Carrie shrugged, then glanced quickly to the impatient customer, now moving his items around on the belt. She heard him clear his throat. "Well, you have a good day, Mrs. Lloyd."

Mrs. Lloyd looked over her shoulder at the man and rolled her eyes, *"You* have a good day." Leaning in the old woman whispered, "Don't sweat the small stuff; September will be here before you know it."

A nervous giggle escaped her lips as Carrie turned her attention away from the elderly woman and toward the man in line; he glared at her.

"How are you doing today, sir? Welcome to Grocery World." Carrie forced a smile to her lips. The man lowered his eyes and cleared his throat again, not responding to her question. She glanced at the items on the conveyor belt—a carton of eggs, a sack of flour and a loaf of Merita bread were among them. Raising her head to meet the man's eyes, he quickly turned away. "How are you doing today?" she repeated.

The man sighed heavily, "humph," as he shoved items toward her. Carrie smiled to herself as she moved the loaf of bread over the scanner.

******

"Oh, what a day!" Carrie slid her legs over the bench of the picnic table and arched her back. "My feet are killing me." She rubbed the small of her back, then pulled her cigarettes from her trouser pocket. Nudging Mindy, she grimaced as she queried, "How's it been going for you?"

Mindy, one of the young cashiers at Grocery World, shook her head, her gaze bounced about from place to place. Nervously she put her fingers to her head and made a motion as if she were pulling her hair out. Releasing a cigarette from her lips, she rolled her eyes, "If one more person tells me that I need to smile, I think I'll choke 'em."

"This is the first time I've seen you with a cigarette. I didn't know you smoked?" Carrie curiously eyed Mindy's fingertips.

"I don't . . . I don't smoke except during tourist season . . . and I'm going to try to quit this summer." Eying the cigarette in her fingers, she rolled it anxiously between them. "You look pooped too."

"My smiling muscles gave out two hours ago," Carrie flicked an ash from her cigarette. "What is this? Asshole day?" she asked rhetorically. "This one man—"

"You try what I told you?" Interrupting, Mindy smiled, inhaling deeply.

"Squeezing the bread?"

"Yeah. I know it helps me," Moving closer, Mindy lowered her voice, "And there's a special way you can pack the groceries in the bags that will keep them on their toes." She motioned with her hands packing a bag, "See, if they want to stand there and watch *you* bag all the groceries, you simply put all the boxes in the corners with the edges out and stuff cans in the middle—over stuff it. And believe me, by the time they get to their car, it will all be on the ground." She feigned a gasp, winked and covered her mouth with her hand. "I mean, it's an emotional roller coaster . . . this one's nice, that one isn't, this one is bitchy, the other one's polite. I tell you it's enough to drive you cray-cray." Arching an eyebrow, Mindy puffed smoke rings, "Know what I mean?"

"Duh." Carrie shook her head in agreement, amazed at how quickly her friend went through a cigarette, "This one man really burned me up. He was so damn impatient–"

"They're either impatient or they ignore you."

"I don't think some of them realize what they're doing." Carrie explained, trying to get a word in as Mindy once again began her rant. It was typical Mindy, all wound up. On busy days Carrie could have sworn the girl was ADHD.

"Well, if they don't know they're being rude, it's even worse." Mindy nervously tapped her fingernails on the picnic table, "We aren't even a second thought." She took a long drag from her cigarette, "I'm a talking ATM," Mindy stood and posed stiffly, making robotic movements as she repeated, "Welcome to Grocery World, welcome to Grocery World." She sat down again and sniggered. "Most of the bastards know exactly what they are doing. They just don't look at us as *real* people. More like robots–servants or–I don't know. But you can believe they look down their noses at us for being lowly cashiers."

Carrie watched as her friend threw her butt into the sand bucket and pulled another cigarette from her pack. Taking a long drag, she seemed to calm a bit, "You heard about that lady that drowned the other day?"

"Yes. Did you find out who it was?"

"Sarah Chambers."

"Hmm, which one is she?"

"Oh, you know her. She's the chunky bitch–fifty or sixty–something like that. She's the one with the blond helmet hair. Always dresses like she's going to a *tea* or something."

Carrie shook her head no and shrugged her shoulders. "I can't place her . . . there's so many helmet heads in the summer."

"She's the one that owns the big fugly yellow and purple three story house up in the dunes about a mile or so north of Surf City Pier."

"I still don't know who you're talking about." Carrie watched as Mindy rolled her eyes in frustration and tapped her nails once again on the table. "How am I supposed to know where she lived?"

Mindy shrugged, "Sorry." An attempt to pull her limp blond hair back into a pony tail had failed as thin strands fell about her face in disarray.

She was another local girl and knew all the gossip and all the old farming and fishing families who had sold their land in the late 1990s, after the hurricanes. Her parents had been farmers and had sold most of their land after crops were destroyed along with the barns and machinery. Still the West family held on to around ten acres where they planted corn, beans and tomatoes and had a few chickens. Carrie smiled to herself as she listened to Mindy continue with the description of Sarah Chambers.

"Okay. I know what will make you remember her. In fact, you hate her guts. She's the one that does the *tsk*. You know. She opens that painted mouth of hers, shows you them 'bleached too white' teeth and goes *tsk*." Mindy shook her head, "Ain't natural, nobody's got teeth that white—just don't look right."

Carrie leaned back and exhaled the smoke from her lips, watching as Mindy calmed with each drag from her Marlboro menthol. "I know who you're talking about now," she chuckled. "What a biddy. I've even quit saying hello to her when she comes in my line."

Carrie checked the time on her cell phone. "What did she do? Fall off her balcony?"

"Nope. Found her wedged beneath the pier in the pilings. The barnacles had torn her to shreds. Didn't have no eyes; some kid that was fishing and snagged her with his line and pulled off part of one of her ears." Mindy spoke matter of factly as she too glanced at her watch. "Break's over . . . gotta go." She smashed the butt of her cigarette into the sand bucket, "Damn, I smoke like a chimney in the summer. I mean it, I'm really going to quit." She shrugged and slid her body from the bench. "I guess they still got me on register seven. If it slows down any I'll fill you in on what I heard from Robby about old Miss Sarah."

Carrie glanced at her watch again. She still had three minutes left of her fifteen minute break. She pulled another cigarette from her pack, lit it and swung her legs around to the other side of the bench.

Yes, she remembered Sarah Chambers very well. Boxy, dumpy, too many face lifts-Sarah Chambers. The one with the rings to her knuckles on each hand, who wore, as if to cover her rolls of fat, a loose, blousy shirt over her matching Capri and glittery knit outfits.

30

She was one of the full time summer tourists that came early and left late.

Where most arrived just after Memorial Day, Sarah came a couple of weeks before and left after Labor Day around mid September. That added another month of having to put up with her obnoxious behavior.

Her habit of breezing into the store, making some kind of gala entrance, as if everyone was to stop what they were doing and notice that she had finally arrived, was not endearing or even funny. It was maddening. Yet everyone smiled and waved to welcome her.

And though Sarah shopped nearly every day, her cart was always full to overflowing.

Carrie wondered where she put all the food; no one could eat a cart full of groceries everyday. She certainly wasn't *that* fat.

Sarah's cart would be stacked with several jugs of water and numerous canned goods, boxed dinners and frozen pizzas. These things, she had explained, must be kept handy in case of a hurricane.

Once, Carrie asked Sarah how she was going to cook any of the food because often there were power outages during storms.

Sarah waved her hand in the air and narrowed her eyes, "I have a generator, dummy."

Carrie forced a laugh as she recalled the times Sarah came to her station. The first items she unloaded were the jugs of water, followed by, "I cannot abide this nasty tasting beach water." She said this every single time she came to Carrie's counter.

Then she'd look at Carrie or whoever was the cashier, as if to blame them for the poor quality of water.

"*You people* just can't seem to keep fresh fruit and vegetables in stock either. Can you?" Sarah would say rhetorically as she plopped sacks of oranges and casaba melons down, usually commenting on their poor condition, as well.

She stuffed bok choy, artichokes and various colors of peppers, zucchini—anything and all went into one plastic produce bag, leaving the cashier to sort it all out and weigh the items separately.

She bought canned and frozen seafood from faraway places like Thailand and Peru rather than purchase from any of the local seafood markets.

This irked Carrie more than anything and the one time Carrie politely suggested that she buy from local fisheries, Sara gave her the infamous blank stare. It lasted an entire minute and was followed by a roll of the eyes, a tsk, and the words, *you people*.

Sarah had a routine when it came to dispensing her groceries. After the water, she barked orders to bag the meat separately by placing each package in a plastic bag and then again in a double paper bag. This would have been fine if she had done it politely.

Then halfway through her cart of groceries, Sarah would stop and search through her handbag for the cell phone, if it had not already rung. At this point, she would begin a loud conversation filled with laughter as she slowly lifted one item at a time from her cart. If there was no bagger to empty the contents of her cart for her, a tilt of her head to the left and her infamous *tsk* let the cashier know it was time to come from around the register and unload it for her.

One time Paula Weldon happened to be in line behind Ms. Chambers. It was well past Labor Day, and Paula was taking her regular off-season hiatus. Familiar with Sarah's routine and having witnessed it herself several times, Paula spoke out, "You're not from around here, are you sweetie?"

"I'll have you know I've been coming to Topsail for ten years. What business is it of yours?" Sarah snapped as she turned her boxy frame to face Paula. "And my name is not *sweetie*."

Turning away, she continued slowly pulling one item at a time from the cart as she reached for her cell phone.

"Then it must be *bitch*." Paula moved even closer behind Sarah.

"You people..." Arching her back and pursing her lips, Sarah raised her hand and pointed a finger in Paula's face, "I'm so tired—"

"You look tired," Towering over the older woman, Paula grinned, "why don't you go home and put some more hair spray on your hair. It doesn't look hard enough."

Sarah's face reddened as she puffed out her chest, "I'm having a talk with the manager about you," She snorted.

"Be my guest," Paula retorted. "I don't work here now."

"Humph," Sarah's nostrils flared as she tossed more items onto the belt.

Nothing more was said between the two women and Sarah, after her order was completed, rushed through the doors and out to her Jeep.

Chapter Three

"Robby says they really had a time fishing her out of the water. I mean, she was wedged in there tight and her clothes were all shredded from the pilings and barnacles. Man, they really tore her face up good. Even her arms and legs were all torn up. Hell, she was a mess."

Carrie listened intently to Mindy. "I bet," she nodded.

"She weighed ten pounds less than an elephant. No wonder they had such a hard time getting her out." Mindy's eyes grew wide. "You know what was keeping her wedged? What was holding her on to that piling?"

A puzzled look crossed Carrie's face as she shook her head no.

"She had on a body girdle. You know, one of those things that's supposed to hold your tummy in and smooth your figure." Primping as she moved her hands down the sides of her body, Mindy giggled. "They're all latex, you know, thick, and hot as hell, too. My momma's got one."

Mindy leaned against her counter and stretched to peer down one of the aisles where customers were shopping. "How she can wear one of those things in the summertime beats me. They're thick and heavy-why, she could have been there forever if that kid hadn't hooked her with his line."

"Ugh," Carrie grimaced and crinkled her nose, ending the conversation as a customer came to her register.

She greeted him, rang up the liter of coke and twelve pack of beer. "Thank you for shopping Grocery World, "she said, leaning toward Mindy for more information.

The man nodded and smiled in return.

"Yeah, the crabs really got to her. Robby says he almost upchucked when they were dragging her to shore. Even the fish were picking at her."

"Yuck, what a way to go." Carrie shook her head.

"I didn't like her, but I wouldn't wish that on my worst enemy," Mindy scowled as she turned her attention to the customers with loaded grocery carts lining up at her register. It was Friday, four o'clock and between then and closing time the aisles would be full of vacationers purchasing supplies for the week.

Carrie watched in amazement as Mindy seemed to shift into high gear—she was most certainly the fastest of all the cashiers.

******

Morgan Simpers rested his elbow on the car door; a half-opened hand cradled his chin. It was nearly eight o'clock and still light outside, but he had parked far enough away from the entrance of the store so as not to be noticed. Summertime made that much easier; the parking lot was constantly full of cars.

He reached a hand to pet the dog sitting in the passenger seat. It panted loudly, then slurped a wet tongue across his cheek. "Good boy." He patted the dog again before turning his attention back to the store entrance. Carrie would be ending her shift and leaving soon. He would wait until he saw her walk through the sliding glass doors.

Morgan pictured her strawberry blonde hair; she usually wore a clip to the side to hold it back, but still it framed her oval face and drew attention to her light blue eyes. Morgan sighed as he thought of her.

He liked the way her navy trousers and yellow knit shirt fit her, although he had seen her in shorts and a tank top before. But for some reason he liked her better in a uniform.

"Ah, there she is," he whispered to himself. Her quick steps made her hair bounce as she made her way past the soda machines and small shops of the Grocery World Shopping Center.

Morgan knew where she lived, not quite a half mile from the store. One time during the winter, when Carrie had to work late, he'd given her a ride home. She trusted him, he knew. And he knew she liked him. How much, he wasn't sure. But during the winter when business was slow, Carrie always greeted him with a smile and hello. And yes, she even inquired about him: 'How are you doing today?' she had asked so many times.

The question felt genuine coming from the pretty woman.

Once, as he lifted a forty pound bag of dog food to be scanned, Carrie asked, "What kind of dog do you have?"

The moment she spoke the words, Morgan felt encouragement—encouragement beyond measure. Especially since he'd felt as if no one like her could ever be interested in him.

He felt nervous answering her, "Lab," he smiled back.

And she didn't stop there either with the questions, she went on about how she herself loved dogs; her face beamed and gestured with smiles and giggles going on about her Yorkie and chihuahua.

"Is your Lab Black or Yellow?' She tilted her head a bit to the side.

"Chocolate," he responded.

"What's his name?"

"Lucky," Morgan felt giddy as he responded. He smiled broadly.

From then on whenever Morgan came through her line, Carrie asked about his dog. And as the winter progressed their conversations began to vary; anything from recipes to politics. They seemed to agree on just about everything. Or at least Morgan tried to make it so.

Yes, there was no doubt in Morgan's mind that the pretty woman must like him or she wouldn't talk and smile at him so often.

As he watched Carrie from his car, he ran a forefinger the length of his neck and uttered aloud, "I bet she kisses really good too."

His eyes following her, Morgan bit into his lower cheek. "She sure is pretty," he moaned.

Morgan would not follow her home this evening. Instead he lowered the car windows a bit, patted the dog again and exited the Subaru Baja, gently closing the door. There was a list of items his wife had asked him to pick up on his way back from delivering the seafood he'd caught that day.

******

As she walked home, Carrie recalled the conversation with Mindy about Sarah Chambers. Gruesome was the only word for it. She would not have liked to have seen the condition Sarah ended up in. The images of an empty eye socket and torn flesh caused her to shudder and she tried to erase them from her mind. "Better things to think about than that," she said aloud as she made her way down the path to her home.

Nearing the small wooden structure, Carrie could hear her pets yapping. She pictured them jumping up and down as they did all the time. They seemed to be in a perpetual state of excitement. Shaking her head, Carrie tittered a thin laugh and called out, "Mommy's home!" Their barking increased as she spotted their heads through the window of her cottage.

Bobbing up and down, the faces of the Yorkie and chihuahua seemed comical; she laughed again and felt the love well in her heart.

Her little doggies had been with her through thick and thin. They were the epitome of the unconditional love she needed since her divorce two years ago.

"Joey! Bella! How are my babies?" Carrie called as she opened the screen door, inserted the key and turned the doorknob. "Mommy's got some goodies for you today." She waved a plastic bag of bones from the butcher. "Come on out to the back porch."

Carrie kicked off her shoes and slid them next to the front door, then led the way as the small dogs jumped and whimpered.

Opening the door to the sun porch, she placed two large bones on two separate mats in opposite corners of the porch. Joey circled his, then finally growled, glared at Bella and began gnawing.

Bella timidly sniffed her bone, laid down as she glanced at Carrie, wagged her tail and began pulling on the little strands of meat still left.

"It never ceases to amaze me how stereo-typically male and female you two are," Giggling she removed the clip from her hair and tossed it free, then flopped down on the divan with the purple upholstery and gold tassel trim.

She still hadn't quite figured out why Bella and Joey hadn't chewed the tassels off, they had chewed every other fluffy thing coasting near the floor.

Of all the pieces of furniture in her home, the divan was her favorite. She'd found the couch one Saturday morning as she and Paula browsed the yard sales in Tern Shores, an exclusive gated community where many of the wealthy people lived. Carrie had fallen in love with the piece and immediately she and Paula strapped it to the top of her car.

There was one tear on the foot of the couch, easy enough to mend. It was barely noticeable; even if it had been, Carrie wouldn't have minded. The divan was the most comfortable thing she had ever laid on.

As she loosened the yellow shirt from her trousers, Carrie situated the pillows to her liking and lit a cigarette. "What a day," she sighed. "I don't know if I can go through three more months of this crap."

She rubbed her brow, then rose and padded her way to the small kitchen to pour a glass of iced tea from the refrigerator. The leftover cold chicken and green beans from yesterday would warm up nicely in the microwave.

She took her plate of food to the porch and sat at the small table near the south wall. Joey and Bella were still gnawing ravenously at their steak bones; Bella raised her head for a moment and wagged her tail, then resumed gnawing. Joey tightened his paws around his, turned his head slightly to eye Carrie's plate and growled before turning his attention away.

Carrie hated eating late dinners but during the busy summer months her work schedule would include later than normal working hours at least a couple times a week.

*At least I'm **making** forty hours a week*, she thought.

And she needed to take advantage of that since after Labor Day, when the tourists left, her weekly schedule would barely total twenty.

The green beans, though not as crisp as they had been the day before, were yummy—she'd have to remember to thank Paula again for the recipe. Spearing several beans with her fork, Carrie raised them to her open mouth just as the phone rang; she looked at the lighted display, it was her ex-husband, Jim.

Her gaze slid from the phone to the view outside the window. "I'm not answering that," she muttered as she placed the forkful of beans in her mouth.

Chapter Four

It was all a compromise. Make a little money in the summer and even less in the winter, but at least she was at the beach.

Life was supposed to be about quality not quantity, wasn't it? And what better quality of life could there be than living at the beach? Despite all the crap she had to put up with at her job during tourist season, she wouldn't complain, shouldn't complain; at least life was better than it had been with her ex, Jim.

Lazy, beer-swilling Jim. After eighteen years, it had been easy to leave him, easy to leave Florida where she had lived her entire life.

"Eighteen years, humph." *What an idiot I was.*

Her eyes wandered to the photograph of her son and daughter. Both in college-she was optimistic for their futures.

She was happy for them.

Looking about her home, Carrie thought of the first day she had come to Topsail. It was October and she and her friend, Betsey, had driven from Florida.

They had planned to go to Cape Hatteras and Ocracoke Island. They'd heard a lot about the Outer Banks , but a wrong exit left them taking a lonely road toward Highway 210.

One sign pointed toward Wilmington, another pointed toward Jacksonville and Topsail Island; they took the latter.

Carrie remembered perusing the internet on her cell as they drove along. "Topsail Island is twenty-six miles long and has three townships, North Topsail Beach, Surf City and Topsail Beach."

"Sounds good to me. Why don't we check it out?" Betsey was game and they proceeded on.

As they drove across the little green swing bridge in Surf City, Carrie fell in love.

"This is the place for me." She drank in the view of boats moored at docks dotting the landscape and small shops with their doors wide open, welcoming the fall breeze.

Along the nearly empty roads people were riding bikes and walking leisurely. She could hear the roar of the ocean.

"Not named for the surfing here that those young boys and girls are always doing. It's named for the fishing—for the surf fishing," one old-timer told her as they leaned against the railing of the ocean front Welcome Center. "Even the fishing on the pier is good, damn good," the man boasted, "best place on the east coast for fishing."

The temperature was still in the high seventies. She liked that. And she liked the pace of the small coastal town, it was slow, yet there were doctor's offices, grocery stores, clothing stores and plenty of restaurants.

For five days she and Betsey spent hours in the many gift shops, enthralled by the local art; Betsey bought a sea glass necklace and Carrie bought a set of glass bottle wind chimes.

They drove down to the south end of the island, Topsail Beach, and ate lunch at the Breezeway Restaurant; Carrie found a Nicholas Sparks book to read at the Quarter Moon Book Store. Then the two women sat and listened to the island's history in the local Missiles and More Museum.

She fell even deeper in love with the place as she learned of how during World War II the island had been part of an expansive military base called Camp Davis. Located in a town a few miles west in Holly Ridge, the Army camp was home to thousands of young men preparing for war in the early 1940s.

After the war, the island slowly began developing; today it was quaint, unhurried and friendly.

The romance of the past, as well as the present-day charm enamored Carrie and she felt the pull to become part of the somewhat bohemian community.

"Looks like home to me," Carrie's eyes twinkled as she turned to her friend.

"Really?" Betsey queried as they drove on to North Topsail Beach. It was quiet there and when they parked to venture out onto the beach to search for sea shells, they noticed the dolphins.

"That one spun in the air when he jumped," Betsey cooed.

"There's six of them," Carrie pointed, amused and filled with lighthearted youthfulness. "I love it here." She turned to her friend, "I might . . . "

"I know, you're thinking of moving here. Aren't you?"

The third day of their visit to Topsail, Betsey and Carrie walked out onto Surf City Pier and watched as fisherman reeled in fish after fish.

It was spot season and as the fish migrated southward every year, they schooled past the barrier islands of North Carolina.

Carrie looked at the fish; the biggest were possibly six or seven inches in length and couldn't have weighed more than a few ounces.

"How in the world can that have enough meat on it to feed anybody?" she wondered.

Betsey shrugged, but that evening at Batson's Galley, both women ordered spot dinners.

While waiting for their orders, Carrie browsed the pictures on the knotty pine walls of the restaurant: one was a man and woman pulling a huge net full of fish from the back of a boat; another was of a man standing next to an enormous fish hung from a scaffold.

There was a photo of a dilapidated building surrounded by mounds of sand and wooden debris; small print on the bottom read: Hurricane Hazel, 1954. There were many pictures, all black and white—obviously from a time when the coastal town was truly only a fishing village.

Carrie was enthralled by the down to earth quality of the local business and when she sat down to eat her meal, she was pleasingly surprised by the mild taste of the small bony fish. She understood why it was so popular.

The next morning the women ate breakfast at Batts' Grill. Then they walked to Herring's Outdoor Sports, rented a kayak and paddled out into the sound; it was similar to Florida, home to egrets and herons, turtles and alligators.

Various reeds, cattails and grasses stood staunchly In the marshy shores rife with sea life. It was beautiful, and not yet spoiled by development. The next day she and Betsey rented bikes and toured the small town. It was quaint, it was slow and laid-back. And that was just what Carrie wanted.

Life is too short, she thought as they pedaled about the island. At that moment she made the decision.

Within two weeks of her return to Florida, Carrie rented a small trailer and packed what she could. The rest she left to the past as she moved forward with her life.

She put a down payment on an old run-down house, put in an application for work at Grocery World, and the rest was history.

As she lay on the divan thinking of how she had come to Topsail, Carrie's lips broadened into a smile. Life *was* getting better—she owned her home—or was on the way to owning it—even though there were some structural problems.

The roof needed repair and it needed a new water heater; since the house was so old, it had no central heating and air. During the summer she used the small air conditioner she had purchased at the hardware store and during the short winter she used space heaters. These would have to do until she could save the money to install a central unit.

She bought curtains, sheets and throw rugs at consignment shops and found a dinette set at a yard sale—it only needed a little sanding and some varnish—she did that.

Carrie decorated the bathroom with sea shells and dried flowers and beach grasses set in the vases she found at yard sales too.

Painting the outside of the house had been fun. Several of her new friends at Grocery World pitched in, along with one of the customers.

******

Hank Butler was a regular at Grocery World. He was a local man who now lived comfortably from the sale of most of his family's farm land. It had been a rather large estate of five hundred acres that now was home to the community of Southern Breeze, with its own swimming pool, tennis courts and club house.

Butler still owned a beach house on the island and around fifty sound-front acres on the mainland.

He had traveled much since the sale of his land; the Bahamas, Virgin Islands and even to Europe for a six months stay. France, he said, was his favorite place: "Not because of the people there or even the sites . . . the place is dirty as hell, but they have the best food in the world," he'd been heard to say.

Carrie liked him from the first time he approached her counter with a cart chock-full of exotic melons, fleshy gourds, obscure mushrooms and anything else he could persuade the produce manager to stock or order personally for him.

Initially he appeared to be quite restrained, reserved—never wearing jeans and never a tee-shirt. It was button-down cotton shirts and khakis for him. He dressed a bit less leisurely than most that lived in the area and it set him apart, making him a bit more unapproachable.

But as he came more and more to her register, Carrie began to notice his rather charming personality. Though quiet and unassuming, his humor was subtle and dry. In many ways he was boyish.

Once Carrie had seen him walking behind a tourist, mimicking him. Carrie laughed and laughed.

Another time she noticed how he stood aside, hands on hips as he watched a tourist park his cart in the middle of an aisle and walk about looking for a particular item.

She couldn't hear what words were exchanged between the two men, but Hank's must have been powerful because the tourist immediately moved his cart, apologizing as he did so. She could hear those words, "So sorry, my mistake, won't happen again, sir."

Hank had slid his eyes to catch Carrie's, he must have known she was watching, since he raised his eyebrows and grinned.

"I guess I shouldn't do that," he smiled as he approached her. "They just act so . . . entitled."

"What did you say to him?" Carrie asked.

"I simply and politely asked him to move," Hank spoke the words tenderly as he caught her eyes and held them. Carrie felt her face redden; Hank leaned in a bit.

"It's bad enough that they haven't got a clue that they're rude and arrogant, but they don't even know how to prepare seafood properly. You need to come to my home sometime and try *my* coconut shrimp . . . puts the restaurants to shame."

He had segued so smoothly into the proposal; it took Carrie's breath away.

"I have a friend that goes spear fishing and brings back the best *local* grouper, you'd love it."

Dumbfounded, Carrie lost all track of what she was doing. It took a few seconds for her to realize she was supposed to be checking his groceries; nervously she pulled another item over the scanner.

She felt her face flush and her pulse quicken. It had been so many years since a man had paid this kind of attention to her.

Avoiding his eyes, she tried to regain her composure, "Sounds delicious." She waited for the invitation, a day, a time. He had sounded as if he were going to ask her on a date, but the words never came.

Embarrassed at her assumption, Carrie lifted her face, Hank was smiling gently at her, and she could not help but return the gesture.

For the next few weeks Hank always checked his groceries at Carrie's register. She got to know him better and better, enjoying his subtle humor and flirtatious manner.

The attention was a welcoming factor and made her feel vulnerable, young and wanted.

Hank was fit and handsome, his walk-crisp and light as he held his broad shoulders back and head high. His close cut salt and pepper hair lay neatly against his scalp.

Always clean-shaven he once teased as he lay down a package of Schick razors, "Gotta keep it smooth for the ladies." Brushing his cheek with the back of his hand, he comically distorted his face in pain as he drew a hand near his chin.

Once he was even suggestive—unintentionally Carrie believed—"The most delicious of the melons is the Sharlyn. Full and round; moist . . ." She watched as he lowered his head and blushed; his Adam's apple jerked as he swallowed hard. Lifting his head to hold her eyes for a moment, he quickly changed the subject.

Carrie wondered if the innuendo was intentional, still, his demeanor was so self effacing, that Carrie found it endearing.

Chapter Five

"I can't believe ol' Fern scheduled us all to come in at the same time." Mindy pulled a strand of hair behind her ears; as she leaned into the flame of her lighter, the strand fell back into her face, a quick sizzle and pop followed as her hair singed.

"Shit—I'm cutting this mop." Mindy once again pulled her hair behind her ears. "And I'm quitting smoking too."

"Yeah, yeah, we've heard that before," Paula shook her head as she watched the girl.

"It is strange, Fern never schedules us at the same time, usually there's at least a couple hours between us." Mindy sat on the picnic bench, crossed her legs, swinging one as she pulled a stick of gum from her pocket.

"She says we talk too much, that's why she never schedules us together." Carrie flicked her ashes toward the bucket of sand next to the table. "Besides, Terri is out—she called in sick—and that new girl, Winnie, didn't show."

"I didn't think she would," Paula shook her head, "she just had that look about her—you know, intimidated by the whole thing—all the people, all the rules, all the hours on your feet."

Glancing at her watch, Paula continued, "We've got fourteen minutes before we all clock in, so fill me in quickly on the murder, Mindy. Your boyfriend, Robby, seems to know everything."

"He says there's nothing new on ol' Sarah Chambers; for sure she did not jump off the pier— someone would have seen that. So they're thinking that she happened to wash up to the pier over night and got stuck. I found out that the kid that hooked her has a dad who's with the police department."

"Um," Paula and Carrie grunted in unison.

"Who's the dad? Which cop?" Paula asked.

"Oh, you've dated him." Mindy tittered.

Releasing a sigh as she closed her eyes, Paula shifted a stern look to the young girl. "Belkin?"

"Yep, it's Blondie."

"I only went out with Don a couple of times," Paula shrugged, "and he's the detective."

"The hunka, hunka, burning love—you know— Don." Mindy giggled.

Paula leaned against the table; her lips formed a broad smile. "He sure is good looking." Releasing a sigh, she added, "But there just wasn't that spark, you know," She looked quizzically at the two women.

"Hey, seems like you've dated just about everyone around here," Carrie raised an eyebrow.

"Feels like it." Paula popped her gum several times and shrugged. "Just haven't found the right guy I guess and sometimes I don't even think I want to."

Quickly Paula stood, thrusting her hands in the pockets of her trousers. "Speaking of *hunks of burning love*, what's going on between you and Hank? He's always coming over to your register. I won't have a soul in my line and damn if he won't rush on over to yours where there's three or four waiting."

Carrie blushed. "Nothing's going on. I've been hoping he'd ask me out. Maybe he's shy."

"Shy my butt. Honey, he's the Casanova of Topsail—that's just the way he operates." Mindy took a long drag from her cigarette.

"I've been out with him," Paula cocked her head to the side and sucked her teeth. "I think he likes to keep the girls guessing and the prettier the girl the longer he likes to have them wonder."

"So, if you've been out with him, what's he like?" Carrie's eyes lit up.

"He's smooth." Casting her eyes downward, Paula relaxed against the table.

"He's been doing the guessing thing with Carrie for about a month now," Mindy giggled. "Hank must really like you. Usually he makes his move within a couple of weeks."

"Really? Sounds like you know him pretty well." Carrie's brow furrowed a bit as her interest grew. "And you, Paula, you seem to know him real well."

"Yeah, pretty good," Paula said, "but I've known his family, the Butler family, all my life.

55

They're good people. He's just like I said . . . *smooth*."

"Well, how did the date go? You said you'd been out with him," Mindy blurted.

Curling her upper lip, Paula shrugged, "So-so. Wasn't meant to be."

Mindy slid her eyes to the side, "Really."

Paula sniggered, "I do know that he's gaga for you, Carrie. I think he's set his sights on you-but be careful." Glancing at her watch, Paula continued, "Don't let that sweet act fool you, he goes out with lots of women. And he's nice, polite and charming and he'll get your britches off before you can count to twenty."

Carrie's eyes widened as she caught her breath.

"How far did you make it, Paula," Mindy chided.

"Fifteen," Paula glanced Mindy's way and winked. "Believe me, it was weird."

Bewildered by Paula's admission, Carrie said, "So you don't think I should bother with him?"

"I didn't say that. Just make him come to you. Don't be pushy with Hank, play hard to get."

"Oh poop," Mindy chided, " Don't be an old fuddy duddy, Paula. This isn't 1990; we're in the twenty-first century now. Things aren't like they were in the old days when men always made the first move. Haven't you heard of the *women's movement*?"

To Carrie the thought of going out, dating, was confusing and scary. It had been years—decades—since she'd opened herself to that possibility. She

56

supposed that things had changed—it appeared so as she listened to the words of music playing on the radio and the things she had glimpsed on MTV. Girls did seem to be the aggressors these days.

However, she could not deny that there *was* a sexual tension between her and Hank, maybe *that* was just what she needed. But the thought of being with a man after so long scared her. Hadn't she been taught that sex only came with a long term relationship . . . with marriage?

As she contemplated the idea, Carrie curled her lip, for a moment the choice between letting herself go and walking the straight and narrow weighed in favor of the former. Her mind raced spastically to thoughts of skin and touching and physical satisfaction; she felt her face redden.

"Good grief, look at her face. It's red as a beet." Paula laughed. "You *are* thinking about *being* with Hank." Paula laughed, glancing at her watch once again. "You naughty girl." Still smiling, she turned to walk toward the back entrance to Grocery World.

"I say you go for the gold before he gets away." Mindy snuffed her cigarette in the sand bucket as she followed Paula to the door. "He's a good catch, sweetie—has lots of dough and a beautiful home on the island. You could have it all if you play your cards right or you could be another one he's tossed to the side of the road—the beach is littered with Hank's old girlfriends."

Paula laughed, "You make up your own mind. Do what you want."

That afternoon during a lull in customer traffic, Hank just happened to overhear a conversation between Mindy and Carrie about painting the outside of her house. Immediately he volunteered his services.

He wasn't really asking her for a date, but it did present an opportunity for him to spend real time with her.

"Oh, the way he makes me feel when he looks at me," Carrie said to Paula. "I don't know if I'm going to be able to control myself when he comes over to help."

"They'll be at least eight of us there." Paula rolled her eyes. "You'll do fine. Just don't give in— don't look so wanton."

"But—"

"Make him work for it. Men like a good chase."

"It's been years." Carrie sighed heavily.

"Oh, you poor thing," Paula laughed, "Quit whining. We've warned you that he's a player, but . . ."

"He's a whore dog," Mindy interrupted.

Paula ignored the comment, "Well, I don't know if he's been to bed with everyone, but he has been around. None of it lasts very long." She added, "But he is a nice guy and he ain't bad to look at either. *Maybe you're the one,*" She added snidely.

"Has he ever been married?"

"Once, she died about twelve years ago in a boating accident. She was pregnant . . . and they'd gone sailing on his sloop. Boy, was it a nice one, a Cheoy Lee, teak decks and trim," Paula sighed. "They were coming through the south inlet . . . and you know that one can get really rough at times . . . somehow she fell overboard and drowned.

"Poor man, must have been horrible for him."

"Yeah, after that he . . . well, he was still living on his parents' land . . . he and his wife lived in a real nice brick home about a half a mile from the family place. After that he sold nearly everything, his parents' house and most of the land there."

"What about his parents? Aren't they still here?" Carrie asked.

Paula lowered her eyes, "They were killed a year earlier—a horrible wreck on Highway seventeen in Wilmington."

"Sad, huh?" Mindy pulled a strand of hair behind her ears and leaned forward, "He's had bad stuff happen to him one thing after another."

"Sounds like it."

"Selling his parents' place left him with some acreage and two or three sound side houses next to the boathouse he has out by the dock. I'm pretty sure he rents the houses-at least two of them."

Paula nodded, "Yeah, I know an old man and his wife stay in one of them."

"But Hank stays in his house over on Ocean Drive on the island," Mindy added. "It's a nice house, great ocean view and . . . '

Carrie chuckled, "You've been there?" Sliding her eyes to meet Paula's, she added, "Don't you think he's a bit old for you?"

Mindy lowered her eyes, "Good looking is good looking . . . and I was twenty when we got together."

"So it couldn't have been that many years ago."

"I just couldn't resist his *southern charm*," Mindy bit her lip and shrugged. "He's got this cat, and believe me, it's all about the cat. It was like, here kitty kitty—I roll over and he pets the cat. It was stupid, I know—but hey, it is what it is—or was."

"Lots of girls, you say?" Carrie queried, curious as to if she really wanted to get involved with such a ladies' man. "I've never seen him in here with anyone."

"He usually doesn't keep them around long enough to bring them shopping, sweetie," Paula rolled her eyes. "Too bad, I feel sort of sorry for him—maybe that's what he uses to bed his women, sympathy."

"You make him sound horrible."

"Scorned woman syndrome, I guess."

"I thought you were too smart for that," Carrie giggled as she turned to Paula.

"Oh, the heart does what the heart wants." Shrugging, Paula welcomed a group of teenagers as they approached her register.

They stood anxiously in front of her as she ran the twelve pack of Miller beer across the scanner, Paula paused for a moment, "May I see your ID?"

The tallest boy reached into his wallet and removed a license and handed it to her.

"So today's your birthday, huh?"

"Yes ma'am." The boy took the card from Paula's hand and slid it back into his wallet.

"We're all having a party to celebrate," one of the girls in the group chimed.

Paula grabbed the boys hand, "I know your Momma so you better behave yourselves; the cops around here just might check that ID better than I did."

"I think you scared the pee out of them," Carrie tittered, watching as the group walked through the sliding glass doors.

"That ID is as fake as Gilda Mathis's boobs and those kids weren't anymore twenty-one than my dog is."

"Maybe you should have called the cops."

Shaking her head, Paula explained, "I know the boy's family—I'll have a talk with his mom. Besides, if I hand him over to the cops he'll get a record. He needs a chance." She raised an eyebrow, "Anyway, that bunch of kids rents a little house right across the road from here."

"If Paula didn't sell it to them, they'd get it from somewhere else," Mindy chimed in. "Bobby Scaggins, that's the tall boy's name—he was a couple of years behind me in school so he's not far from being twenty-one. And as I remember him, he was a pretty good guy but his daddy is mean as a snake and if that kid got in trouble with the law the old man would beat him to a pulp."

Carrie stood by her register, checked the time on the display and thought of just how little she really knew about her friends and co-workers.

They had both been willing lovers to Hank, yet they had warned her against him. And the boy— letting him buy beer, it was clearly illegal.

The longer she lived here the more she became aware of the dichotomies, the old ways and the new clashing. Customs long held were being challenged by new ways; newcomers to the area were changing things.

Carrie understood all that, and she was beginning to understand some of the animosities between the locals and newer residents.

"Hey," Paula called, "You look perplexed there, gal. Are you all bent out of shape because I let that kid walk out of here with beer?"

Carrie shrugged, "I guess I just don't know this community as well as I thought."

"No, you probably don't, Carrie." Mindy spoke defensively.

"Every place has its little tics and idiosyncrasies – just like a family." Paula turned the light to her station off. "Time for me to go home," she said as she walked to the time clock and slid her card through the slot.

"We kind of watch out for one another," Mindy added. "We may not like everybody, but we understand that nobody is perfect."

"Does that include Hank?" Carrie asked. "It seems like y'all don't care if I get bedded by him or not, even though you admit that he's a player." She looked questioningly at them, "Didn't he hurt you? Didn't he take advantage of you?"

"Everyone around here knows how Hank is—we had to learn for ourselves. But that's not to say that we don't feel for him or understand why he does what he does." Mindy toyed with the pack of cigarettes in her pocket.

"Speaking for myself, I thought that maybe I would be the one to mend his broken heart." Paula shrugged and walked toward the large glass doors, "See y'all tomorrow."

A puzzled look crossed Carrie's brow, "Well . . . what about Hank?" She looked intently at Mindy.

"After his momma and daddy died, he changed–he found Emma, he loved Emma. And then when she died we thought he'd . . . you know– kill himself, or something. He never touched the sailboat again–just built a big bonfire and burned that gorgeous sloop down to the ground." Mindy pursed her lips, "He just hasn't been the same since then, or so I hear. I was just a kid when it happened. But Paula remembers him and so do my mom and dad and that's what they say."

Still fidgeting with the pack of cigarettes in her pockets, Mindy continued, "So, don't go falling in love with him–more than likely he'll only break your heart."

"Well, maybe *I'll* be the one to change that," Smiling, Carrie tossed her strawberry blond locks and wiggled her hips.

"I hope so. He needs some real love in his life."

Carrie thrust her chin high in the air. "He just hasn't met the right chick yet."

"Maybe not."

Shaking her head, Carrie smirked, "I know, I know. He only wants one thing."

As Mindy fumbled with her pockets she winked, "I'm just letting you know the odds."

"Hey, I'm not ever getting married again, so maybe a good roll in the hay is all I need. You know, something to smooth out all the rough edges . . . settle my nerves."

"Smoking's cheaper," Mindy reached into her pocket and pulled out her pack of Marlboro Menthols–I need a cigarette. I'm taking a break."

Chapter Six

Paula showed up for the house painting party around two o'clock, so did a couple of the bag boys. Marsha, a fairly new girl at the store brought her boyfriend and Mindy came dragging in with Robby about an hour later.

"Where's the pizza!" Mindy hollered as she reached into a cooler of beer and soft drinks.

A crisp *whoosh* escaped the can of Budweiser as she popped the top. "I'm hungry!" she called out again as Robby grabbed her from behind and wrestled the Bud from her hands.

Laughing aloud, Carrie walked from the porch and settled her phone on a small round table. "Just called it in-maybe thirty minutes. Is that fast enough for you?" Tilting her head to the side, she chuckled and tossed a paint brush to her friend. "You came here to work, kiddo, not eat."

Carrie was pleased as she scanned the group of co-workers who had come to help. Seeing them all there reassured her that she'd made the right decision to move to Surf City.

Even with it being summer terrorist season, this makes everything worthwhile, Carrie walked down the few steps to the front yard eager to join in with the painting and partying. She wondered if Hank was still at the side of the house where she'd last seen him diligently, yet meticulously dipping a brush into a can of *mystic sea foam* paint.

As she rounded the corner, she was blindsided and fell softly to the ground; Hanks arms cushioning their fall.

She struggled against him, "What!" she giggled, "You're going to get paint all over me."

"That's the idea, my dear." Hank growled teasingly and pulled her close to where he had been working. "You sure look pretty with paint on your nose."

"I don't have—"

In a flash he swiped her nose with his brush, "now you do."

As she and Hank worked on the little wooden home, they teased and flirted, chased each other around with the water hose—splattered each other with paint—did the things kids would do—and felt like kids doing them.

Again he grabbed her and they tumbled to the ground; Carrie thought he was going to kiss her and she waited a moment as he brought his face close to hers. She could feel his warm breath against her lips.

It didn't matter what Paula and Mindy had said, Carrie was smitten with Hank and her desires were doing the talking, not her head.

"Come over to my house tonight, I'll fix you a fantastic seafood dinner." Hank pulled away, he did not bring his lips to hers; rather he held her at a distance, studying her face. "Maybe after we eat I'll take you out on the Robalo for a midnight cruise."

Pushing her gently from him, he picked up a paintbrush and wielded it like a weapon.

"Say yes," Hank teased as he flicked the paint-laden brush in the air.

Carrie laughed. Her cheeks hurt from laughing so much and she readily said yes to his dinner proposal.

Later that afternoon she showered, washing the paint from her body, and shampooed and coiffed her hair to look natural; tonight she let her strawberry tresses hang loosely—no barrettes.

The dress she chose to wear was mid-thigh and not too low cut. The soft orange color she thought went well with the color of her hair.

As she pulled her car into Hank's driveway, Carrie felt a nervousness sweep over her. Was she going to go to bed with this man?

She felt the color leave her face and heard a resounding *no* echo in her head. At the same time she knew the true answer was up to Hank.

As she climbed the stairway to his home, indistinct feelings swirled about inside her. At once she felt as if she should turn back and not even go through with the date. After all Mindy and Paula had told her, Carrie was now growing anxious and afraid of what might happen.

Was he going to take advantage of her vulnerability? Was she vulnerable? It had been so long since she had even liked someone other than her husband or even wanted to spend time with another man.

Having someone cook dinner for her, dressing herself up in something besides work clothes, or jeans, having someone smile when they greeted you and show interest in who you were—who you are—these thoughts pushed her forward and she moved gingerly up the stairs to ring the door bell of Hank's home.

Through the glass door she saw him make his way to her and nodding, he reached a hand forward to take hers, "Welcome to my modest beach home."

Certainly, the house wasn't fancy and was not oceanfront as were the majority on Ocean Front Drive.

Small dunes separated Hank's home from the Atlantic, but still a spectacular view could be seen from the veranda.

Hank handed Carrie a glass of Zinfandel and one long stemmed white rose as he led her into the living area. The glass doors were open; breezes from the ocean gently roused the thin curtains. The view beckoned Carrie to move outside; Hank followed her as she stood near the railing looking out into the night sky.

"You certainly have a lovely home, Hank—and the view is wonderful." Carrie gazed out at the darkening expanse before her, making out the movement of the waves by the light that shown from the rising moon. Giggling, she recalled the afternoon of play and found herself anticipating a similar evening.

Hank leaned against the railing and raised a finger to touch Carrie's bare arm. It surprised her— the look on his face seemed so serious. Yet he did not speak at all as he gazed steadily into her eyes.

Gently his fingers caressed the inside of her arm, running its length from shoulder to wrist, his hazel eyes still staring into hers. The look was not menacing nor leering, but gentle and filled with desire—so overwhelmingly that the intensity frightened Carrie a bit.

Hank moved his body closer to hers, barely brushing her skin.

"Have you lived here long?" Carrie's feeble attempt to initiate some sort of conversation stopped him for a moment.

"Um hum," Hank raised his hand again to caress the nape of her neck.

"Going a little fast, aren't you?" Carrie asked nervously.

Hank slowly shook his head no and continued running his fingers along her neck and then to her jaw line.

"You promised me a fine seafood diner." Stepping back, Carrie touched where his fingers had been on her face. She turned to walk from the veranda and into the kitchen.

Hank leaned against the doorway and smiled, "I did promise you a fine dinner, didn't I?" Setting his wine glass on the kitchen counter, he walked leisurely to the refrigerator, sliding his hand gently along Carrie's shoulders as he moved past her.

"We are going to prepare mahi mahi almondine style. How does that sound?"

"Sounds delicious," she replied, almost in a whisper.

"I've already got the ingredients for the sauce," Hank tapped the counter next to the range. "Why don't you peel those lemons for me?"

Grabbing a lemon, Carrie searched in a drawer close by and retrieved a paring knife.

Hank sifted the flour, oregano, garlic powder, paprika and other spices into a glass pie plate. "Darling, why don't you reach into the fridge and get the mahi mahi for me?"

Carrie could smell his faint masculine scent. It was intoxicating. She turned in response to his request, meeting his passionate gaze. Her stomach fluttered and she felt her pulse quicken. "Okay." The breathy reply escaped her lips as she reached to open the refrigerator door.

"Hmm," Carrie sighed as she studied its contents.

There were two plates of fish, one on the second shelf next to a container of fresh snap beans and another on the bottom shelf situated behind a large bowl of grapes. Both were in plastic zip lock bags.

"Bring out the grapes too, if you would Darling."

Carrie felt odd being called *darling*. It had always been *sweetie*, or *dear* or *sugar* by her ex-husband. But darling sounded nice, more loving.

She bit her bottom lip and reached for the bowl of grapes and the fish behind them.

"Here." She placed the fish next to Hank and settled the grapes on the counter, plucking one and popping it in her mouth.

"No, sorry my love, but this is not the right fish." He smiled gently at her, "Would you mind putting these in the freezer and getting the others?"

Carrie, opened the side door of the freezer and set the fish on an empty rung.

"It looks like you're out of food, Hank. Except for a bottle of Vodka, the freezer is empty."

"Oh Darling, I'm just not much for freezing things and I never freeze fish, it's always best fresh."

Carrie agreed, there was nothing better than fresh caught fish, and she loved mahi mahi.

Opening the refrigerator door she caught a glimpse of the photo of a young blonde haired woman. *Must be his deceased wife*, Carrie thought as she reached for the plate of filets on the second shelf. They looked a little pinker than the other bag of fish; she shrugged, considering that Hank must know a lot more about seafood than she did.

"I should have been clearer. I should have told you to get the plate on the second shelf," he said as he lifted the light pink filets and dredged them in the flour and spice mixture.

Helping Hank prepare the dinner was almost as fun as painting the house earlier that day. They teased and flirted, held hands and brushed against one another.

They talked about everything, beginning with the tourist season. Each agreed that the *terrorists* made life unpleasant during the summer months.

"Let's not talk about them," Hank winked, "I can tell it makes you unhappy." He touched his hand to cup her face, instinctively redirecting her mood with compliments–how he'd noticed how well she related with other people and how patient and tolerant she was.

Carrie laughed, confessing the bread squeezing she often felt compelled to do.

"Sometimes a little vengeance goes a long way," Hank grinned. "Other times it just doesn't seem that satisfying."

Reaching to caress her cheek again, he added, "Just be your own sweet self, don't let the small minded people get to you."

"I keep hearing that," Carrie bit her lip.

"It's true, Darling."

They talked a bit about places to go on the island, things they found fun to do, like clamming and walking the beach. Finally Hank asked about Carrie's life.

She mentioned Jim, though tried not to linger on his bad habits or their loveless marriage. And she spoke lovingly and proudly of her children, David and Sue, wondering all the while if she was divulging too much information. But Hank listened intently as Carrie expressed how proud she was of them.

As she talked, thoughts of asking him about the photograph on the refrigerator crossed her mind, but Hank must have anticipated those questions

72

and moved the conversation to compliments of how brave she was to make such a daring move to a place she knew nothing about.

As they sat at the small kitchen table across from one another enjoying the mahi almondine, Hank reached a hand to caress hers. He held it gently but firmly, stroking her palm and wrist.

Carrie knew what all the talk, the touching and the teasing was leading to, she could feel it and she knew she could not resist.

"It's been such a long time since anyone has ever said such nice things to me."

"Uh huh," Hank stood and gently pulled Carrie to her feet.

Was she ready for *this*? She asked herself.

Hesitating, Carrie felt Hank's hand caress the small of her back, she leaned into his touch. Closing her eyes she breathed a soft sigh as his fingers gently brushed the few wisps of hair from her face. She set the glass of wine on the table and touched his bicep. She could feel the tense strength and could smell the light aroma of his natural scent. It was clean, yet warm at the same time.

A thin smile graced her lips, Hank grinned gently in response. Carrie waited for the kiss as he moved his face toward hers, but there was none. Rather his lips gently brushed her earlobe; she could feel his warm breath against her.

His fingers gently pushed her chin to face him; the intensity of his gaze pulled all thoughts of resistance from her. She exhaled nervously as his fingers touched her collar bone—*what was that look in his eyes?* It aroused in her a desire for him to touch her more; it had been so long since any man had been this close.

She'd only had a few sips of wine; certainly that was not enough to loosen her defenses, so the drunken state of her emotions could be attributed to nothing else but Hank's touch and the overwhelming desire sweeping uncontrollably over her. The *no* she had planned on saying, was swept away in a blur of feelings she didn't think she'd ever experienced before.

Everything seemed surreal as she acquiesced to his will and she was not surprised when she realized she was lying on the bed with him, consumed with want and amazingly aware of her own body and how he made it feel.

It seemed he avoided her most intimate parts, caressing only the inner softness of her thighs. He pressed an open palm against her soft belly, moving his hands toward her breasts; he cupped them for a simple moment before nuzzling her belly again.

He pulled her nearer for a deep kiss. She felt his hands, his fingers dig gently into the softness of her buttocks pulling her in closer, nuzzling her neck, and drawing her sweat drenched body into him.

All reasoning, all thoughts of anything at all left her as she wallowed in the experience of total pleasure. Carrie let herself be drowned in all that she had ever imagined physical love could be.

Exhausted, still tingling from the lovemaking, Carrie sighed with utter joy. No one had ever aroused her senses to such heights; she felt complete and turned to search his face for the passion she herself was feeling.

Hank's eyes were closed; a soft grin lay on his lips.

He looks so peaceful, Carrie thought, *this is so good, so wonderful to finally find someone who is capable of the love I need.*

Touching his cheek with her fingertips, Carrie stretched her neck to kiss him softly. Hank turned to find her welcoming eyes.

"Sure was good, wasn't it baby—bet you've never had it *that* good."

The words jolted her and she wondered if she had heard him correctly, "What is that, dear?" She asked meekly.

"Really didn't expect for you to go down so easily." He reached to pat her bottom. "But it sure was good, I could teach you a few things more though."

The winding, spiraling journey back to reality was most certainly only a few seconds, but to Carrie it seemed so long and drawn out that she was sure Hank noticed her disappointment; she scrambled to regain her composure. Pulling the sheet around her, she suddenly felt bare.

"Aw come on now, a sheet? No need for modesty after all we've done tonight." He looked gently at her for a moment, "You're a fantastic girl, Carrie. I really do like you."

Setting the urge to slap him aside, Carrie mustered the courage to act as if everything was normal—that *this* was what she expected all along.

Hank's demeanor had been switched to another mode as if one might turn a lamp on and off. Gone was the mesmerizing pull of his eyes, the slow, tender allure of his touch—he even seemed to smell differently—the spell had been broken.

Carrie could hear her friend Paula's response, *Got in your britches, didn't he? Told you not to fall for it.*

Now was a different Hank, still teasing and playful, but different.

As the man rolled to his back and laced his fingers, laying them against his chest. He turned his head to look toward the carpeted floor of the bedroom. A squeaking sound came from his pursed lips and he patted the side of the bed, "Come on kitty."

A lean calico cat jumped up and positioned herself on Hank's chest, immediately it began purring loudly.

Carrie reached to pet the animal, it growled and hissed as the hairs of its tail bushed.

"Don't worry Tango, this lady is nice, she'll share me with you." Hank winked at Carrie and whispered, "She won't scratch you." He continued to stroke the cat, "Will you, sweet Tango?" Stroking the cat's fur, he turned to Carrie and commented nonchalantly, "She's old. I've spoiled her."

"That's okay, I've spoiled my dogs too." A sick feeling rose in her stomach as she realized the ambiguity of her feelings. *I ate the whole damn cake and now I have to work like hell to get back to being me.* Closing her eyes, she swallowed hard, *It was so good. Didn't even think about the consequences.*

"Hungry? I've got a nice lemon meringue pie in the fridge." He winked, "Just for you."

"Sounds good," Carrie said, forcing a broad grin to her lips. She felt like a fool, used. But had she been? He certainly had made her do nothing she didn't want to do.

It was all the *wooing*. As if he truly desired *me*. She could feel the cheeks of her face flush as she held back her feelings. Carrie didn't know if she wanted to laugh or cry.

Watching the cat as it purred loudly on Hank's chest, a consuming feeling of disillusionment overwhelmed her.

But what had made her think it would be otherwise? She had been warned.

Please get up. Please go. She thought, as if she could will him to do so. *Please go get the pie.*

Carrie could barely contain herself as she lay next to the man she had just been so intimate with. The uneasiness consumed her; but she pushed herself to appear relaxed and propped herself on one elbow.

"I'm really hungry after all that."

"Me too," Carrie added enthusiastically.

Hank slipped a pair of running shorts on as he stepped from the bed. Patting his thigh, he encouraged the cat to follow.

As they padded from the room, Carrie heard Hank whisper, "You're still my favorite Tango."

Carrie immediately dressed, feeling cumbersome and nervous the whole while. Yes, she had been a fool, a big fool. No buts about it—her guard had been down.

She imagined Mindy remarking, telling her that there was nothing wrong with a good roll in the hay, but Carrie knew better than that. There was no fooling herself, she couldn't settle for *rolls in the hay,* intimacy required respect and trust and at least the hope of love.

Oh, *he* was good in the sack; magnificent, earth shaking, even. Where some people developed wood working to a high art, Hank had perfected his own craft of love making to palpable perfection.

Closing her eyes, she felt the queasiness rise in her stomach; the evening of passion had been no more than that—a super, fantastic *roll in the hay*— Hank's well honed craft. But it just was not enough. Carrie's heart sank a bit. She was not used to being so very intimate with someone who did not love her or at least expressed feelings for her.

Hank had not even offered a pretense of love. At least with Jim, she suspected that somewhere in his heart he had held some sort of love for her.

Isn't it funny, she thought, *how sometimes lies are easier to live with than truth?*

Hank made no mention of her spending the night. And he made no mention of seeing her again.

And for whatever reason, Carrie was glad he had not.

"You're not happy," Hank spoke as he stood by the entrance to his home.

Carrie shrugged.

78

"I know you liked it—I could tell."

Carrie said nothing; she could not even meet his eyes. "I can't just . . ."

"But you just did, Darling," His words sounded accusatory.

The words wouldn't come and Carrie simply shrugged.

"We're still friends, okay." Hank reassured her as she turned to leave.

But weren't friends confiding, caring—weren't friends supposed to be open with one another—try to get to know one another? She had divulged her life, but he had offered none of his.

The romance, if that is what you could call it, fizzled just as Paula had warned. The moment he got her, the game was over. Carrie had heard of things like this, but then again, he was only the second man she had ever been with.

Chastising herself, Carrie considered that if this was what the dating scene was like, she would simply put *love* on the back burner and get her own life in order before looking for Mr. Right.

As far as she was concerned there were more important things to get *right* in her life and she found herself glad that the affair with Hank was simple and short.

There was still the matter of getting her house fixed and buying a decent car. She needed shoes and a new wardrobe. There were lots of things she needed beside a man in her life.

Chapter Seven

"I only want one item."

Carrie heard the man speak softly to the woman with the high-piled cart In front of him. He smiled politely, gesturing a move ahead of her. She nodded and grinned, letting him step in front of her cart.

"I'd like a can of Coyote Peppermint Snuff," he spoke.

There were a gazillion kinds of snuff and they all came in different colored tins. Brands were always changing and often depleted from the inventory. It made it difficult for Carrie to keep up with the assortment of chewing tobacco and snuff.

"What color tin is the snuff in, sir?" She asked politely.

His shoulders squared as his face contorted in a rubbery sneer. "Coyote Peppermint Snuff," He repeated, this time more loudly.

"Yes, sir, but what color tin is it in? We have so many kinds. It will help me find it faster if you tell me the color of the tin."

Again the man repeated his order, only this time he rolled his eyes and placed his hands on his hips. "Coyote—Peppermint—Snuff," He spoke slowly and louder as he glared at her.

Oh, how Carrie had wanted to say, *Look, butt head, what color tin is the damn snuff in? You obnoxious bag of poop, chewing tobacco is disgusting. But I'll get it for you if you'll tell me what color tin it's in.*

But she did not. Instead, she smiled and said, "Yes, sir," then turned, more slowly than she would have normally, and began looking through the nearly forty different kinds of chewing tobacco for the man's order.

Several minutes later she handed the round tin to him and quoted the price, the man quickly swiped his credit card through the machine, "If you don't know how to do your job, you need to find another one." He shook his head from side to side as he waited for the receipt to be printed.

Crap I wish you had a loaf of bread, I'd squeeze the living daylights out of it, Carrie thought as she glared into the man's eyes and handed him the receipt. "Thank you for shopping Grocery World."

Carrie turned her attention to the next woman in line, looking for some sort of understanding gesture or sympathy for the way in which the rude tobacco chewer had treated her. "Thank you for being patient ma'am," She apologized to the lady with the high piled cart.

"If I'd have known you were going to take so long, I wouldn't have let him go ahead of me," the woman spat.

Carrie swiped the items on the counter in silence as quickly as she could and thanked the customer.

"Uh huh," the woman sarcastically responded as she moved her cart full of bagged groceries.

Leaning against the register, Carrie closed her eyes and shook her head; she was ready for a break and a cigarette.

"You look like you're having a bad day, gal." Morgan Simpers' lean frame rested against the counter.

Startled, Carrie responded with a breathy, "Oh, hi Morgan. How are you doing today?"

"Pretty good, thank you, Carrie. Busy day? Are some of these customers giving you a hard time?"

"Ah, you know how the summer goes."

"Yep."

Smiling, she eyed the large bag of Purina Dog Chow in Morgan's cart. "No need lifting it, I'll just use the hand scanner." Leaning over, she took the wand and beeped in the price.

"Two buttheads in a row, huh?"

"You saw that?"

Morgan chuckled, "I saw. That man was so rude to you."

Carrie nodded in agreement.

"I've seen him around. He's another one of those Yankees that's always got on a pair of shorts —doesn't matter if it's ninety out there or twenty degrees-Yankees think they gotta make a statement about how it's warm enough to wear shorts." Morgan sucked his teeth. "Hell, thirty is thirty no matter where you're at and thirty degrees is not shorts wearing weather." Morgan shook his head and sneered, "People like that really get to me. Looks like they get to you too, Carrie."

Nodding her head, Carrie rolled her eyes. "I don't care what people wear, just as long as they're polite . . . and try to be patient."

"Well . . . "

"Geez, I wish I could find a way to let it roll off me—not let it bother me." She looked questioningly at Morgan.

"Wish I knew what to tell you, Carrie. I know I couldn't put up with snotty folks like that. But then I don't have to." He chuckled again. "I take that back . . . I'm married."

"It can't be that bad." Carrie taunted.

"Naw, just joking," Morgan slid his gaze to the floor.

"The thoughts that go through my head and the things I'd like to say to some of these people, Morgan, you have no idea."

"I can imagine." Slowly moving his eyes upward to meet Carrie's, he winked. "You just don't worry about it." Morgan was silent for a moment as he placed a few more items on the conveyor belt. "Oh, I heard about your *favorite* customer."

Looking up curiously, Carrie held his eyes for a moment as she moved the items across the scanner.

"Remember? Sarah Chambers."

"Oh, yeah, Sarah Chambers. Sure was terrible the way they found her."

"Did they ever find out what happened to her? I mean, did she fall off the pier or something? Or did somebody kill her?" Morgan asked curiously.

"Mindy's boyfriend, Robby, says they're still investigating it. But she didn't fall off the pier. There's somebody out there around the clock this time of year and not one person says they saw a thing until that kid snagged her on his line."

"I bet that shocked the heck of him." Morgan sniggered. "You know whose son he is, don't you?"

"Detective Belkin's son, wasn't it?"

Morgan nodded, "Yeah. The kid just came out here this summer to live with him, looks like he's going to stay."

"Really?" Carrie eyed the customer next in line. It was a local who didn't mind the banter between her and Morgan. Smiling gently to the older man, she nodded acknowledgment, "Hi, Mr. Sanders."

The man smiled back, leaning into the conversation, "I hear his mother was some sort of drug addict and that Belkin got custody of the boy. Guess he's going to try to straighten him out-make sure he doesn't end up like his mom."

Morgan and Carried nodded in unison.

"Yes," Mr. Sanders sniggered, "The kid's a brat, got a smart filthy mouth. His father has his work cut out for him."

"That's too bad, Mr. Sanders," Carrie responded.

"Yeah, my neighbor Joe was out on the pier that day fishing right across from the kid," Sanders grimaced, "he said it was one cuss word after another and that the boy was a real smarty pants."

The older man snorted, "I hear the little snot vomited all over the place and when his father came to question him, he bawled like a baby . . . not so tough, yeah, acted all high and mighty until a dead body shows up."

Morgan guffawed as he slowly placed canned and frozen items on the conveyor belt, "Yeah, sounds like the kid needs to do a little growing up."

Mr. Sanders added that he wished the best for the boy and that since he was young maybe there was hope for him yet. Morgan and Carrie nodded in agreement.

"I guess this means you won't have to contend with Sarah Chambers anymore—huh?" Morgan grinned.

"Ha, ha, ha—I guess you could say that. It's terrible what happened, but I can't say I'm going to miss her."

"Maybe we can hope for a hurricane to scare the rest of the tourists away."

"They aren't all bad, Morgan. *Some* are nice," Carrie chuckled. "But they sure know how to put a kink in my day. And we sure as heck don't need a hurricane, that makes them even nuttier.

"Every time they hear something on the news about a hurricane they come in here and buy more beer. Hurricanes are party time for them."

"You can say that again," Mr. Sanders joined in. "You should have seen that bunch next to my home last August when Hurricane Lillian grazed us. You'd have thought it was New Year's Eve—they were running in and out the doors, whooping and popping fire crackers and throwing beer cans out in the lawn.

"A couple of ladies, if that's what you want to call them, came running out the top floor buck naked," he blushed and laughed at the same time, "bouncing down those steps—ran out in the yard in all that wind and rain saying they were getting close to Mother Nature—I made myself a couple of fish sandwiches and sat by my picture window and watched them all—dinner and a show—you know."

"Lillian was only a category one," Morgan chuckled. "Well, we can always hope for a big one," he laughed again.

Carrie tittered delicately and, in an effort to change the subject, asked about Morgan's dog.

"Ol' Lucky's doing just fine, caught a rabbit yesterday and dragged it up on the back porch."

"He loves you," Carrie giggled. "Now, if it was Joey or Bella, it would be the rabbit dragging *them* to my back porch."

Morgan chuckled, "My sister's got one of them little ankle biters, runs and hides every time I come around."

Carrie looked up at him, "That will be one hundred and forty-seven dollars and twenty-eight cents, sir."

He laid the money in her hand, then moved to bag his groceries.

"Wish some of my other customers were as nice as you, Morgan. You always bag your own groceries, even if I've got a bagger to help."

"My pleasure, Carrie." He grinned at her again and turned to leave. "You take care of yourself, now."

"Bye," Carrie nodded.

"I always see him out and about with that dog, little gal," Mr. Sanders pushed his five items closer. "I think he spends more time with Lucky than with his wife."

"Dogs are supposed to be man's best friend."

"I think ol' Lucky might be Morgan's only friend." The man pulled a wallet from his trousers pocket as Carrie checked his items, "What's the damage, young lady?"

Pulling a strand of coupons from the machine, Carrie sifted through them until she came to the one that offered fifty cents off a can of Del Monte stew. "Here you go—this will save you a few pennies."

"Young lady, I appreciate that." Sanders nodded. "You have a good afternoon, now. Okay?"

Chapter Eight

Detective Donald Belkin felt the crunch of the gravel beneath the wheels of his car as he pulled slowly into Sarah Chambers' driveway. Taking a deep breath, he rolled his shoulders and drew his lips in tightly.

As he exited the faded black Dodge Charger, he leaned against it, feeling the nervousness in his belly. It seemed that everything was closing in on him or was *this*—the murder—a good thing? At least now he wouldn't have to contend with Chambers anymore.

"Humph," Don sighed, *I need to be careful as hell*, he bounced a curled knuckle against his mouth.

The warmth of the car felt somewhat comforting and he relaxed against it, recalling his first meeting with Sarah Chambers—it had been both surprising and unpleasant.

Within the first week of his move to the Surf City Police Department three years ago, Don had been assigned to patrol the area across the island bridge—the mainland and sound side of the town. It was always especially quiet with acres and acres of mostly old vacant farms waiting to be sold and developed.

That second week, on a Tuesday night around ten, while making rounds with then detective Seth Milton, they drove down Old Landing Road. The dim light of a crescent moon lit their way as they drove toward the oyster shell lined shore.

Don was amazed at just how untouched the area was. There were no houses, no piers, not even a park. There wasn't even any trash around to suggest that people frequented the area.

The only sign that humans visited there were the small skiffs tied to old steering wheels, swaying with the tidal movement and the long slender sticks that jutted intermittently out of the still waters of the sound.

"What are those sticks standing out in the water?" he asked Milton.

"Those are the markers for some of the locals' oyster beds." Milton put the patrol car in park and turned the ignition key off. He lowered the windows to let the natural breezes sift through the car. It was high tide and the usual pungent smell of the marsh and the sea life there were barely noticeable.

They sat in silence for a while, Don gazing out into the tranquil sparkling moonlit waters. After nearly ten minutes of silence, Don turned to his partner, "You know, this is nice and enjoyable, but shouldn't we be patrolling the area?"

Milton kept silent, ignoring Don's question.

For about five minutes longer they sat quietly; a couple of fish jumped in the waters.

"Bet there's some good fishing here."

"Uh huh," Milton grunted, his face turned northward as if searching the distance for something.

"If we're on surveillance . . ." Don began. Then he heard a low buzzing sound. He listened too as it grew louder and until it sounded as if it were nearly right in front of the patrol car.

As the sound stopped, Milton stepped from the vehicle, Don followed, still wondering what was going on.

"Is this one of your contacts?"

"You could say that." Milton's words were barely audible over the crunch of his shoes on the oyster shell covered ground.

"Reggie, this is going to be your new *contact*," Milton chuckled as he took a brown paper grocery bag from the man. He then stepped aside to allow Don to shake hands with Reggie.

"Once a month, second Tuesday, at this exact time, Reggie will be here." Milton moved close, too close, to where Don could feel his breath as he spoke. "Understand?"

Suddenly he did understand.

"What!" Raising his hand as if to sweep away the suggestion, Detective Don Belkin walked to the passenger side of the vehicle. "Hell, I want no part of this! I'm getting out of here . . . I'm calling this in." Don reached for his cell phone.

Reggie sniggered as he pulled a long filet knife from its sheath, "Ain't this guy new, Milt?"

"Sure is."

"And he's the one I've been meeting here the last couple weeks."

The two men grinned at each other and then at Don.

"Buddy boy, you ain't calling nobody." Milton rested his hand on the holster of his side arm.

Reggie stood shoulder to shoulder with him running the blade of his knife along his arm, "Hell, this is sharp, cut the hair right off my arm." He rubbed his finger along the skin and presented the arm to Don. "See cuts like a razor," he nodded. "It'd be a mistake—two against one and you really don't want to cause any trouble. It's just a little snort and sometimes some hash or weed. Stuff needs to be legalized anyway."

In a flash the knife flew from his hand, piercing a hermit crab as it scuttled along the spongy shore.

Don sneered, "If it was legal, how would you make a living, scum."

Straightening his back, Don felt his pulse quicken and his jaw tighten. He did not like being forced into anything. But at this moment he really didn't have much choice. Milton would probably shoot him and then say how surprised he was to find out that the new rookie cop was so rotten—was dealing drugs.

Don didn't have a choice.

"You've got to understand, Officer Belkin," Milton began, "I'm leaving the force in a few months—Chief said you were interested in detective, so you're *next in line,* so to speak." He chuckled. "You'll be head of any investigations.

Patting Belkin on the shoulder he glared at Don, "You did say you were interested in making detective, didn't you?"

Don turned his head a bit to the side, "Yeah, but I haven't even been here that long—that takes a while."

"Not around this little burg," Milton patted Don on the shoulder again.

Raising his eyes to meet Milton's, Don shrugged sharply to remove the man's hand.

"Hey, buddy boy, you're just getting some really good on the Job training. Besides, we need someone we can trust. You're perfect."

"Why not one of the other men on the force?"

"Nobody else wants to be a detective," Milton grinned.

Don could feel the heat on his face, he wanted to pull his gun, take them in—tell it all—take his chances.

"Come on now, Don. This makes sense. You're the new kid on the block. Most of the other officers have been here for years. They have families here— the community knows them."

Reggie moved in to shake Don's hand. "Hey man, welcome to the party." He smiled broadly, waiting for Don to extend his hand in return. "There's some dough in it for you. You could use a little extra money, couldn't you?"

Glancing at the man's outstretched hand, Don gritted his teeth and cursed, "Damn you."

"I've been doing this for six years. Never an eyebrow cocked, never any suspicion. Nobody around here gives a damn or a dollar . . . so just play it cool, man." Leaning against the patrol car, Milton shrugged then winked, "and remember, we know where you live and all about that wife and kid in California."

Four months to the day, Milton left the force. As he boxed the few items in his office he called out to Don as he passed in the hallway.

"Tuesdays, you got it man."

Stopping in the doorway, Don leaned in, "One day . . ."

"Not my problem anymore. I'm outta here." Milton grinned and walked from the room.

Detective Belkin didn't care where the bastard went, though later he heard he was down in Florida somewhere.

Don figured that Milton had built a nice big nest egg in the years he had been dealing drugs on the island and probably had enough for a nice boat — wasn't that the dream?

He'd overheard him yukking it up with some other men at the station— bragging that when he retired he was going to spend the rest of his life sailing around the world.

It all sounded good, maybe he would do that too someday . . . and yes, the money had come in handy; as of last September, after hiring lawyers he shouldn't have been able to afford, he'd been granted custody of his son Phil.

He wondered now if he'd done the right thing—the boy was lost, messed up. Don had no relationship to speak of with him.

He was constantly skipping school, and Don was sure he smoked weed. The last time he'd spoken with the school counselor, she'd told him he would have to be held back a grade for having missed so many days.

So yes, the extra cash had come in handy, and he'd been able to get his son, but had it helped at all? Was it too late for the boy?"

He pondered the questions daily.

Don shivered as he thought of how comfortable meeting Reggie had become. And he didn't like himself for It, but the money had been put to good use and he did have his boy now.

Hanging his head against his chest, Don rubbed the back of his neck then glanced up at the huge three-story house before him.

It was odd, he thought—very odd—Sarah turning up dead now.

Hadn't she invited him to dinner last night with that a-hole Reggie? Wasn't she going to have a friend of hers prepare some extraordinarily fancy meal?

Anyway, that is what she said. 'You simply have to be here, it's an order'. He remembered her stressing that it was an order.

"Maybe if she hadn't ordered me to come, I would have." The words fell almost silently from his lips.

"Then who would be investigating *my* death?"

He didn't call–hadn't even bothered to come up with some kind of excuse. He just didn't feel like having dinner with the boss lady, so he simply didn't show up.

Kicking the gravel beneath his feet, Don glared at the house of the now deceased Sarah Chambers.

It was as ostentatious as Sarah, with its stained glass windows and shark weather vane mounted on the roof.

At least the partial darkness of the night subdued the bright yellow and purple colors.

Thank goodness it was not a windy day because he couldn't have stood the loud clanging and obnoxious tinkling of the many wind chimes mounted about the eaves of the structure. They annoyed him to no end.

Pushing the thoughts of Sarah and her pretentious behavior out of his mind, he walked steadily to the side door of the victim's home; it was locked and there had been no key on Sarah's body.

Don reached into a pocket, pulled a pair of latex gloves out and stretched them to cover his hands.

Hunching over, he picked the lock; twisting the knob, he entered on the ground floor.

A flip of the switch revealed the garage; a faint odor of gasoline lingered in the air, sandy tread marks still stood untouched on the cement.

He looked slowly about the nearly empty room. Obviously the garage was used mostly for beach paraphernalia–chairs and umbrellas were stacked neatly in one corner. He walked over to them and peered about, moving a few items to the side.

To the back of the garage was a door slightly ajar; Don opened it to reveal a small room, possibly used for house guests. A single bed and small dresser were the only pieces of furniture there.

As he left the room, Don noticed a second door in the far corner of the garage. *Stairway,* he thought grinning to himself. He walked the flight that led to the second floor of Sarah's home.

It looked untouched as had the garage. Starlight filtered into the room, illuminating it dimly. Nothing was in disarray.

HIs eyes followed the layout of the room; It had been decorated with beach style rattan furniture with teal and mauve sea life print upholstery. A glass coffee table and end tables accented the rattan. Randomly set on them were mauve and teal vases and knickknacks depicting nautical scenes.

On the walls, whitewash wooden frames held pictures of sailboats and dolphins.

As he slowly moved about the living room, the aroma of seafood tickled his nose. Whatever it was, it was a light smelling fish. He glanced toward the kitchen but continued down a wide hall to the other rooms; he would save the kitchen for last.

A spacious full bath with a walk-in shower was next to what Don assumed was another guest bedroom—much larger than the tiny room in the garage.

As he entered, the first thing to catch his attention was the painting of a mermaid hanging on the wall. It resembled Sarah more than just a little; he let out a muffled guffaw and continued studying the room and its contents.

A small balcony stretched from the sliding glass doors. Opening them he walked out; the roar of the ocean, though ever present anywhere on or near the island, seemed to fill his head as he watched the waves pull and push their way to shore. The breeze was refreshing and he breathed in deeply, washing away the fishy smell from the kitchen; turning he re-entered the guest room.

A queen size bed sat centered along the south wall; the bedspread was teal and the pillows piled high were mauve. The mirror frame was etched in mauve and teal designs of waves and sky; the lamp and ceiling fan were mauve and teal, as well.

She sure likes teal and mauve, Don smirked as he walked slowly to the rattan dresser; he opened the drawers. They were all empty.

Moving into what appeared to be an office; he flipped a light switch and scanned the room. It was similar to the living room only rather than pictures of sailboats and dolphins, the pictures were of sand dunes and sea oats. On the far north wall was a long sofa—a sleeper sofa.

The house could have been nice, he thought, *what in the world was she thinking with the colors and pictures.*

Don sneered, *well, anything oceanfront is nice.*

He shook his head—*what a price. How much dope would I have to sell to get a house like this?*

Thoughts of how he could be living oceanfront if he had not spent all his money trying to save his son from his drug addict ex-wife, played in his head.

Cursing himself for the thought, he left the room and moved toward the kitchen.

It was huge; a large wooden island stood in its center. Shiny silver appliances stared back at him. A pan with remnants of some kind of sauce sat on the front left burner of the range. A larger empty pot was on the rear left burner. Pinpoint spatters of grease dotted the top and splash guard. A muffin tin with crusted bits of cornbread lay on the counter next to the range.

Opening the overhead cabinets, Don eyed the measuring cups and mixing bowls stacked on top of one another.

As he gently closed them, Don moved to the refrigerator; it was large—one of those that had side by side front doors. Don opened them wide; the side door shelves were lined with condiments, the crispers were full of fresh vegetables and deli meats. A huge roast beef, covered in cling wrap sat in a ceramic serving dish; Don was tempted to slice a piece off.

Expensive cheeses, wines, grapes, melons and other fresh foods lay on the shelves. "Wish she'd invited me over for dinner some time," Don laughed as he closed the doors. "Oh, that's right— she did." He chuckled again.

As he walked steadily past the appliances he ran a gloved finger along the edges of the sink—a few used pieces of silverware sat in the basin along with a couple of bowls.

He pulled open the drawers of silverware and utensils. Another drawer was stuffed with measuring cups and rubber spatulas. One more held odds and ends and a stack of receipts from Grocery Word paper clipped together with items circled in red on many. He would have to stop by the store and see if they were of any significance.

His eyes searched all nooks and crannies, looking for anything that may have been out of place or out of the ordinary.

Remnants of the meal, the one with the lingering seafood smell, were on the table. He was surprised that the smell was mild; various kinds of fish circulated in his mind as he thought of lesser pungent types of seafood.

Three dinner plates, three silverware settings—askew-and crumpled linen napkins sat on the far end of an oak table large enough for a seating of ten.

"No serving platter," he thought aloud. "Why?"

A half empty bottle of Chablis stood next to the muffin basket; the cork lay next to it.

With his gloved fingers he moved the bits and flakes of fish about on one of the plates.

A basket of corn muffins sat in the center of the table; a bit far from where the dirty plates were placed. Don thumped them lightly. The leftovers had grown stale and hard.

Some kind of pasta dish and asparagus with what looked like hollandaise sauce sat in stoneware bowls between the place settings.

Three long stem wine glasses, nearly empty, posed next to the dinnerware.

Who else had Sarah been entertaining? he wondered. *It could have been me if I'd shown up as requested.*

Drawing his lips tight, he knew Reggie must have been there. Where was he now?

Don felt the chill of impending disaster—his disaster. *That could have been me tied up in those pilings.* He felt his pulse quicken.

"Hell," he said aloud, "you're just winding yourself up." He took a deep breath and eyed the table once again; everything, the plates, the silverware, glasses—it would have to taken in. He'd come over later with Abbott and pick it up.

Leaning against the kitchen counter, Don rubbed a finger across the bridge of his nose. Something about the kitchen bothered him. But he wasn't sure what it was.

Not many people left fish or seafood out for any amount of time. Most cleaned it up within an hour—maybe less. But Sarah had left everything out.

This was not like her; she was too meticulous to leave food out.

Thumping the side of the table, Don turned to examine the flakes of fish once more. If he tasted it, he'd know what it was.

He shook his head, *they'll know at the lab.* Sighing lightly, he stretched his hands behind his head to rub his neck.

Turning his head quickly to the right, he heard the bones pop. For a moment the corners of his mouth turned upward as he glanced at the stairway leading to the third floor.

He walked up them slowly, studying the knickknacks and pictures mounted on the stairway walls.

As he reached the top floor, the fragrance of perfume filled his nostrils. He wasn't sure what perfume it was—or was it air freshener?—but it smelled as if the whole room was filled with flowers.

Standing at the top of the stairs Don slowly eyed the room before him; the whole top floor was Sarah's king sized bedroom. It was almost too big—too spacious. But the view was spectacular.

He could see everything from where he stood—the ocean, the shore, the fishing pier. His eyes quickly caught the pair of binoculars situated on the small table in front of one of the north side windows; he scanned past them.

Heavy aqua colored draperies hung from the sides of each window.

"Well, she sure wasn't planning on going to bed anytime soon," he whispered to himself.

As Don stepped a few feet into the room, he eyed the large seventy-inch television hanging from the center of one wall. Speakers had been placed discriminately in the corners.

A long hand-carved chest lined another wall. Don walked over to it and studied the engravings so exquisitely sculpted into dark wood.

Scenes of the ocean, of ships and whales were cut deeply into the grain. Certainly someone had spent hours, days or even months to make it so elaborate and striking.

What in the world was Sarah doing with something so nice? Don thought as he ran his fingers along the engraved wood. "Humph," he sighed lightly. He never could figure that woman out–he had never wanted to.

Running his hands through his short hair, he continued his investigation of the room. In one corner was a tall ornate étagère. It too was carved, but not quite as intricately as the chest; it looked manufactured, busy–like the carvings had been assembly lined. Don shook his head–he had never understood or liked Sarah Chambers and now, her taste in furniture befuddled him. She was inconsistent, annoyingly so.

If coincidences were made in hell Don was surely getting paid back for his wild and wooly youth. He and Sarah went way back, so far back that he wished he could forget it.

He'd met her over twenty years ago, the summer before joining the Marines. A high GPA and interest in humanities afforded him the opportunity to study a semester at Oxford University in England. However, the only class available to him was Art History.

Don never thought he would find it as interesting as he did and when not enjoying a pint at the Eagle and Boar pub, he spent his time buried deep in relics of centuries past in the basement of the Ashmolean Museum.

Samuel Palmer had held his interest more than any other as he delved into the wood carvings and drawings of the lesser known artist.

Moeris and Galatea–the work done in sepia–
had fascinated him. It had been his favorite of
Palmer's drawings.

However, on such a tight budget he was only
able to purchase a reduced size printed copy at the
museum gift shop.

If he remembered correctly, he had it tucked
away somewhere in a picture album, or maybe it
was one of the things he'd left behind with his ex-
wife. He couldn't remember. Drawing a sigh, Don's
thoughts drifted back to when he was a college
student in Oxford.

On weekends he and other American students
took day trips to Blenheim Palace or Bath and
London where he visited the Tate Museum and
took in a few Shakespearean plays. He didn't care
too much for the plays, he'd never really cared
much for Shakespeare, but the girls did and so he
tolerated the performances.

One weekend a group of students journeyed to
Paris, another weekend they visited Ireland. But the
last weekend of his stay in England–the weekend
he was supposed to fly to Germany–a trip he
strongly anticipated because of his German
heritage, he overslept after a late night at the Eagle
and Boar, and missed the flight.

Don had planned to look up long lost relatives
in Germany. Disheartened, he packed a small bag
and took the bus to Edinburgh, Scotland, instead.

The castle there was cool, especially the
dungeon. All the old torture apparatus fascinated
him as did the whole city itself. The cobblestone

streets, ancient buildings and the greenness of it all was captivating.

Wandering about, he found a little Russian restaurant where he experienced Borscht for the first time. It was okay. The salmon was good too.

After eating he ventured out into the city, so different, he thought, of typical American cities. Here large metropolises seemed more relaxed. Maybe that was because Europe's cities were much older.

Whatever the reason, he was enjoying the differences and the experiences.

He climbed Calton Hill and looked down at the red door of the Russian restaurant where he had just eaten and hiked along the narrow paths near the edges of the hill. It was very picturesque; he could see nearly the whole of the city.

Wandering along the outskirts of Edinburgh, he found himself in the countryside. It was as if he had stumbled onto a different world, one quaint and very pastoral. He thought of the scenes Palmer had penned and etched—it all reminded him so much of the artist.

Eventually he came upon a road sign, Blue Nose Road—he chuckled at the name and decided to wander down to see what lay further.

Flocks of sheep were fenced on either side of the road; they grazed peacefully as the fog rolled across the stone street and into the rolling hillsides.

He continued down, walking about a mile before he came upon a small fishing community; dories, cat rigged sailboats and a few trawlers were moored at the docks. The pictorial beauty was breath taking and he stood for several minutes drinking in what resembled sights he had only seen in the books he had been studying.

There, at the brink of the Firth of Forth, little houses dotted the hilly land stretching up from the water's edge. The slapping of tidal waters echoed from the moorings. His eyes scanned the landscape again and again, drinking it all in-committing it to memory.

On a low rise sat a rustic pub; he stepped along the cobblestones and stairways to the entrance.

Dimly lit, yet glowing with hospitable warmth, the room emitted an ambiance of comradeship and community—immediately Don felt drawn to the group of people within.

The patrons nodded as he entered, some smiled as he walked up to the bar and ordered, with a German accent, a pint of dark ale.

Why he did so, baffled him. His German was not that good. But the game of it all was too enticing to pass up. Years later, as he recalled the event, he referred to it as youthful exuberance—it was the only thing that made sense.

A woman, maybe in her late thirties sat at one of the tables. She was sipping her own pint and listening to the men gathered around her tell bawdy jokes; the woman laughed loudly with the men.

When she beckoned to Don to join her he did so. "Guten tag," he nodded as he pulled a chair near her.

"Ah, a German lad, they sure know how to build you there in Deutschland. Sarah tousled his thick blond hair and leaned close enough for him to smell the Chanel she wore.

"Bist du diejenige, auf die ich gewartet habe?" He smiled broadly

"Hey babe, sprechen ze English?" the woman retorted.

Don shrugged and nodded then responded with his best German accent, as if struggling with the English words, "only a little, bitta."

The neckline of her pheasant blouse was loose and exposed breasts overflowing from the red push up bra she wore. Her hair was bobbed short just above the neck. Her make-up was applied too thickly and her blue eye shadow too boldly above her mascara laden lashes.

The woman rubbed her hands across her breasts bursting over the low cut neckline of her blouse, licked her lips and moved her hand to Don's thighs, "I bet you're good. Aren't you, honey?"

The bewildered look on Don's face encouraged her to talk even more and she whispered explicit sexual acts in his ear and rubbed his thighs all the while believing he had no idea of what she was saying.

Smiling back at her, Don nodded.

Very aroused and feeling the buzz from the dark ale, Don growled, "Es wird ein lustigen abend, fettsack." He thrust his face into her breasts and shook back and forth, "blub, blub, blub—Da kommt freude auf—ha, ha."

By the end of the evening he found himself wrapped neatly between her dimpled thighs and more than ample breasts.

The next morning as he awoke, Don lay confused, trying to regain any memory of the previous night's events.

He glanced about the room; the skylight above him allowing excellent lighting to study his surroundings. They were simple, a bed and sink. A half opened door revealed a shower stall and toilet.

Slowly the memory of the previous evening became clearer. He grinned to himself and turned his body toward Sarah's. She was awake, lying on her back, her eyes focused it seemed on the wall directly across from her. She reached for the ashtray on a bedside table.

"You talk in your sleep, sugar." Propping herself against the headboard Sarah picked a marijuana roach from the ashtray and lit it. Rubbing her eyes she barked, "Shut the curtains, Herr American, and what's the idea of pretending you're German." She sucked loudly on the roach, inhaling the smoke and slid her eyes over Don's naked body, "I could have gotten that in the states."

Don sighed, as he recalled the first time he ever met Sarah. A curse word fell silently from his lips as he shook his head.

If he had known he would ever run into her again he would have traveled to Tasmania to avoid doing so. He scowled ruefully, "Oh my God, why me, why me?" Saying the words aloud, Don leaned against the étagère.

"Too much," the detective spoke loudly as he tried to wipe the images of the younger Sarah and the Sarah he had seen last, disfigured and swollen, from his mind.

He pulled open the glass door to the balcony and walked out, breathing in the salty air.

The breezes had kicked up a bit and though warm, they refreshed his thoughts. Turning to re-enter the bedroom, Don walked back to the étagère.

Displayed inside, on the three glass shelves, were assorted figurines. On the top shelf was an ivory carved elephant, a jade Buddha, and several glass dogs held together by a tiny chain.

A couple of tall thin vases stood toward the back of the shelf.

On the center shelf were some ceramic birds; a shorter, more stout vase, another set of animals—this time elephants, strung together by a thin chain.

Studying them, he noticed the dust particles on the glass; he moved a figurine, beneath it the glass was clear.

Don's eyes wandered to the bottom shelf; it held five Hummels, nothing else.

Don recognized them; one of his aunts had been a collector. Aunt Helen, that was who he remembered, she owned three Hummels. The boy in the apple tree looked vaguely familiar, so did the girl with the umbrella and the one that looked like a hobo—those stood in his mind as figurines he recalled seeing in his aunt's knickknack shelf those many years ago.

But he wasn't sure. All he recalled was how big a fuss his mother and his aunt had made over him trying to touch them and how the women scolded him, warning that if he broke one it would cost him at least a year's allowance to replace it.

He was not familiar with anything more about Hummels, As far as he was concerned, they were little more than trinkets old ladies loved to look at.

He moved closer to the glass of the Sarah's cabinet and examined the figurines more closely. One of them, the one of the boy in the apple tree had a small chip at its base; it was barely noticeable. The others were in perfect condition as far as he could tell.

Perhaps someone entered her home with the intention of stealing her assets, Don considered as he shook his head. "No, there's really not enough there to amount to more than a few hundred, maybe a thousand if you're lucky . . . but then again," he continued, "to someone it just might be enough."

Fashioning a scenario of an intruder entering the house and being surprised by Sarah, Don squinted, "No, there were no signs of struggle, no signs that would indicate an intruder -not on this floor-not on any of the floors."

"Sarah was too smart to fall prey to an intruder. And besides, maybe it was an accident—maybe she went swimming at night and had a heart attack."

He thought for a moment as he looked about the room once again. "No. This is murder."

"Sarah got herself killed because of drugs." Don spoke aloud as he walked about the master bedroom. "Hmm. . . " His eyebrows furrowed and then quickly released, "It wasn't Reggie who killed her," his voice softened. "Three plates, Reggie,

Sarah . . . there was a third person . . . Reggie's bound to turn up any day."

Still studying the figurines, Don considered both of his "partners." Sarah was the smartest of all the trash he had been associating with since he came to Topsail.

She was the one in control of everything. Reggie worked for her, so did Milton.

Don wondered who else did. He considered that since Sarah was not greedy she was content to enjoy the relatively small amount of money that her "business" earned.

He had learned that Sarah's little group of bridge players In New York were the same ones who visited her in the summer months. These were her only clients—and as she had explained, it kept things small and therefore safe.

Reggie, on the other hand, took his cut with the understanding that he supplied *only* the local big dogs—the shop owners and high dollar realtors. There were only a handful of them—the same ones that had been there from the beginning.

Sarah did not want to dirty her hands by cutting the coke down, that was Reggie's job.

What she sold was the highest quality, and only her clients were entitled to that.

But recently, in the last few months Reggie had been talking about wanting to take his portion and stepping on it again, cutting it even more and selling it by the gram.

Sarah had been adamant. She wanted no more cutting than was already being done and she wanted no more clients.

Don recalled Sarah's words—*If you don't like the way things are and you think you can do better, you're free to leave.*

She'd complained about Reggie's nagging to him. She complained about a lot of things to Don. It seemed to him that complaining was one of her favorite things to do. So he assumed that after a few weeks had passed without Sarah mentioning Reggie and his request, that it was over. Or at least Reggie had decided to go behind her back and cut the coke without her knowledge.

Don suspected that the New York know it all, had done just that.

After all, Reggie was a spoiled brat.

Why he had moved to the barrier island was beyond Don. But like many other rich brats, Reggie had come for the low-key lifestyle available to those who could afford it. It was typical, even common on the island.

Don's s brow furrowed as he thought of the two people he despised yet was forced to do business with.

He thought he'd seen it all when he was in the military and stationed in Iraq and Afghanistan. He'd met all kinds of liars, and cheats—thieves and other low lifes who didn't give a damn about anyone but themselves.

But Sarah and Reggie took the whole cake. Maybe that was so because they were the two people out of all the others he had met that he could not simply walk away from. They had him by the nuts.

Who would have thought he would be standing in the house of some woman he met twenty years ago in Scotland? It was all too surreal.

Who would figure that a New York tramp would be the Lieutenant of a drug ring in such a tiny town in North Carolina?

Who would believe that a dumpy old nobody would have so much power? Yes, she had the obnoxious arrogant personality that went along with power—he had learned that those who have never been used to power often abuse it. Sarah wielded her power like a baton.

He smirked, irritated that Sarah, even in death, would not leave him alone. Her image came to his mind again.

From afar she had appeared to be dressed as a queen holding a scepter. But as he pulled the car into her driveway he realized it was just a overweight woman in a bathrobe holding a plunger.

Don laughed aloud, recalling that evening several years back as a novice drug dealer. He hadn't recognized her at first then, but she had known him. And when she smiled and batted her lashes, the image of her decades before came swirling back.

When he handed her the package, she squinted her eyes, jerked her head back in a loud raucous laugh and roared, "Herr American."

It seemed the events of the past were now humorous and she waved them away with a sweep of her hand saying that it was all water under the bridge and that the two of them had been young and foolish.

But a few weeks later dispatch called and he was instructed to check out a complaint of vandalism at her home. He wondered if she had purposely called at a time when she knew he was on duty.

He remembered that night so vividly, driving up to her house on Ocean Front Drive, thick humidity hanging in the night air.

"Someone has pulled up all my pampas grass." She had barked, "Find out who it is and make them pay me back. That stuff is expensive." Her condescending tone annoyed Don as he stepped from his car.

She eyed him curiously as he walked toward her. "See that it's done, *Herr Officer.*"

Don stared at her, "I thought that was all water under the bridge."

"Humph. Maybe it is and maybe it isn't."

He squared his shoulders, and peered deeply into her face. Stepping back a few paces he captured the full view of her. In the evening breeze her loud brightly colored muumuu belied the bulges and sag of her aging body. Raising his head his gaze met hers and the corners of his mouth turned upward. She looked like an old joke.

"You think this is funny?" Sarah asked.

His eyes found the gravel at his feet and he shook his head, "No ma'am."

As he scanned the ground near Sarah's feet, he noticed how black with dirt her bedroom slippers were. It occurred to him that perhaps she had pulled the grass up herself.

He lifted his eyes to meet hers.

114

"I was trying to put it back," she hissed.

Raising an eyebrow, Don shrugged. "It's awfully late to be outside checking out the shrubbery, is all I'm saying."

Sarah ran her thumb and forefinger around her mouth, wiping away the crumbs of some left over tidbit. Settling her hands on her ample hips, she lifted her chin. "I heard something earlier but just thought it was the wind–the chimes were going nuts."

She ran a hand along the loose skin of her neck, and lifted her chin even more. "I was watching an old show on Turner Classic Movies– Double Indemnity, you know, that old movie with Barbara Stanwyck and Fred MacMurray."

The names sounded familiar to Don, he vaguely remembered watching an old television show with an actor by the man's name.

He shook his head, "Never heard of it . . . what's that got to do . . ."

Interrupting him, Sarah licked her lips, "you kind of remind me of MacMurray, except you're a blond." She rubbed her upper arm and licked her lips again. "I was just thinking about all this trouble around here, and *you* being so involved with *things* –maybe we can take a little of those *things* out in trade."

Don leaned against his car and crossed his arms, "I don't think that's a good idea, Miss Chambers." His tone was dismissive and abrupt, more so than he would have liked it to have been. Still, his eyes met hers with a certainty that could not be ignored.

To his surprise, Sarah backed down. Laughing, she touched her heavily hair sprayed coif and slid her eyes from his to the gravel at her feet.

Her lips curled into a sneer. "I know I've gotten dumpy in my old age, but I thought it was worth a try. Anyway you have improved with time . . . and I guess it is always best to never mix business with pleasure."

She lifted her face, her eyes held the steely gaze Don was familiar with.

"Anyway, what are you going to do about all this pampas grass?"

'I'll look in to it." Don's jaws tightened as he brushed a mosquito away from his face. He asked a few questions regarding the times she heard the noises outside and told her she needed to report any strange behavior she might notice.

Sarah chuckled, "*Nobody* bothers me, Detective Belkin . . . nobody. I've got these two men that are always by my side," she patted the pocket of her dress where her thigh bulged. "Smith and Wesson," Sarah winked. "Two best men I've ever known."

Nodding, Don grinned, "Well, it's more than likely some kids around here are just having some mischievous fun, Miss Chambers."

She looked smugly at him, eying his frame. He *had* kept himself in shape over the years.

Pulling her muumuu loosely from her skin, she drew her eyes from his, "Little snots have no respect for anyone anymore."

Since then, Sarah had never mentioned the Scotland incident or tried to make advances to Don.

116

That was one thing he was grateful for.

"I can't change the past," Don muttered as he focused on the contents of Sarah's bedroom; the bed was laden with stuffed animals and pillows, his eyes followed the wall—*no teal and mauve pictures here*, he thought as he walked closer to a framed picture.

"And here's my past staring me right in the face again—damn."

His eyes studied the drawing on the south wall next to the huge king size bed—*Moeris and Galatea*, his favorite of all the Samuel Palmer etchings.

It was hanging on *her* bedroom wall—but unlike the copy he had purchased so long ago in Oxford, this picture was not a reprint—it was the real thing or a really good fake—who knew with Sarah. Either way, it was fantastic.

Without knowledge of the artist, Samuel Palmer, and the period in which he lived, no one would have known the value of the drawing.

It seemed childlike but upon closer inspection the intricacy was profound. He had fallen in love with it then, seeing it up close, he fell again.

Palmer had drawn a scene of a slow rolling hillside thick with hanging trees and shrubbery before an ocean; sunrise shimmered across the water. It was intricate, painstakingly so.

The picture reminded Don of the north Inlet of Topsail Island—or at least what it used to look like decades before when he had been stationed at Camp Lejeune as a young Sergeant in the Marine Corps.

117

He'd been working in the Criminal Investigation Division and often had the opportunity to go there when off duty. Usually he brought his new wife, Maggie there for picnics.

Those were happier days before their move to California, before her drug addiction and before hordes of developers descended to demolish much of the island's natural beauty.

At that time low hills and dunes graced the north end of the island from the ocean to the sound. Merkle bushes and scrub oaks stood thick, providing hammocks here and there.

There was a fresh water pond located among the wide expanse of grasses and sand; Don recalled filling a jug of clear water there as he walked the sandy paths askew with driftwood and sea shells.

He often thought that if they had stayed at Topsail rather than moving to California, as Maggie had insisted, their marriage may have had a chance.

He'd never gotten Topsail out of his mind and when things took a turn for the worse, the island was the first and only place he'd considered for refuge.

He sighed heavily as he perused the drawing. It had been a long time ago since the island looked like that-so peaceful.

Studying the picture less intently, Don considered that peace may have been the reason so many people had moved here.

Sarah, maybe you did have some redeeming qualities.

Chapter Nine

"Two within a week. Kind of odd, ain't it Belkin?"

Shaking his head as he walked through the tall marsh grass, Buck Butler grimaced as he bent to move the grasses aside, providing a better view for the detective.

"Seems to be an epidemic." Leaning a bit to the side, Don Belkin straightened his baseball cap to fit more securely on his head.

Quietly and without hesitation, the detective waded into the marshy waters of the sound. The dark blue of his jeans was now wet above the knees. He peered intently at the body resting against a fallen scrub oak log and scribbled notations into his notebook before stuffing it into his back pants pocket. Leaning forward and reaching into the murky sound waters, he felt around.

"Whatcha lookin' for? Drop your watch?" Buck guffawed, his thin body bouncing as he stuffed his hands into his pockets.

He watched as the detective breathed a heavy sigh and blew a "humph" from his lips.

"Did you touch this man or anything around here?" Belkin asked solemnly as he studied Buck's lopsided straw hat. Eying what looked like the butt end of a roach peaking through the raggedy headband, Belkin shook his head.

"Nope, not a thing." Buck straightened the hat, "You don't think this is a coincidence do you?" He moved aside as the detective leaned in again. "I mean, with that Chambers woman and now this. You thinking they're connected in any way?"

"Um." Ignoring the question, Don raised a hand to rub the back of his neck.

"Whatcha think?" Buck asked again, his overbite resting on his bottom lip.

"I think he's dead." Belkin glanced up, sliding his eyes sardonically toward the man.

"Ya think," Buck guffawed. "Shouldn't you turn him over or something?"

"Do you really want to see a face with no eyes?" Annoyed, Don glanced toward Buck. "What were you doing out here so early in the morning?"

Buck's lips parted as he shook his head in response to the first question—he looked quizzically at the detective to answer the second, "Fishin'— Don, now—you know I ain't got no part in this. I just found the damn Yankee."

"How do you know he's a Yankee?" Trying to hold back a grin, Don gazed down at the body once again.

"Ain't nobody 'round here wears them plaid Bermuda shorts like them. They all do it—wear plaid shorts like they're the biggest fad on earth," Buck's brow furrowed, "and you know it." He looked deeper into the murky sound waters; he could make out the small crabs and fish scurrying around the head of the dead man. Mesmerized, he could not look away until the sound of cars motoring down the rutted path to the landing startled him back to reality.

"Exactly what time did you find the body?" Don ignored the slamming of car doors and crunch of shoes on gravel from the police officers as they neared the site.

An ambulance pulled alongside the patrol cars; Buck lifted his head and waved to a familiar face, "Hey, Mary Lou."

The woman nodded, "Hey Buck, "Who'd you kill now?"

"Huh?" He turned apprehensively toward Belkin, "I ain't—"

"Oh, I'm just picking on you Bucky," the driver chuckled.

Detective Belkin lowered his head, "Never mind that. Now, tell me—when did you find our friend here?"

"Let's see. I left the house around five thirty this morning," Buck answered nervously, his thoughts tangled between the dead man and the marijuana cigarette in his pocket.

Detective Belkin glanced once more at his head. Suddenly Buck remembered the roach in the hat headband.

Immediately his hand drew to his head and his eyes grew wide as he tried to avoid Detective Belkin's gaze.

"Where do you live?" Don knew where Butler lived, but he loved rattling Buck's cage. He could tell by the man's fidgeting, that he was getting nervous; he nearly laughed out loud when Buck backed up several steps.

Nodding a welcome to the officers as they stepped from the patrol car, Buck smiled, then answered Don's question.

"Down Mill Creek Road, you know that Don–Detective Belkin." As he rubbed the thighs of his jeans, Buck stammered, "I just–I just wanted to get out and do a little fishing this morning before all the tourists got on them jet skis and–and started tearing up the water." He smirked. "Damn idiots-damn Yankees–scaring the fish away–messing up everything."

"Um." Don muttered. "You never told me what time you got here."

"You never gave me a chance!" Pouting, Buck thrust both hands in his pockets and toyed once again with the marijuana cigarette. "I just set out with my cast net. I was planning on catching some pogy for bait. My cousin Hank wanted me to get him some 'cause he was planning on going out to the Gulf Stream today." Buck rubbed his forehead. "So, I'd say I got here around six this morning . . . or near 'bouts that time. Didn't think to check my watch when I called you."

"Okay, Buck." Don met the man's eyes, then turned his attention toward one of the officers, he motioned with his arms, "Okay, cordon off this space."

Nodding to the photographer, the detective called out, "You know what to do."

He turned his attention to Buck once more, "Did you leave the body at any time, Mr. Butler?"

So it's Mr. Butler now, Buck thought to himself as he tensely eyed Don. "Nope, just waited right here for you to arrive—and I guess my cousin ain't getting' his bait."

"Nope . . . I guess not." Don grinned, sliding his eyes sharply toward Buck's hat. "When you see Hank, say hello for me." The detective nodded and moved from the water.

Buck stood quietly watching the officers as they sunk narrow slats of wood into the marshy ground and cordoned off the area near the body with yellow tape.

The photographer was snapping from various angles, some of which Buck considered bizarre. But then again, he thought, he'd seen actors on television behaving similarly. He sniggered and drew his shoulders back, inhaling deeply, *I found it—him. They're probably going to want to take me in for questioning—like they do on television—maybe put me on the news.*

He heard someone clear their throat and suddenly he felt self conscious. His eyes studied Officer Abbott—he'd talked with him just the other day at the grocery store.

Buck leaned to get a better view of the name tag pinned to the officer standing next to Abbott. *C. Rosell*; he knew that name. He used to go fishing with a man named Rosell. It was a familiar name in the area. *I bet I know that boy's kinfolk.* Buck mustered a grin and nodded to the policemen, but they behaved as if they'd never seen him before.

They're all acting weird—showing off their big shot police skills, Buck thought as he shrugged and curled his upper lip.

He continued watching the officers as they pulled the body from the marsh. "Ugh!" A queasiness rose from Buck's stomach, "Geez, hell!" He bared his teeth and growled, "Damn!"

A single crab clung to one eyelid of the body; Buck shuddered and watched as Detective Belkin reached a hand into the back pocket of the dead man's plaid Bermuda shorts.

Don flipped open the leather wallet, brushing away droplets of water from the picture ID, "Reginald Bourne, age forty-eight, North Carolina resident," he said aloud, "Not anymore."

"He's a bit waterlogged, wouldn't you say?" Buck sniggered, trying to hide the nausea as he gulped vomit back down his throat.

Stepping back as the men brushed silently against him to lift the body onto a gurney, Buck stared. His mouth fell open; he could feel beads of sweat popping out on his forehead. The men seemed so reticent in their duty; they appeared as strangers. It bothered Buck that local folks would treat him so.

Why were they acting like they didn't even know him now? He expected that kind of behavior from the transplants, former military guys that joined the force. But the local boys, the ones whose families he'd grown up with, they seemed like strangers in the presence of their Detective Belkin. He wondered just what had been said to make them so rigid and distant. He didn't understand why they all were treating him like an outsider.

Buck felt Belkin's eyes on him as his thoughts wandered from the dead man to the officers; he looked quickly toward Belkin, and then just as quickly turned his eyes and body away. Did Belkin know? Did Belkin suspect that he had pot on him now? That he sold a little on the side? Did he care? Was Belkin going to arrest him? Was that why they were treating him like a criminal?

Hell, I just grow it for myself. Hell, I don't really sell it. It's more like a donation when I give a buddy a joint or two—they leave a few dollars, that's all.

Buck felt his face redden. He placed his hands in his pockets and felt the cigarette deep in its corner. *Oh boy, they're going to arrest me. I'm going to jail.*

Immediately his hands went to his straw hat, he pulled it tightly against his scalp as chill bumps covered his arms and as he backed further away from the crime scene.

"Need me anymore, Don?"

Belkin eyed him curiously, his lips turned downward, "I don't know. You're acting pretty nervous this morning." He stepped a few paces toward Buck and watched as his eyes grew wider and wider. Again, he could hardly keep from laughing out loud, "Nope, I don't need you anymore, Buck. Just don't leave town." As he turned his back to the man a broad grin crossed his lips and he chuckled to himself. He knew he'd just scared the crap out of the man.

Don doubted seriously that Buck had anything to do with this murder—or any other. Buck was known simply as the local ne'er do well with barely a penny to his name. He eked out a living from fishing, shrimping and oystering, and sold his seafood from the tailgate of his Chevy pickup at the side of the road. No, Buck Butler was not a suspect.

This was drug related—the drugs *he* had been dealing—he'd bet his next paycheck on it. And he was certain that Sarah and Reggie had pissed someone off enough for them to be killed. But who was it? He had to find out who before anything led to him.

******

Leaning back in the chair, Don propped his feet on the desk; he settled his arms on the faux leather armrests and stared out the window of his rented beach cottage.

The image of Reggie floating face down in the water filled in his mind. His body was not nearly as grotesque as Sarah's barnacle-mauled corpse had been, but it was still unsettling.

A couple of days had passed since finding the bodies and gathering information on Sarah had not been difficult. NCIC reported she was clean; not even a speeding ticket.

As for her personal life, the first marriage ended in divorce. She received alimony until she married Navy Corpsman, Chief Petty Officer Greg Chambers.

CPO Chambers was seven years younger than Sarah. They'd met in New York City and lived there until his transfer to Camp Lejeune in Jacksonville, North Carolina.

Locals in the back-gate town of Sneads Ferry area alleged that the move had pleased both CPO Chambers and his wife; they seemed happy and excited about southern coastal living.

They bought a small soundfront house a few miles from the back gate to the Marine Corps base, made friends with neighbors, had cookouts and parties. They bought a nineteen foot Grady White and on calm days motored over to Topsail Island; Sarah spent the time sunbathing while Greg fished.

Life looked good for the Chambers'.

September 11, 2001 changed everything for the couple, as it did for many military families, and by June of 2002 Greg received orders for deployment to Iraq.

Two months later Sarah heard the news that her husband had been killed in action. She moved immediately back to New York City.

Her life there, since her husband's death, was lead quietly.

She met a couple times a week with friends to play mah jongg and she was a member of a book club.

In the winter months she rented an apartment in Zephyrhills, Florida and every October she traveled to Europe for a two week stay.

She led a pretty predictable life and appeared to have become a creature of habit since her late husband's death in 2002.

Even during the months on Topsail she continued her mah jongg and book club gatherings. Sometimes she would have lunch at one of the beach restaurants with one or more of the northern visitors. She was never seen with any locals and had earned a reputation, among the waitresses and clerks of various businesses, as being condescending and arrogant.

Leaning back in his chair, Don propped his feet on the desk, "Humph, that's Sarah, she was the nouveau riche Yankee who treated locals like crap."

For a moment he felt the glow of finality—the feel that retribution had been accomplished.

"No more Sarah, no more Reggie, I'm a free man," he mumbled silently to himself.

His sense of relief was short lived though, as he wondered just who had killed the two people he disliked most and if the killer knew about him. Was he next on the list?

Don shook his head, *I have to find out who did this.* Folding his arms across his chest he nodded, *yes, drugs are involved, I am certain of that.*

They argued over the last shipment. Reggie was stepping on it too much?

"Sarah didn't trust Reggie—she didn't trust anyone. Everyone was a means to an end, for her.

"It must be awful lonely not having anyone you can trust and not having any friends," Don ground his teeth as his jaw tightened.

Of course, since I got involved with Sarah, I've been in the same boat.

His thoughts rambled back to his own plight, *don't hardly go out or hang with the other guys on the force . . . And Phil, my own kid, I don't really even know him. Maybe I'm not so different than Sarah.*

Inhaling a long breath, he tried to focus on the crime–on Sarah–on Reggie.

"Crap," Pushing himself from the desk, Don rose, "I've got to get out of here and clear my head."

It was late In the day and only a few couples lingered, strolling along the shore. Don studied them all, it was habit. They looked benign, harmless. *What evil lurks in the heart's of men?* The thought brought a smile to his lips as he recalled the line from THE SHADOW, an old radio show his father used to tell him about.

I came to the beach to clear my head, now do it. Beleaguered steps to the shore belied Don's troubled stated of mind. Again his eyes scanned the people walking along the beachfront.

The laughter of a family, caught his attention. It seemed to break the rhythm of the waves and all at once he felt distant from the things he once believed he wanted. Turning his face into the breeze, he thought of his son, Phil. Their relationship was nonexistent. There was no bond and he found himself wondering why he had ever gotten custody of the boy–it was obvious that Phil couldn't stand the sight of him.

Don studied the shells at his feet. Spying a shark's tooth, he stooped to pick it up. Instantly it reminded him of the one Reggie wore around his neck.

The last time I made a delivery to Sarah's house, they were standing outside arguing about cutting the coke.

"What was that he said?" Belkin searched his memory.

'It's not fair, for the less fortunate to do without,' "That was it," Don heard Reggie's voice from a few weeks prior.

'I've got friends that would buy—maybe they can't pay as much, but that's where I could cut things. That way everybody wins.'

Reggie had insisted that he needed to step on his portion at least once, maybe twice.

But Sarah was adamant; there would be no more cutting, no more clients. She wanted no variations and no growth.

Don kicked at the sand beneath his feet and lowered his head to study the swath of shells he had come upon.

For a moment his mind left the gritty crime events as he slowly scanned them.

Bending, he reached to pick up an olive shell. It was perfect. Rubbing the sand from it with his fingers, he pushed it into his pocket and continued walking along the beach, his thoughts returning to his former associates.

Sarah thought Reggie was getting greedy—Don nodded as he placed one foot in front of the other into the sinking sand.

He should have kept his mouth shut about it, but he had to tell Sarah what he wanted to do.

"Should have just gone ahead and done it," Don spoke aloud into the rising wind. "Because, the moment he was told no, I knew—and so did Sarah— that he was going to do it anyway."

Maybe that's what happened—that made sense. Maybe he sold to someone and they were dissatisfied. Maybe Sarah killed him when she found he disobeyed her. But who killed Sarah? Maybe they killed each other. No—the third plate— someone I don't know about killed them both over the cocaine.

Don considered all the maybes—there were too many. But he was certain the deaths of Sarah and Reggie were over the drugs and that made him very vulnerable.

Feeling the warm breeze as it played with his short cropped hair, Detective Belkin stuffed his hands in his pockets, found the olive shell and turned it around and around, *I've got to be damn careful*, he cursed beneath his breath, frustrated with his own life . . . and then there was his son.

"Some damn father I am."

There was a chance he could right things. Sarah and Reggie were dead. "Yes, I can concentrate on the boy now." *But I was supposed to be at that dinner. As far as I know—I'm supposed to be dead too.*

Was he really a potential victim? In the years he'd been involved with Reggie and Sarah, Don had never felt as if his own life was in danger. But now? It most definitely was.

He felt the encroaching tide lap at his shoes; the sun was at his back, warming it as the sky before him dimmed. The beach was empty now and he walked slower.

What if I admitted it all. Told them what I've been doing since I got here. Just the thought brought a sense of relief to him. He could feel the tension leave his shoulders.

It would make things a lot easier, but then again, it would probably end up in prison.

Don rubbed his forehead; he wasn't prone to headaches, but in the last few days it seemed he kept one. *What is so odd about this case? Is it because I'm tied to it? Is that why?*

Everything he felt, everything he'd been taught as a youth, as a Marine, and as a policeman was utterly opposed to what he was doing. Before moving to Topsail *that* man, the one who held to those ideals had been searching for a better life—a less complicated life. "Ha," Don smirked. "What was I complaining about? Look at things now."

Topsail is a great place to live—still small enough to enjoy that feel of community. I like that. And sometimes it feels like home—but damn Reggie—damn Sarah. He shook his head, *the girl—. Carrie. I like her.* For a moment the corners of his lips began to lift. *What if I could be with a woman like that.*

He laughed at himself and the daydream, indulging it a bit farther: *With a woman like that I'd leave here. Maybe go north back home to Pennsylvania. Now that Sarah is gone . . .*

"I'll take the boy . . . "He began aloud, then shook his head as he considered his brat child whom he knew was a pot smoker and who knew what else. The kid was a mess and what woman wants to take on a messed up kid who is always high?

Was it Buck that was the boy's supplier? Don thought about that and sniggered. Or could it be Reggie who was selling to him?

It sounded like something the bastard would do.

Suppressing his rising anger, Don stopped for a moment and gazed out into the darkening sky. It was not a well lit night; clouds obscured most of the stars and the moon too, as it hung eerily in the sky above the deep green waters. A few whitecaps jumped here and there as he felt the wind kick up.

He noticed, in the dimming light that the people had left the beach; he was alone.

As Don struggled between the calm and peace the ocean offered and the chaos of his life, he chose the latter and began sifting through the information he'd gathered about the man he detested.

Reggie had been a low-life even up north. The National Crime Investigation Center related that he had a couple of misdemeanors for possession of hash and that he had been arrested once for assault and battery.

Since dropping out of college, he'd had a progression of menial jobs that only lasted a few months each. And despite coming from an upscale

New York family, Reggie had found his niche among petty thieves and other slackers.

Don speculated that there had probably been a rift in the relationship between him and his family; the report stated that his parents had not heard from him in nearly a year.

One would have never guessed that he'd attended one of the finer prep schools or that his family was worth several million dollars from the way the man dressed. Usually he wore plaid shorts, flip flops and raggedy polo shirts. Most of the time he was unshaven.

Reggie would have fooled anyone. But, there it was. For some reason Reggie had chosen crime over the comforts his own family could have given him.

Who knows what makes people do things, Don gazed out to the ocean once again. "It's not my job to find out why. The fact is, he made his own choices."

Since moving to Topsail, Reggie had worked as a dishwasher, prep cook and on occasion went fishing and shrimping with friends. Aside from those occasional jobs he had no source of income, other than what he procured from the sale of drugs.

Don wondered how Sarah and Reggie had met. They were total opposites. Granted, they were both condescending and arrogant—*class has nothing to do with being an asshole,* the detective sniggered. *But Reggie wasn't half as pretentious and condescending as that old bat.*

She placed herself above locals. Reggie did not. He melded right in. He'd become a tobacco chewing, crotch-scratching good old boy—except for his penchant for plaid shorts and his northern accent.

On paper there was nothing to tie the two together. They were never seen together and neither frequented the other's favorite places. They were as different as night and day and there seemed no connection or suggestion that they even knew one another—except for one thing.

Officer Abbott reported that a barmaid at the Brass Pelican had commented on an event that occurred several months earlier. According to the barmaid, Sarah had entered the Brass Pelican looking for Reggie. She described Sarah to a tee and had overheard Reggie call her by name.

'She pushed the door open and stood for several seconds looking out at everybody—didn't say a single word. She had her hands on her hips and she looked mad as hell.'

The barmaid went on to describe how Sarah had walked toward Reggie once she spied him and how she'd grabbed him by the arm and pulled him toward a vacant table in the back.

'Her finger was just wagging,' The tall blonde girl shook her head. *'Then she walked on out after a couple of minutes—he just stood there—then it wasn't long after and he left—you know, he always tipped me good, real good.'*

The moon had risen by now, and a cooler breeze now played with the hairs of his exposed arms, *salty air always feels so fine.* The thought brought a smile to Don's lips.

Running his fingers through his short blond hair, Don swallowed hard, "What a tangled web we weave," he spat as his eyes slid to his feet; a devil's shopping bag lay in the sand just to the left of his weathered loafers. He leaned to pick it up.

Once, while flipping through the channels on television, he'd seen a documentary on sting rays and skates; he flipped the black egg sack from side to side, "devil's shopping bag, huh. I got just the stuff to fill you up."

Chapter Ten

"They roll up the sidewalks around here after ten." Morgan Simpers guffawed, mimicking a conversation he had overheard while waiting in line at the grocery store.

Stepping from the small skiff, he grasped the lip of the prow, and pulled the boat into the thick marsh grasses.

He kicked off his rubber boots and slid on a pair of sneakers, then tucked his pony tail beneath his ball cap.

Leaning back into the small boat, he pulled an oblong canvas bag to his shoulder then rubbed his thumb between the strap and where it settled against his body.

He cocked his head to the side and breathed in the strong pungent smell of the marsh.

Glancing around at the now quiet community that lay just beyond the marshy area of the barrier island's sound side, Morgan took a deep breath and stepped forward.

It was quiet. It was two-thirty in the morning; no one was around.

He'd been watching the last day or so and had figured out the routine of the local cops; every night between ten and midnight they checked out the Chambers' place, driving by slowly.

Then they drove by once again between four-thirty and six in the morning when the sun was up.

Morgan was confident he would not be caught. Taking a deep breath, he tried to reassure himself of that.

The lights of Surf City Fishing Pier shone hazily in the distance and though the moon and stars were out, the clouds hid most of them. He watched as the night sky peeked from behind the moving clouds.

The roaring of the Atlantic seemed to keep beat with the thumping of his heart; there was no denying he was a little nervous, he had reason to be. He sure didn't want to get caught in Sarah Chambers' house.

As he walked from the marsh to the highway, a single car passed, he could hear music drifting from its open windows.

His eyes followed the car as the tail lights grew smaller and smaller—no, they wouldn't have noticed him.

Dressed in dark jeans and a dark sweat shirt, Morgan made sure to move among the scrub oaks as he made his way toward Sarah's house.

Once he heard loud laughter followed by a drunken request for Suzy to get her clothes on.

He turned toward the commotion in the distance and chuckled at what he knew was youth run amok.

Do not walk on sand dunes–fine of up to $300–the sign next to a wooden beach access stairway announced.

Morgan shook his head in dismay, recalling how as a child he had played among the dunes, using the sea oat stalks as swords when he played pirates with his friends.

All the daggone tourists screwing up and trashing the place ruined all that, he thought as he made his way among the foliage and rental houses toward Sarah's tall beach front home.

The last thirty years–picturing the small fishing village that once was Surf City, Morgan felt his tension ease–it was a simpler time. He nodded and smiled.

A scowl quickly reached his brow and his lips tightened into a line as he stepped toward the pavement where row after row of houses glared at him. Their windows were all dark. No cars were in the driveways. "No one is renting this week." Morgan smiled.

Everything had changed; everything on the island had changed and in his opinion it was now overbuilt and overrun with people who didn't give a damn about the island itself.

Palm trees and pampas grass lined the driveways and skirted the perimeters of the summer rental homes; *there's no need for all this,* he thought as he moved among the foliage–it was easy now to hide among all the grasses and other

139

non-indigenous plants that home owners had planted along the driveways of their houses.

Making sure to avoid the cedar ground cover and loose pebbles that surrounded the pretentious trim, Morgan moved toward the side door of Sarah Chambers' summer vacation home.

He had watched Detective Belkin leave the house a few days before, the same day her body had been found. Since then he'd been watching and waiting for the perfect time.

He'd heard about the other body found in the sound too. "Somebody's got the right idea," Morgan whispered to himself. "Now, if we just had a good hurricane."

Morgan muffled a belch as he rounded the building to the north side. He could care less about the man in the sound or the woman whose house he was about to break in to, neither one of them had ever been nice to him and he'd seen how rude—how demeaning—they both had been to Carrie.

As far as he was concerned, they deserved what they got.

The north side of Sarah's home escaped the lights of the fishing pier, leaving Morgan engulfed in near darkness. With measured steps he moved along the edges of the big house, being careful not to disturb the shrubbery.

As he stooped in front of the door, he pulled the latex gloves from his pocket and stretched them over his fingers. His hand slowly slid across the door to find the knob.

Picking the lock easily, Morgan opened the door and gently closed it behind him.

The garage had the familiar smells of gasoline and beach sand. Tread marks were visible where once a vehicle had been. He recalled the Willis Jeep in which Mrs. Chambers often cruised the island.

He pictured her in his mind's eye; both hands on the wheel, her head tilted upward and that hair, always unmoving, held like cement against the breezes that whipped about as she drove.

"What a bitch," Morgan whispered to himself, "treats Carrie really bad."

The skin around his eyes gathered as he smiled, "Oops, I mean *treated* Carrle."

His eyes drifted to the beach chairs, stacked one on top of the other in one corner of the large room; a few lay on their side as if someone had toppled them.

He eyed the umbrellas and array of beach toys and coolers scattered next to them.

Glancing at the door in the rear of the garage, Morgan mumbled to himself, "Just that little room she had us add on."

He knew exactly where to go; he had helped build this house a decade or so before when he was working in construction—so he walked immediately to the other door in the far corner that led to the stairway. This one was not locked and he slowly grabbed the railing and moved upward.

Upon reaching the second floor, Morgan kicked off his sneakers and padded across the thick carpet of the living room; he could just make out the furniture. He moved toward the entertainment center.

Kneeling down to open its doors, Morgan pressed the switch to his flashlight and examined the contents of the outdated piece of furniture. Inside were stacks of dusty DVD cases; he recognized some of them that dated back several years.

Rising, he moved slowly throughout the room shining the flashlight along other shelves and tables.

"Humph, where are you?" he sing-songed.

The lingering aroma of fish wafted from the adjoining kitchen and he moved there, taking deliberate steps; his hand grazed the furniture as he did so.

The appliances reflected the glare of the moonlight and pier lights that seeped through the large oceanfront windows. The muted lighting dimly lit his way as he settled next to the large dining room table.

"Where's the fish?" Morgan raised an eyebrow and lifted his nose to smell the air.

"I can smell it." He scanned the table top; small flakes of crusted fish rested there. It was obvious that plates and silverware had been removed, leaving a ring of crumbs around where they had been.

Greasy smears reflected against the sheen of the wood. Rings marking where glasses had been were left. Morgan shook his head and guffawed as he recollected what his wife, Roz, would have said-'*You're going to ruin my table, dummy. Put a damn coaster or at least a napkin under your stupid glass.'*

"How can a glass be stupid?" Morgan rolled his eyes. "She's the one that's stupid and she'll find out just how stupid she is when I throw those divorce papers down in front of her. She's going to get the surprise of her life—that old biddy."

Morgan puffed his chest and continued searching. He remembered the layout of the building and he padded toward the other two rooms on the second floor. Their doors were wide open and he peered inside.

One had only a bed and dresser, no display case was in sight.

The other room appeared to be some sort of office—again, no display case.

"Darn." Curling his lip as he sneered, Morgan lumbered toward the next flight of stairs that led to the master bedroom of the house.

"Gotta be up there," he muttered. "They have to be there. Where else could they be?"

Closing his eyes, he pictured the figurines he had studied on the internet site. They must have been the same figurines Sarah had been talking about in the grocery store.

"Tsk." He sneered as the image of that day came to mind. "Wasn't that the day before she showed up at the pier, the day she bought the farm, kicked the bucket, and met her maker?" Morgan chuckled.

Loud and ostentatious Sarah had prattled on and on as she held the cell phone to her ear.

He remembered thinking that she should just turn on the speaker so the entire store could hear both sides of the conversation.

He listened to her voice; suddenly the inflection became less pronounced as she began to whisper—as if Sarah could ever speak quietly. Still, it was the best she could do.

Humbles? She was talking with someone about *humbles*? *Humble, humlet, humbol* – whatever the word was, he did not quite understand what Sarah meant but whatever she was talking about cost four hundred dollars. And yes, she had five of them.

Then he remembered Carrie's reaction as she listened to Sarah; her eyes had sparkled and a faint smile had crossed her lips.

"My mother had Hummels . . ." Carrie began. Morgan watched Sarah raise her hand as the cashier spoke the words.

"You probably mean she had copies, lots of dime store and cheapy dollar stores have things that look like them."

Carrie lowered her eyes and continued checking Sarah's groceries. When she was finished, she waited for Sarah to swipe her card. Sarah flipped it onto the counter, "I hate these things—you do it."

Oh, how he had wanted to swat her once across the head and dislodge her helmet of blond straw.

He watched Carrie politely take the card, swipe it and then thank her.

And then he watched Sarah waddle, pushing her cart toward the sliding glass doors.

The wheels in Morgan's head started turning.

Sarah had something Carrie liked. Sarah treated Carrie like whale poop. Someday he would make things right and could get those *hubbles* for Carrie.

As he looked into her eyes, Morgan smiled. "What is a humble–hamble, homble?" He shrugged.

Carrie giggled in response, "No, no–not a *humble*, it's a *Hummel*–H-u-m-m-e-l. They're little glass figurines-about this high." She stretched her thumb and middle finger to give an estimate of their height. "My mother had two, the one with the little boy in the apple tree and another with a little girl holding an umbrella."

She held her smile for several seconds, then sighed as she lowered her eyes, "I always liked them, and Mom said when she passed on they would be mine."

Taking a deep breath she continued, "but they got broken one day, long ago." She shrugged, "Just wasn't meant to be."

Later that evening Morgan looked up *Hummel* on his computer. He liked the figurines too–they looked old timey and childlike–innocent, just like he believed Carrie to be.

He wished then that he could get them for her. He *would* get them for her.

The top floor of the monstrous house smelled of perfume; it was a flowery scent and it seemed to attack Morgan's nostrils. He crinkled his nose, rubbed the side of his head and cleared his throat as he felt the first tingles of allergy begin.

Blowing a breath from his lips, he whispered, "Stinko." A brief glance from the bedroom window captured the silent sights of stillness along the island shore. A thin outline of the waves as they rolled in to caress the sand, and tiny lights in the southern distance that curved gently with the outline of the island caught his breath. No matter how long, no matter how many houses, sights like this roused his soul.

He nodded to himself—the clouds had moved on and the night sky was clearing, making room for the stars and crescent moon that shone above. He could see nearly to the southern end of the Island where the lights of Jolly Roger Fishing Pier flickered.

Morgan exhaled deeply. There was business at hand. He pulled his cap more tightly against his head and walked lightly to the large glass étagère that stood against the wall of the master bedroom of washed pine furniture.

Against the center wall was the king sized bed; he rolled his eyes at the mountain of pillows covering it. A large stuffed manatee sat amidst them. Morgan shook his head in disgust. "There are no manatees in North Carolina, there are no damn palm trees in North Carolina and there's no freaking pampas grass; they're not indigenous to this area," he shuddered, "stupid, stupid, fake, pretentious, ignorant, self-absorbed, buttheads."

Drawing his lips to purse, Morgan closed his eyes for a moment, gaining his composure. "I shouldn't let them get to me—they just make me so angry." Calmly he took another breath, this one more shallow.

"Okay, I'm okay now." Morgan flipped the long strap of his canvas carrying case from around his neck and placed the bag on the bed, opening it to reveal swaths of thick cotton padding and five small boxes, each containing cheap figurine—ones he had purchased at the local dollar store.

He unwrapped them slowly and set them carefully on the bed.

As Morgan pulled gently on the glass door of the étagère, he pushed his tongue behind his teeth, "Tsk." He smirked, recalling Sarah's habit of making the sound. "Freaking people come here and try to make it something it's not."

Pushing the glass door open, he wrapped his fingers around the small statuette of a boy swinging from an apple tree; he gently wrapped it in cotton and placed it in a box.

"Ah, what else have we got here?" He muttered to himself, "*Apple Tree Girl, Merry Wanderer, Cheeky Fellow* and *Umbrella Girl*." Each statuette he gently wrapped and set in a small white box.

Each box he tenderly settled in more cotton batting within the carrying case.

Then, mindful to make it appear as if nothing was missing from the étagère, he placed the five dollar store figurines in the exact places where the authentic statuettes had stood; the replacements fit nearly into the dust free spaces.

Closing the door to the étagère, he stepped back and admired his handiwork. "Can't tell the difference." He grinned, then gathered the carrying case, smoothing the bed where it had lain. He turned to leave.

"What's this?" Morgan drew his chin backwards as he eyed a framed drawing over the headboard of Sarah's bed. To him it looked odd–child-like even–similar to one of those pictures you see on someone's refrigerator door. But this picture looked faded with age.

"It's old as the dickens." Raising a finger to the drawing he shook his head and grumbled to himself, "probably something she drew when she was in the first grade."

With his fingers to his chin he studied the drawing; to him it looked silly; his top lip curled as he discarded the idea of taking it.

Morgan flipped his hand in the air. "Garbage," he muttered as he secured the case and settled the strap to his shoulder.

Chapter Eleven

The two bodies had been sent to Chapel Hill for autopsy; so far it had been determined that even though Reggie's body was found a day later than Sarah's, the time of their deaths was approximately the same. It looked as if they had died within only a few hours of one another.

This knowledge only supported Don's belief that the two had been murdered by the same person.

Contemplating the circumstances that could have led to their deaths, Don drove slowly along the road to Sarah's home; he groaned as he anticipated another search of her house. He felt his stomach tighten. *Everything could come crashing down*, he thought.

Small beads of sweat dotted his forehead.

Collecting his thoughts, endeavoring to diminish the fear, Don focused on the job at hand as he pulled into the gravel driveway. He turned off the ignition and sat in darkness as his thoughts wandered.

He already knew most of the information collected on Reggie and Sarah. Luckily, none of it pointed to him.

Don wiped his damp brow and brushed away a buzzing mosquito. He hated the damn things though this time of year they were not normally so bad; it would be late summer and early fall when they really became a problem.

Eying another mosquito settling quietly on the steering wheel, he cautiously raised his hand. Thwap! "Gottcha," the word spilled from behind his gritted teeth.

Feeling the quickened rise and fall of his chest, Don brought his hand to his brow, *Why did I let this happen? Why didn't I immediately go to the Chief when it all started with Milton?*

The times he had asked himself these questions in the last few days was in the hundreds.

He answered his questions aloud, "I was new on the force, brand new – no one would have believed me. It would have looked bad; I would have been the one to be suspect."

******

Detective Belkin rested against a wooden stool next to the long granite counter. Still feeling as if something was amiss, he studied the kitchen slowly.

The smell of seafood still lingered and he walked to the table where the place settings had been.

A few crumbs of corn muffin was all that remained of the earlier dinner. Officer Abbott had bagged everything; it wouldn't be long before the results came back from Raleigh.

Turning, Don eyed the stairway to Sarah's master bedroom; he climbed the stairs and made his way to the sliding doors.

Taking in the view, he reached to unlatch them, then stopped and turned toward the étagère.

"Curious." His brow furrowed as he bent to examine the figurines. "Weren't you Hummels the other night?"

He opened the glass door to examine them more closely.

"Ha! I'll have to see who has been patrolling Miss Sarah's home," he said sarcastically. "I wonder who has been visiting?" As he picked up one of the small statuettes, he noticed the dust ring and how it did not quite fit over it.

Reaching into his back pocket he extracted a plastic bag and placed the ceramic statues inside.

******

Today the results from forensics should be in, thought Don; he buckled his belt around his trim waist and pulled a tee-shirt over his head.

Turning his head to the muffled sounds of his son in the next room, Don lifted his head skyward, "please help that boy, I've got no clue how to."

"Phil, I'll drive you over to the Sea Gull Restaurant if you want to fill out an application for dishwasher. I know they need one." Don called as he ran a comb through his hair.

"I ain't washing nobody's dirty dishes," the boy called back.

"Any one of these restaurants around here could use a busboy . . ." Don heard the bedroom door slam before he finished the sentence; he sighed again and shook his head.

"If I didn't have all this crap coming down on me I'd take care of that brat—his mother sure did mess him up." The mumbled words flew from his lips.

As Don slipped his bare feet into a pair of worn out Topsider shoes he reached for the car keys on the hook above the kitchen counter.

Glancing back at his son's door, Don watched as Phil opened it and walked across the linoleum to the kitchen. Pushing open the screen door, he let it slam shut behind him.

He had on flip flops, "he's not going job hunting." Anxiety over the boy's hopeless future welled inside him and Don slammed a fist against the small kitchen table. "What in the world am I going to do with that kid?" he asked rhetorically.

Scrubbing a hand across his face, Don watched from the window as Phil slowly walked along the beach road. Ever since the boy had hooked Sarah's ear, he'd become even more distant.

He wondered what was going on inside his son's head. And though the boy had put up a front, Don knew that finding the body had disturbed him;

Phil had cried when he'd first arrived at the pier and the crime scene.

But right now, there wasn't much he could do about Phil—every effort to communicate was thwarted by sarcasm or silence.

Not bothering to lock the door of the little block beach house, Don placed an old soft drink crate in front of the screen door, then glanced quickly to make sure it was exactly over the two nearly invisible spots in the cement floor of his porch.

He slid into the seat of the Dodge Charger, backed out of his driveway and motored slowly next to Phil as he walked along the paved road.

It was too tempting to resist taunting his son as he passed the teenager and he gently tapped the horn several times.

"Hey kid. Getta job!" he called as he passed.

From his side mirror Don watched Phil flip him the bird; unintelligible words moved from the boys lips.

As Don popped a knuckle against the steering wheel and drew his lips into a tight line, part of him wanted to stop the car, grab the boy by the shirt and punch his face.

His heart sank at the thought immediately. "The kid is a mess," he said aloud as he sped up a bit; "I'll have to get to that when I get my own ass out of this sling."

* * * * * *

Forensics *was* in. Both victims had drowned. Both bodies contained tetrodotoxin, a poison found in a fish from the Far East. *Fugu*, it was called. He typed the letters and waited for the site to pop onto the computer screen.

The fish looked nearly identical to the blowfish found all along the southeastern seaboard.

"it's bigger, that's about the only difference."

Someone—a friend of Sarah's—must have fixed dinner and served poison fish. How well did she know that person—the cook—chef? Did she know she was eating blowfish? Was it an accident? "Hell no." His own voice startled him as the questions poured. *Who would serve poison fish? Why would someone want them dead?*

They were the same questions. Who? Why?

He read further-*attacks the nervous system within ten minutes, there's a tingling sensation throughout the body-loss of muscle control*.

Imagining Sarah experiencing the symptoms, Don pictured the overweight woman trying to stand as dizziness overcame her. Sarah would have felt increasingly warm, and in an attempt to cool herself she would have walked into the water and then swam out into the ocean. Finally, losing the ability to control her muscles, she drowned.

"Maybe . . . more than likely."

Reaching for a folder on his desk, He studied the photos that had been taken at Sarah's house.

There it was, the table set with three place settings, napkins, silverware, pasta, asparagus—no platter of fish—and the wine and muffin basket.

He had found it a bit odd at the time when he first went to Sarah's—but now, no platter for the fish—"That way, each piece was placed on the plate of the cook's choosing, no one could select from a platter."

"The third person was the killer. That someone knew Reggie and Sarah well enough to cook for them—it was someone they trusted—this was planned—premeditated." Speaking aloud, the detective's thoughts raced to various cooks and chefs at local restaurants.

"Where would they get the fish? It's not a local species."

Who was that third person? And did they know about him?

It wasn't as if Reggie and Sarah were pulling in millions every year from their drug trade—maybe close to a hundred or so thousand, tops. But that money kept Sarah in her nice beach house and afforded her a trip abroad once a year.

It kept Reggie in women, beer and flip flops. That seemed to be all he was interested in.

There were plenty of reasons to kill Sarah and Reggie—hell, nobody liked them, and they were drug dealers. So the *why* was not so hard to figure out. It was the *who*. But just who *would* or who *could* murder Reggie and Sarah was beyond his reach.

Maybe somebody from back in New York got greedy or maybe someone felt they got shorted? Or maybe there was another reason that had nothing to do with drugs or money.

And why would someone risk coming back to Sarah's house to steal little German figurines?

It made no sense.

Not a local—not one of the older locals anyway, Don thought. *Maybe someone who's been here a few years—maybe.*

Maybe someone like me who just got sick and tired of being manipulated.

Damn, he was glad they were dead.

******

A thorough search of both victims' homes had turned up absolutely nothing.

Reggie's home, a small block soundfront house, was a typical beach bum house. An old wooden pier jutted out into the water where a Grady White skiff was moored.

Don assumed it must be Sarah's old nineteen-foot boot. He looked at it with disdain, it seemed so unfair that the lawless had nice toys and he was stuck scraping to pay rent.

Walking about the living room area of Reggie's home, Detective Belkin stepped over discarded pieces of clothing laying on the floor along with a couple of pair of flip flops.

Sea shells were displayed willy-nilly on cluttered end tables and Foster beer cans were stacked in a pyramid in one corner. Empty Crown Royal bottles stood empty as if on display on top of the refrigerator amidst dust and wadded paper towels—Reggie was a slob.

Still, there was no sign of drugs—or of a struggle; nothing seemed out of the ordinary—no signs that Reggie was involved in cocaine or anything else illegal.

Officer Rosell was with him today, and as they walked about the house sifting through drawers and shelves, Don worried. Had he left something there during one of his very seldom visits— something, a note, or a telephone number . . . *anything that linked Reggie to him?*

Scanning the room as thoroughly and quickly as he could, Don clenched and unclenched his fists; a knuckle popped.

It was an annoying habit—one he was not aware of. And a sure sign that thoughts were running amok in his head.

Rosell cleared his throat, "Detective?"

Don popped another knuckle.

"Detective Belkin," the officer spoke again.

Don turned to catch the man's gaze, "Yes?"

"Got something on your mind?"

Quickly Don shook his head, "Just thought we'd find something here—guess not."

The younger officer looked at the detective's still fidgeting hands.

What, Don thought; he followed the Rosell's eyes and raised an eyebrow as he searched the officer's face. "What are you looking at, Rosell?"

The officer chuckled, "Sir, you pop your knuckles when you get anxious."

Half smiling in response to Rosell, Don chuckled, "Oh."

Chapter Twelve

"Has he talked with you yet?" Mindy leaned far over the counter and called to Carrie.

"He who?"

"That detective," Mindy nodded toward the office door where Detective Don Belkin stood talking to Fern West, the store manager. "Hunka, hunka, burnin' love," Mindy cooed. "Now that's my kind of man."

"What about Robby?"

"Robby who?" Mindy batted her eyelashes and laughed.

"He is so *fine*."

"Why, thank you Carrie." The familiar voice startled her. "I didn't know you cared." An elderly gentleman lifted a jug of cat litter to the conveyor belt, "but I really don't think my wife would approve."

Carrie blushed, "Oh, Mr. Allen, I–."

"Don't worry about it," Mrs. Allen giggled, "I think the officer is dreamy too." She nodded in Belkin's direction as her husband rolled his eyes.

159

As the couple picked up their bagged groceries and left the store, Carrie whispered to Mindy, "Is he questioning everyone?"

"Yep, and I'll tell you, when he was questioning me I couldn't think straight for looking into those dark blue eyes . . . youza!" Mindy swiped make-believe sweat away from her brow. "Doesn't he just make you go gaga all over?"

Her thoughts were somewhere between Mindy's humorous comments, Detective Belkin and Hank Butler, who had just walked through the sliding glass doors and was making his way toward Belkin and Fern.

The two men smiled at one another and shook hands, Belkin edging away from Fern as Hank leaned forward to speak to him. They laughed about something—Carrie wondered what it could be.

Feeling the heat rise to her face, she imagined that everyone knew of her and Hank's *night out*.

She watched as Hank turned to retrieve his shopping cart and pat Belkin on the shoulder. She overheard the exchange of words: 'Six a.m. at the dock, buddy.'

"See you then, I'll bring the beer." The detective raised his hand in a partial wave, nodded, and then resumed his conversation with Fern.

Does Belkin know about Hank and me—about our—fling? Carrie considered that everyone did, after all Surf City was a small town.

A loud clang and jolt of the counter brought her attention to an obviously annoyed woman standing before her.

"Are you out of pimento or do you carry it at all?"

Perplexed, Carrie eyed the woman, realizing that she had purposely rammed the cart into her station. Fumbling with an answer, Carrie responded, "Yes ma'am, we carry pimento in the jar on aisle two. It should be next to the hearts of palm."

"I didn't see it. Would you get it for me?"

"I'm sorry ma'am, but I'm not allowed to leave my register," Carrie answered apologetically. "But I can call someone for you."

"Don't bother, just ring this up for me." The woman pushed the few items. "That is, if it's not too much trouble."

Quietly Carrie checked the items and bagged them. "That will be seventeen dollars and forty–two cents."

Searching her handbag, the woman found a twenty and flipped it onto the counter.

Carrie picked the bill up and slid her eyes to meet the woman's. She was so tired of being polite to rude people. But she took a deep breath and counted out the change from the twenty.

"Two fifty-eight." She placed the change on the counter and stood with her hands resting on her hips. "Thank you," she pushed the words sarcastically from her lips, "for shopping Grocery World."

After watching the woman leave the store, Carrie caught her breath. *I almost lost it that time, I shouldn't have been so short with her,* she thought to herself.

As she shook her head and sighed, Carrie leaned forward to whisper to Mindy, "Is the detective here about Sarah Chambers?"

"Yeah, he asked me a bunch of questions about her during my lunch break. And he asked me about some man named Reggie something, uh . . . Reggie Bourne, some guy that comes in here. You remember him?"

"Hell, Mindy. *Everybody* comes in here. We're the only grocery store in town. "

"Yeah, but he's the one . . . he smiles all the time . . . always buys a twelve pack of Rolling Rock . . . has brown hair and sort of stout." Mindy looked up and squinted her eyes, trying to recall more descriptive details.

"Is he the one who wears those plaid shorts all the time, even during the winter?" asked Carrie.

"Yeah, he's the one. Lots of them wear shorts all year long, but he's the one who wears the plaid. I hate those damn plaid purple ones he wears. Looks like such a dork." Mindy stuck out her tongue and blew a raspberry.

"What about him?"

"Found him dead too," Mindy grimaced. "I asked him last winter why he was wearing shorts in thirty degree weather and he said that it felt like summer here compared to New York."

"Butthead. Thirty degrees is thirty degrees. I don't care where you are."

"Hey lady! Are you open? Can you get this bag of dog food for me?" A tall woman of about thirty stood near the front of Carrie's aisle. She was thin,

162

too thin, and she wore a gossamer broom skirt over her low cut one-piece swim suit.

French style manicured fingernails tapped on the handle of her cart. "I don't want to have to lift this again. Get it for me, will you." She added a condescending "please."

Carrie eyed the fifty pound bag of dog food, "I can hand scan it for you." She picked up the scanning wand.

"No, no. I want you to pick it up. My boyfriend is standing by the ice machine and he's bringing his cart over here now. Can you put it in there for me?" She dotted the sentence with another sarcastic "please."

"No problem." Carrie eyed the woman, curled her lips in a sneer, then looked to the young man who must have been the boyfriend, his hands pressed deeply in the pockets of the cool white Bermuda shorts he wore. A pastel sweater was tied around his shoulders and he wore a pastel golfing hat on his head.

She saw him wave to the skinny woman and point to the bag of ice in his cart. "Got it!" he called out.

"Could you ask your boyfriend to bring the cart over here so I don't have to carry it so far?"

The woman glared at her, "Isn't that your job? Aren't you supposed to take care of the customer?"

"I just asked . . ."

"Don't get rude with me, Miss."

"Sir," Carrie called to the young man in the white Bermuda shorts, "could you roll your cart over here, please?"

The young man moved his cart forward toward Carrie; she picked up several bags of groceries on the counter to place them in the cart.

As she stooped to pick up the bag of dog food, the man interrupted her.

"No, no, I can lift one side if you get the other. He grabbed two corners of the bag and lifted, Carrie grabbed the other two.

Pulling upward, the man seemed to be ready to place the dog food on top of the groceries.

"No, you'll squish everything. The bag is too heavy," she called excitedly.

"If you don't want my help, the heck with you," the man snapped as he released his corners of the dog food.

The full weight of the bag fell against Carrie, but she deftly leaned in and scooted the bag to the bottom rung of the cart, then rose up and dusted her hands against her trousers.

"Darling, that bag was just too heavy for you. She could have helped more." The thin woman rubbed her boyfriend's shoulder.

"The darn bag is on your cart," Carrie spat. "And I'm certainly glad neither of you dirtied your clothes lifting it."

She heard the "humph" in unison from the two as they rolled their cart toward the sliding glass doors.

Mindy, who had been watching from her register the whole time, quickly raced to her side, "Man, I saw that. What a couple of giant genitals."

Carrie shook her head and scoffed, "Yeah, they deserve each other."

She looked quickly to the office where the detective and Fern were still chatting, "You think that guy—Reggie what's his name—you think he and Sarah got murdered by the same person? Whoever did it, I'm going to sic them on that crappy couple." She nodded toward the sliding glass door where the couple still stood perusing the grocery receipt.

"Looks like Fern and the detective are coming over here. Guess it's your turn now." Mindy mindfully grabbed the spray bottle and paper towels to busy herself as she cleaned her counter. Fern nodded to her and grinned, then turned her attention to Carrie.

"Go ahead and take your lunch break, Detective Belkin would like to talk with you about these people that have, well, been killed this week."

"Okay." Carrie switched her register light to off and grabbed her purse as she moved from behind the counter. "You don't mind if I get a soda and a sandwich first. Do you?" She felt the detective watching her—a quick glance into his dark blue eyes quickened her pulse, *No, no. I'm not going to be a fool. Anyone that good looking has got to be self-centered.* "Be mean, be mean," she whispered to herself.

"This won't take long," the detective nodded and stepped aside to let Carrie lead the way.

Carrie straddled the bench of the picnic table and lifted a can of Seven-Up to her lips. She looked at Belkin straightforwardly wondering if Hank had told him about their *fling.* Suddenly self-conscious, she forced a scowl to her face, reminding herself of what a butthead Sarah was.

She prodded herself to remember her last customers—how angry they had made her. She forced herself to think of anything except the man standing before her. There was no denying it, he was attractive.

I never liked Sarah Chambers and I'm not about to act like I did. Detective Belkin can think what he wants.

Tilting her head to meet Belkin's gaze, Carrie spoke, "Well? What do you want to know about the old crow?"

Belkin's lips turned the slightest bit upward; immediately they relaxed as he flipped to a page in his small notebook. "I think you've already answered one of my questions."

"Hey, I'm not going to pretend that I liked her. In fact, I couldn't stand the bitch. She was one of the most—"

Interrupting her, Belkin raised a hand; his eyes met hers with a steady gaze that said he was in no mood for an attitude. "Mrs. Chambers had a reputation for rudeness. We know that."

The bite of sandwich Carrie had been chewing seemed thick and rubbery as she lowered her eyes. She could feel her face redden as she reached for the can of Seven-Up to wash the sandwich down.

"Now, Ms. Adams, I know you ladies hear lots of things and that Mrs. Chambers had a habit of talking on her cell phone while in line. Did you ever hear her say anything that seemed out of place or odd?"

"Well, I never heard her say please or thank you, *that* would have been odd for her. But no, I don't specifically recall any conversations out of the ordinary. But then usually I don't listen to customers while they're on the phone."

"You never overhead anything she said on the phone?"

"That's what I said, nothing that I can remember right off hand," Carrie could feel the man's presence as she met his eyes.

"Oh, there was this one thing a few days ago." She paused to gather her thoughts. "She said something about having some Hummels."

"Hummels?" Don querled.

"Yes, you know, those little German figurines."

Don flashed a grin. It disappeared almost as quickly. "I see," he nodded.

Reminding herself that right now, men were the enemy, Carrie steeled her resolve, "Look, Detective Belkin, I moved here just about two years ago. I've met some of the nicest people I've ever known in my life. But these *tourists*–not all of them, but many of them–are condescending and arrogant. I don't understand that kind of attitude. I don't understand why being polite is out of their realm." She paused, met his gaze and continued, "I really don't like having to contend with that behavior, it brings out a side of me I really don't like." Carrie opened her purse and pulled a cigarette from the pack. "They ruin my day."

Rising from the bench, the detective's voice seemed caring and sympathetic, "You really didn't like her. Did you?"

"Detective Belkin, do you like everyone you meet?"

"I don't kill them."

"What?" Perplexed by the retort, Carrie shot back, "I don't have time to kill everyone I dislike." She smirked and rolled her eyes. "You get to walk away. Or you can intimidate people with your authority. I can't. I can't intimidate or even be the least bit rude to someone who is blatantly rude to me. I'll lose my job. *I'll* get fired."

Belkin rose from the bench and closed his notebook. "I'm sorry . . ."

Interrupting him, Carrie scowled as she threw her cigarette into the sand bucket. "And as far as that Reggie—whatever his name is—I remember him too. He could be flippant, but wasn't always. He'd smile now and then, but would never look you in the eye, know what I mean? Pleasant enough, but I could tell he was another one of those condescending a-holes."

Heaving a sigh, Carrie composed herself, "You know, I just got done being called snippy by someone who talked to me like they just stepped in something—I'm not in the best mood."

A half-smile rose from Don's lips as he nodded. "I understand."

"Well," Carrie continued, "I never saw this *Reggie* with Sarah Chambers. As far as I can remember, but he always bought a twelve pack of beer and he always came in alone."

"Thank you, Miss Adams." Belkin stuffed the notebook in his pocket. Again he smiled gently at her, the thought of reaching out to shake her hand crossed his mind, but he squared his shoulders instead. He was here on business, even if he did like the woman; she seemed genuine, but this was no place and certainly not the time to show any interest.

As he walked away he had the feeling she was watching him and sure enough, as he turned he caught her eyes.

Carrie lowered them immediately.

Nodding, he called out, "Thank you, Miss Adams.

Good. Don thought as he walked toward his car, *so far no one overheard anything that might connect me to them - maybe I'll get out of this thing alive.*

******

Morgan Simpers had been brave that afternoon; he'd parked only a few spaces away from the main entrance to Grocery World. There, as he leaned against the bed of his Subaru Baja, he waited for Carrie to exit the sliding glass doors of the store.

Running scenarios of how he was going to attract her attention, he mumbled to himself, gesturing with his hands. "Hi Carrie," he whispered as he lifted his hand near his waist and waved to no one. "I've got you an early Christmas . . . no, I better say birthday . . . hmm . . . maybe I'll just hold one of the statues in my hand."

Anticipating her happiness, Morgan's mouth spread into a wide grin. "You're welcome, no problem, you deserve them." He gestured again, raising a hand to cover his smile.

"I'll tell her that I found them in a box—one of the boxes in the storage unit I bought at Easy Storage Rental."

He guffawed loudly and quickly covered his mouth again, *I'm sure not going to tell her I stole them from Sarah's house.*

A seagull settled nearby, and began pecking at a bit of garbage lying on the parking lot pavement. Morgan watched, then cleared his throat loudly hoping it would scare the bird away.

The gull ruffled its feathers a bit and waddled to the other side of the space where a discarded McDonald's hamburger lay, squawking as it moved.

Morgan shook his head; he hated how the tourists discarded trash when not fifteen feet away sat a trashcan.

His eyes drifted to the glass doors once again as he eagerly awaited Carrie's exit. No, she had not left yet. He looked skyward, the sun was sinking toward the sound, the west. A slight breeze had kicked up. Morgan liked this time of day when the heat was not at its height.

His eyes narrowed as he grinned and thought of how much pleasure the Hummels would bring Carrie and how grateful she would be.

As he envisioned her throwing her arms around his neck; Morgan could almost feel her body against his as he pulled her close. Her hair would have that just washed scent—a few times he had smelled it while in line at the grocery store.

"Ah, she smells like heaven," Morgan whispered.

Just then, Carrie emerged from the glass doors.

Morgan straightened, his eyes grew wider. Today Carrie was walking quickly, her shoulders were pulled straight back. This posture meant only one thing to him—she was not in a good mood.

Instinctively Morgan's eyebrows turned upward, his bottom lip pouted. And his hand drew to his chest. Oh, how he hated it when Carrie felt like this. It ached him to see her distraught and he felt even more so that he could remedy her cheerless feelings; he called to her.

"Carrie!" He stepped away from the Baja.

She walked briskly past the newspaper boxes and soft drink machines as if she did not hear.

"Carrie!" he called again, this time more loudly. "I've got a surprise for you." Morgan raised his hand and waved.

Still, the woman seemed to ignore him as she rounded the corner of the shopping center and breezed out of sight.

Looking into the passenger seat of his car, Morgan clenched his jaw; a low moan rose from his throat.

"She looked angry; someone made her mad. Had to be one of those damn Yankees."

As he opened the door to the Subaru, Morgan signed, "She won't be mad when I give her these though."

******

The walk home that evening was tedious. Twice she nearly tripped on discarded soda cans. When she reached her home, the first thing she did was pour herself a glass of wine and settle comfortably on the divan.

She thought of the skinny woman in the gossamer skirt, the fifty pound bag of dog food and the jerk with the white shorts. "He looked like he stepped out of Abercrombie and Fitch."

She lit a cigarette and inhaled deeply. "Geez, how I hate snobby people." Slapping her thigh, she coaxed Joey to jump onto her lap. "I think I made a fool out of myself with Detective Belkin." Speaking aloud, Carrie felt the flush come to her face as she recalled the smile and the tenderness in his eyes.

"He was just doing his job, trying to be polite too, and I was royal snot." She shook her head, disgusted with herself. "I get so nervous around men, you'd think I was a teenager."

Relaxing against the divan, Carrie thought for a moment and searched her memory for the exact words the detective had spoken to her during lunch: *I don't kill them*, he had said. *Does he think I had anything to do with Sarah Chambers' or Reggie's death?*

She sat upright, "Naw, he was just being facetious . . . or was he?"

For a moment Carrie felt guilty as she recalled the times the Chambers woman had come to her register and acted so rudely.

"I wished really bad things on her. That's for sure." Carrie recalled the time she told Josh, the bag boy, how she wished the delivery truck would back into Sarah–they had laughed when he commented, "She'd probably dent the damn thing."

"That's just what I need now, that detective, that handsome, polite man thinking I'm involved with killing someone." She rolled her eyes and patted her thigh again for Bella to join Joey on her lap.

"Mommy's not upset with you; it's that store–those rude people. I'm sorry I'm so grouchy." Carrie nuzzled the dogs one at a time. "You're good doggies," she cooed; the dogs curled into sleeping positions on her lap.

Lacing her fingers behind her head, Carrie relaxed as the day's events returned to her thoughts.

She had been in a bad mood since the one obnoxious couple and had even ignored Morgan Simpers as he called to her from his car when she left that evening. "Wonder what he wanted?" she thought. "Lord, I hope he's not getting interested in me. That's just what I need, a married man in my life."

Sighing heavily she thought back to her walk home, how she had seen Morgan in her peripheral vision but kept walking even after he said he had a surprise for her. "Yeah, a surprise in his pants," she rolled her eyes, closed them and nodded to sleep.

Chapter Thirteen

Phil Belkin lowered the window of the 2003 Dodge Charger as he waited for his father to drive them to church.

He hated going to church. His mother never made him go. His mother never made him do a damn thing.

Watching as his father walked from the house to the car, he noticed how much more relaxed he seemed when not on duty. His shoulders weren't hiked about his neck and he lacked the scowl that seemed almost permanent.

He dimly remembered his father from his early childhood, when he would come home wearing his US Marine Corps uniform. Neatly starched and pressed, it stood in stark contrast to the man whose gently rolling laughter flowed so naturally as he picked up his young son to sit on his shoulders.

Back then, Phil was happy and proud to see his uniformed father enter the doorway. He was not intimidating at all, but warm and welcoming.

He recalled playing horseshoes in the backyard and going to Chucky Cheese. He remembered watching his parents dance at backyard barbeques and how they used to laugh together.

But that all changed on September 11, 2001.

Though Phil was sure it must have been longer, it seemed that within days his father left for Iraq, leaving him alone with a mother who became more and more distant.

That had been a long time ago. Phil felt his chest tighten and his face burn; he brushed the hair away from his eyes, shaking the thoughts away, and waited while his father settled himself behind the wheel of the car.

"Well son," Don reached to tousle his son's thick blond hair, "ready to get saved?" Don grinned and winked as he buckled his seat belt.

Phil rolled his eyes and turned his head toward the open window, still lost in thoughts of a kinder, gentler time before his mother lost herself in drugs. He recalled watching her, time and again roll the bills up and breathe in the lines of white powder.

After snorting a line he could have robbed a bank and she wouldn't have given a damn, so he didn't think she'd care about the car he had taken. But boy, was he wrong about that one.

"You seem awfully quiet this morning. "What's up?" Don sensed a distance. Eager to know what his son was thinking, he repeated the question, "What's up, son?"

"Nothing . . . can't I be quiet? Do I have to talk all the time?"

"I was just asking, son," the older man spoke tenderly."

"If you have to know, I was thinking about Mom . . . sorry if that disappoints you," Phil responded snidely.

Don's body tensed, "I can't help what your Mom does . . . neither can you. You just take care of your own life. That's the whole idea in going to church; you'll meet the right kind of people."

Phil leaned back, pulling away from his father's touch, "The right kind of people?"

"Well, at least people who are trying to be better than their vices allow them to be sometimes."

"Humph," As he rolled his eyes, Phil muttered a few words.

"I know, I know—drunk on Saturday, in church on Sunday. They're all a bunch of hypocrites. Right?" Don poked his son with an elbow. "Come on now, its not so bad. It's just one hour."

"Yeah," Phil turned to his father. "So what's the point?"

"I just don't want to see you get in trouble. It's a hard row to hoe."

"A what? Hard row to hoe?" Phil sniggered, "What the hell does that mean?"

"It means life isn't easy, and stealing or getting into drugs will only make it more difficult."

"I don't do drugs, Dad . . . it was Mom that was doing the coke."

"Fries your brain." Don could feel the tension in the car increase and he tried to get back on track, get back to a peaceful conversation between he and his son.

"Maybe, but I've seen dudes, just as wasted on weed and even freaking 'shrooms. Mom told me how you and she used to get high all the time. All this God stuff is a bunch of bull . . ."

Don's face reddened and his arm immediately flew back to slap the boy across the face, "Don't you talk like that and I didn't do . . . you don't understand, it wasn't like that."

He caught his breath and calmed himself, pulling his hand back in time to only graze Phil's cheek; his chest rising and falling as he breathed heavily.

"Sorry," Don willed himself to get control, "what's so important about getting wasted?"

Shrugging, Phil bit his bottom lip. His eyes, wide with fear, narrowed.

"Boy, there are lots of drugs on this island. If you get involved-in any way, I'll let you rot."

"What makes you think I'm going to get into drugs? I've done everything you've asked me to do since I've been here."

"Yes—well, just about. You could clean up that room now and then."

"I did get the dishwashing job you've been hounding me about."

Don nodded, "You did, thanks—now don't screw that up too."

Phil pulled his body in tightly as he slumped down as far as he could in the seat.

"What was that in the car you stole in California?"

"The lady said I could borrow the car, the weed was already in it." Phil rolled his eyes.

"That's not what she told the police. That's not what the officer said." Don's eyes seemed to look right through the boy.

"Son, you don't even have a license, you don't turn sixteen until August. And as for the weed in the glove compartment, hell, Mrs. Wanders is sixty-five years old!"

"I know lots of old folks that smoke a little weed, Dad." He looked steadily into his father's eyes; Don's glared back.

Turning to gaze out the window, a broad smirk crossed Phil's lips.

"You've picked up all these bad habits from that mother of yours." Don pulled the car into the church parking lot and drove to the farthest space. Placing both hands on the steering wheel he looked into a wooded vacant lot. Regretful of the years he had ignored his son and wife, he felt partly to blame for Phil's juvenile behavior, he couldn't put the blame all on Maggie.

"It's almost time to go in." He placed his hands on his thighs, rubbing them against the denim fabric to ease his tension. "Come on, "he nodded as he opened the door to the car.

Phil didn't listen to the sermon as he sat next to his father. Rather, he thought of his parents. *Both of them are full of crap,* Phil thought to himself. *I can't please him and I sure as hell couldn't please my mother and what did I ever do? Pick her up off the floor, wipe up her vomit.*

He was glad to be rid of her just as much as she was of him. But living with his father—the almighty Don Belkin—how could he live up to the tower of strength, the all powerful Marine? There was no way he'd ever measure up to his dad's expectations.

The teenager smirked, *like night and day—from a drug junkie to Mr. Perfect.*

Glancing at his father as he sat next to him in the pew, Phil's face turned upward as he listened to the pastor deliver words he had no interest in, he relaxed, *at least he got me out of jail.* He thought of the cell and the filthy toilet in the corner.

******

"You're late, my friend," the lanky man spoke with a British accent. "You have any idea how odd it looks to be hanging out in the Grocery World parking lot without any groceries?" He pushed his horn-rimmed glasses more securely against his nose and reached his hand to adjust his hair piece.

Phil shrugged, "Sorry 'bout that, bro. But I'm here aren't I?"

"Bloke, you were late, don't let it happen again. Right?" Mick shot the boy an annoyed glance.

"A copper drove by here once already. Gave me the eye, you know, the hairy eye." Mick cocked a thick eyebrow and squinted. "Hey man, was that you I saw riding around with your old man this morning?"

Phil nodded.

"Don't tell me he went and dragged you off to *Sunday School* again."

"It's not so bad." Phil opened the door to the pearl colored Camry as Mick turned the key in the ignition.

"I hope you have the dough this time." Mick slid the car into reverse and raised the volume of the stereo; classical music spilled from the speakers as they drove along the narrow beach road.

Reaching into his pocket, Phil withdrew a fifty dollar bill and placed it on the center console, "Will that work?"

"Yeah man," Mick smiled, bobbing his head. "Is that your allowance, man?"

"Yeah, what of it?" Phil sneered, rolling his eyes, "I hope you take some of this dough and get yourself a new shirt."

"What, my friend? This here is *island wear*," he tugged at a sleeve of the brightly colored floral print shirt.

"Man, that's just bad." Phil chuckled.

"It's my signature, bloke." Mick touched the Rolex on his wrist, "like this," he shifted the watch around, "my signature, like it's hip, man."

Phil guffawed and turned toward the window, shaking his head.

"Whatever," Mick exaggerated a sneer in return. "Look here now, this might be all you get from me in a while, so make it last."

"Aw right, I bloody well will," Phil exaggerated his best Cockney accent. "But whas-sup, bro?" he added.

"I've got a little extra treat for you for another twenty." Reaching into the breast pocket of his shirt, Mick pulled out a bottle of pills and shook them.

"What's that?" The boy asked.

"Oxycontin . . . very relaxing . . . and less expensive if you deal with me."

Phil wrapped his fingers around the bottle, "Pretty good, huh?"

"Yeah, or I can get my hands on some spice for you—but I won't have that for awhile, I'm trying to lay a little low."

The teenager lifted an eyebrow, "Yeah?"

Mick yawned and released his hands momentarily from the steering wheel. "Yeah, my supplier turned up floating in the drink."

"What? What are you talking about, you nutsoid Brit."

"The drink man, the water, the sound." Mick puckered his lips and elongated the word, the *s-o-u-n-d*, "as you blokes refer to it on this side of the pond."

"The guy my dad's been investigating?"

"One and the same, my friend—so no more evil *mary ja wana* for a while." Throwing his head back in laughter, Mick displayed the gold crowns on his back molars. "Besides, you don't want to end up like your poor old momma, do you and you know weed is the gateway drug."

Rolling his eyes, Phil turned away. He wished he'd never mentioned his mother to Mick.

"But on a more serious note-" Raising an eyebrow he leaned toward Phil and released a sinister laugh, "The bloke was selling rock on the side, man. From what I hear he was really racking in the dough."

"This is getting weird, people showing up dead, me catching that lady's ear on my fishing pole. Hell, it's just all getting too close to home, Mick."

"That's what I'm telling you, lay low for a while. Learn to live without the *high*. You need to be like me." Mick reached into his shirt pocket and pulled out a small blue pill. Holding it between his fingers he pressed it to his lips. "This is my baby—keeps all my lady friends happy."

Phil eyed the man as he held the pill in his fingertips. He had no clue why it would be necessary to use such a thing. Hell, he had no problem getting it up with the chick that got high with his mom.

"All I'm saying is that the greatest drug in the world is sex, and this *little boy* assures me that I'll always be a *big* man and that I can have it anytime I want. I'm not suggesting you use it, I'm sure you don't even need it, being a virgin as such."

"I ain't no virgin. I've been with scads of chicks." He grabbed his crotch and slid his eyes sarcastically at Mike. "No way I need *that* . . . that's for old men or men who don't have what it takes."

Sniggering to himself, Mick realized there was no arguing with youth. But then again he'd been relying on the pill for a long time. His inability to perform began in his late twenties. *The shrink blamed it on my mother, or was it my father?* Mick scowled, erasing the thought from his mind and changed the subject back to the purchasing of drugs.

"I do know of one fellow, he's one of your local country boys . . . Buck" Throwing his head back, Mick howled with laughter, "Buck, the country buckaroo. Ha, Ha I can't remember his last name, but I've stopped and bought fresh seafood from him. He grows his own—reefer that is. Doesn't grow his own fish," Mick guffawed.

He leaned toward Phil and whispered, "but be careful, I don't think he's too smart."

Within minutes Mick slowed the car to a stop, pressing a button to change CDs as he did so.

"You like this sound?" Music blared loudly from the speakers, "Duh, duh, duh, duh, duh, woeful countenance." Mick's shoulders swayed to the tune as he sang along with the soundtrack to the *Man of La Mancha.*

"Change the *countenance* my friend. You need to have a better outlook, don't be so worried about stuff—you always look like you're hitting the bottom of the barrel—like you're *so* unhappy, man. And smoking that wacky weed won't make you happy." He winked and put his thumb and little finger to his ear and mouth, "I've got to head back to Raleigh now . . . I'll call you when things are more *copacetic.*"

What a hypocrite, Phil thought as he closed the door to the Camry. *He sells me the stuff and he's telling me not to use it*. The boy shook his head and watched as Mick gently eased his car from the restaurant parking lot and made his way across the bridge to the main highway toward Raleigh.

184

Removing the glasses and hair piece, Mick flipped open his buzzing cell phone, "Hey man, what's up?" The British accent was gone, so was the effervescent demeanor.

Listening as he nodded, the phone resting between his chin and shoulder, Mick responded to the caller, "Naw, told the kid I was going to Raleigh."

Chapter Fourteen

"You think with Sarah and Reggie out of the way that Belkin will be any problem?" Mick leaned back in the rattan chair, propping his feet on the foot rest.

He drew an e-cig from the chest pocket of his bright orange shirt and filled it with liquid nicotine. The aroma of apples filled the air.

Casting an annoyed glance toward Mick, Hank walked to the kitchen. "Would have been a lot easier if he'd have croaked when they did. What happened anyway? I thought you said he was going to be there that night too."

"I can't see into the future, my friend." Mick inhaled from the e-cig deeply. "What Reggie told me was that all three of them would be going over some *business* that night and I reassured him that I would be there too and prepare mahi almondine for everybody." Mick laughed, his mouth wide, revealing his teeth as he slumped deeper into the chair. Closing his eyes he began whistling the *Man of La Mancha;* his hands making the motions of wielding a knife filleting meat.

Annoyed with Mick's whistling, Hank reached to turn on the CD player. A flood of Barry Manilow burst loudly into the room.

"All right, all right, I'll quit the whistling. Just turn that elevator music down." Tilting his head back to release a plume of vapor, Mick closed his eyes as Hank lowered the music. "Almondine, almondine–I showed her the recipe, the one you gave me–made a fuss over it. I told her how wonderfully it *sat on the palate,*–just like you told me–hell, I don't understand why you didn't fix the meal yourself."

Mick took another long drag on the e-cig and grinned, opening only a corner of his mouth, he let the vapor escape.

"I gave her a list of what I would need to prepare–the one you gave me–the side dishes, the muffins–told her that I would bring the fish, and then I stressed that she had to serve a white wine with it.

Mick slid his eyes to Hank, "I told her that she had to have a good quality wine. You know Sarah had no real class–white trash with money."

His back to Mick, Hank rolled his eyes; his shoulders rose and fell as he released a breath.

"I was over there at six thirty–the *special* fish in my cooler . . . she had everything, the asparagus, sauce, almonds–and you know she bought *muffin mix*–Sarah bought *muffin mix!*" Mick struck his brow with his fingers. "That dummy bought muffin mix instead of cornmeal–expecting me to prepare a fine diner with store bought *muffin mix*.

"That just shows you that the woman had no sense of decorum or class–no class at all."

Hank listened as Mick continued degrading Sarah's social standing and choices of foods. He grinned as Mick derided her use of packaged hollandaise sauce, and bow tie pasta as side dishes.

"At least she didn't buy canned asparagus." Mick sucked on the stem of the electronic cigarette and stretched his neck back to follow Hank as he opened the kitchen cabinet doors.

"I did the best with what I had and if I say so myself, I think the meal was pretty damn good." Forcing a laugh, Mick ran his fingers along the buttons of his flowered shirt.

"The fish was to *die* for." He laughed loudly again.

Standing behind the granite bar of his kitchen, Hank reached for two long stemmed glasses from the overhead cabinet and poured white wine into one.

"No wine for me, remember–just the sparkly stuff," Mick tittered as he watched Hank pour sparkling grape juice into his glass.

"Sounds as if the meal was delicious, I can say that," Hank chuckled, "obviously she never noticed , well, maybe she had no clue what the difference is between mahi and oriental fish–fugu– isn't it called fugu?"

"Both are white meat, aren't they?" Mick asked.

"Mahi is light pink. Blowfish, any kind, is paler. It is almost white." Hank spoke gently as he looked to Mick, "never said a word, huh, never even considered that it wasn't mahi? "

Mick shook his head slowly, "Nope, my friend," his hands once again slicing the air with a make-believe knife, "ovaries, liver and skin, just like you said. Of course, I cut off the skin, it's tough you know." He smiled as Hank handed him the glass of grape juice.

Mick grasped the stemmed glass and nodded a thank you. "You ought to take up diving, my friend. It's the most beautiful, peaceful thing you'll ever do in your whole life," Taking another gulp from his glass, Mick rose from the chair and walked toward the counter where Hank stood.

"Yes, my friend. You need to go diving with me sometime. All kinds of things in that ocean—and let me tell you the day I saw those fugu swimming around I nearly busted a nut and I knew right then that I was about to become your new best friend."

"I'd say that, you certainly became more important in my life that evening you showed up with Reggie." Rubbing the lip of his wine glass, Hank raised an eyebrow. "You never did tell me how you and Reggie became such good friends."

"I've known Reggie since we were kids, we actually went to the same prep school in New York," Mick brought the e-cig to his lips and inhaled loudly; vapor curled about his head.

"He called me up one day a few months back and told me of this lovely little island and how well he was faring."

"So you two have been friends since you were boys?" Hank queried.

"I wouldn't exactly say friends, *my friend*. You might say good acquaintances or even rivals—at least I was his. Reggie always liked having things his way, mind you it was over the strangest things. He never wanted the biggest car or the hottest chick, but when he decided he wanted something—well, damn it he made sure he got it."

Pausing to take another drag from the e-cig and gulp from the grape juice, Mick continued, "That's what he called me for. He said the old bat was being greedy and that he wanted to get out from under her and do his own thing and I was just the man to make it happen for him.

"I was to take the old bag out in his little boat after dinner—she was a horny old broad—make her think I was hot for her, and then dump her out about twenty miles.

"But then I met you, my friend," Mick raised his glass in a toast then held it out to be filled again, "and well, the rest is history.

"You did a good job, Mick." Hank raised his glass; swirling the liquid about. "I've prepared fugu several times at the Chez Louis in Paris. I would have loved to have been there to see how Sarah's and Reggie's turned out."

"Naw, you would have loved to have been there to see how they reacted when the effects started to get to them." Mick laughed, his mouth wide.

Hank took another breath. "Tell me, why do you wear a toupee, talk in that accent you do?

191

"But not around you, Hank. I'm the real thing around you." His eyes focused solemnly on Hank.

"But why at all?"

"Just part of the game, bloke. Got to play the part, confuse the masses."

Hank cocked his head to one side, "Hmm, I guess if that's the way you feel you have to be."

"Makes things more interesting, more fun." Mick rested his long frame in a nearby chair, and then turned quickly to Hank, his eyes wide with excitement, "Hey man, I read up online about that fugu the first time I saw it. All kinds of crazy shit happens when it gets in your system. Takes about ten minutes for it to take effect. Then you start feeling a little dizzy and then sweaty, hot. That's how Sarah was feeling. Man, she was sweaty and fidgety. Said she wanted to walk out on the beach to cool herself off. So, I walked out with her. I wanted to see first hand if everything I read was true. Never said a word, never gave her any sympathy—just went along with old Sarah, encouraging her to dip her toes in the water and then pull up her pants legs and go out a little farther." A low chuckle slid from Mick's throat. "Then she was sweating like a pig and I told her that no one would mind if she just went out into the water and got her whole body wet. That's when everything started happening, her muscles started freezing up on her. She couldn't move very well. She sure as hell couldn't swim." He turned a sullen face to meet Hank's eyes. "I watched her go under—glub-glub-glub. And then, Voila! She was gone."

Mick thrust his arms wide and laughed his most sinister laugh, "Nyah, hah, hah."

He pinched his nose with a thumb and forefinger, "glub, glub, glub." Throwing his head back Mick held his side as he laughed. "She was as pathetic as a dog hit by a car, just waiting to die till it gets off the road."

Holding the glass, Mick wiggled it from side to side, "More, please."

As he poured, Hank lifted his head, "Continue," he said with a grin and watched as the man gulped the contents of his glass.

"It probably didn't hit Reggie as quickly as it hit Sarah. But when she and I were walking out the door to the beach, he was still swilling wine. Said he saw *two* bottles on the table instead of one. I told him he was drunk and needed to walk home and sleep it off. Guess he had the same symptoms as Sarah and decided the cool waters of the sound would make him feel better."

Calmly Hank poured more sparkling grape juice into Mick's empty glass. "Are you ready to eat?" As he slipped a padded mitt onto his left hand, he opened the door to the oven, the aroma of almonds and seafood permeated the air. "Now, "I'll show you how real mahi almondine is supposed to taste."

"You sure this isn't real wine you've been pouring in my glass? You know, my man, I'm trying to detox the body, eh? " Mick held the stemmed glass high in the air, peering into it as if he could visually tell if it was an alcoholic beverage.

His accent wavered from British to American, "I feel kind of drunk already and man, you know how I feel about drinking alcohol–dulls the senses."

Hank held up the bottle of sparkling juice, "It says *no alcohol* right on the label." He set the near empty bottle back on the counter. "You're just high from gloating."

Holding the tray with his mitted hand, he slid the slices of fish from the metal tray and placed them each on a plate.

"Yeah, can't say I did a bad job. Can you?" Mick smiled over to Hank. "It was so easy, they ate it like pigs. And that blonde pig was flirting with me all night–and I had to act like I liked it." Thrusting his hips forward Mick bit his bottom lip, "Never liked screwing pigs."

Hank settled the prepared plates of food at the small cherry wood table, turning his back he sneered in disgust at Mick's vulgar gyrations, "The food's going to get cold Mick, you can tell me about it while we eat."

Mick lifted his nose in the air, "Smells good my friend, and you say that this is the way it's supposed to taste. You ain't pulling one on me are you? This ain't that fugu puffer fish?"

"Shut up and eat." Hank speared a forkful of the fish on Mick's plate and placed it in his mouth. "Yum, now eat your fish." He raised his glass to Mick's, they clinked, "Here's to revenge. How sweet it is."

He hated wasting good food, so Hank pushed his fork into the almond crusted fish on Mick's plate; he'd already eaten his own portion.

"You don't mind, do you *my friend?*" His eyes slid to Mick's body, slumped in the chair across from him. "And by the way, that's an ugly shirt."

Rising from his chair at the dining table, Hank kicked Mick's sandalled foot to the side. He leaned in close to the man's face, he was still breathing; his chest rose and fell gently.

"Jeez, you're going to be heavy." Grabbing Mick beneath the armpits, Hank pulled the body across the room and down the stairs and lifted him into the bed of his Ford F150.

He drove silently to a rental property where he kept his Robalo fishing boat tied to the dock.

Sliding a wheelchair from the back seat of the cab, Hank lifted and pushed Mick's body into a seating position."You never should have met me. Reggie made a big mistake that day, introducing someone like *you*, to me.

He settled Mick's long legs into the foot rests and rolled the chair up the ramp to the boat.

"Nice night for a trip down the Intracoastal Waterway." Hank patted Mick on the shoulder, "You don't mind, do you, *my friend?*"

Chapter Fifteen

It was her day off and Carrie really needed a day off. In fact, she could have used a whole week. "If I don't watch it, I'm going to get a permanent vacation," she said aloud, her legs stretched comfortably on the divan. "I hate having to work summers."

Leaning to the side, Carried spied two puppy dog noses sticking out from the gold tassels of the divan. *Still haven't eaten them, huh?* she thought before calling to her dogs; they both hopped onto her lap and curled into balls to sleep.

Taking turns petting the Yorkie and chihuahua, she thought of the day before when Fern the manager had written her up. It was the first time she'd been written up—along with it came a warning to always be polite, regardless of a customer's behavior.

"Psst, hey," a man had called from the end of her counter. "Hey lady, I need a pack of Marlboro Special Blend in the red box."

She should have told the man she was busy—
that he should get in line if he needed to purchase
something. But she had not. She had tried to be
nice and had inadvertently caused other customers
to wait.

Once she paused to get him the pack of
cigarettes he had asked for, he requested chewing
tobacco and then when she got that, he asked for
another pack of cigarettes.

What in the world was she supposed to do?
Here was, *Miss 'I've got big boobs and I'm going to
show them off'*—standing at the counter unloading
her cart, tapping her nails and waiting for Carrie to
begin checking her groceries.

"He wasn't in line, ma'am." Miss Boobs batted
her lashes and placed a hand on a hip.

Carrie looked from the woman to the man,
"I'm sorry sir, you do need to get in line."

"But you have my stuff right now."

"Yeah," *Mr. my beer belly isn't quite big
enough*, hollered. He stood behind Miss Boobs. "It
ain't fair for us to have to wait for someone who
ain't even in line.

As she watched Miss Boobs distance herself as
best she could from Mr. Beer Belly, Carrie noticed
her manager, standing by the office door, her arms
folded across her chest. Carrie knew instantly that
she was going to get a lecture from Fern. She
dreaded those demeaning sermons. And worst of
all, Fern didn't care who was around to hear them.

"I'm sorry," Carrie said as politely as possible.

Mr. Beer Belly snapped loudly at her, "Hey!
We're next in line; we were here before that old

fart was. Ain't that right, baby?" He reached to elbow the buxom woman ahead of him.

She nodded as she took a step backward.

One of beer belly's buddies chimed in, "Don't you dare let *anyone* in front of us. We're in a hurry."

Fern appeared at Carrie's side and walked behind the counter where she stood. "You bag the groceries," she ordered.

Fern lifted her eyes to all of the customers, "I'm so sorry you have all had to wait. Now, who was first?"

No one said a word, rather they all smiled politely and muttered and shrugged.

Phrases like, *it's okay, he can go first, doesn't matter to me*, drifted about the counter as Fern politely nodded and apologized.

She rang the customers up with no fuss or complaints, thanked them for shopping at Grocery World, then shook her head and slid a glare toward Carrie.

"I'll see you in the office at break."

"I bet she's gonna write you up," Mindy sneered from her register. "Sorry."

As she thought of the previous day, the write-up and how foolish she felt, Carrie reflected on the number of times she had squeezed bread, over stuffed bags and broken eggs—all because she felt demeaned.

"Maybe it's bad karma, maybe. Maybe I feel so rotten because of my own stinky Karma."

Carrie glanced at the rooster shaped clock on the porch. "Lunch time," she said loudly, sweeping the thoughts of karma and the grocery store away. Slowly she swung her legs to the floor; the dogs jumped from her lap.

"Kibble?" She questioned the dogs as they pranced about. Their bodies wriggled and brown eyes begged. Carrie poured the food from the bag into their bowls and refreshed their water.

Carrie reached for the refrigerator door, "Hmm." She eyed a cold pork chop and reached for it. Simultaneously, she heard a car horn blare. "Dang." Carrie closed the door and peered from her window. *Morgan?*

He did not exit the car, but rolled his window down, stuck his head out and called, "Carrie, Carrie!"

She walked to the edge of her front porch."Hi Morgan, what's going on?"

"Whatcha doing?" he asked.

"Trying to relax." She tried to hide her irritation as best she could.

"Oh, I'm sorry. It's just that I tried to get you yesterday when you were walking home but I guess you didn't hear me."

Morgan opened the door to the Subaru and leaned against the car. Scratching his arms and biting his lip, he shifted his eyes from Carrie to the yard. "Maybe I shouldn't have come . . . I'm sorry." He moved to open the door to his car.

"No, no," Carrie smiled apologetically. "I just wasn't expecting anyone and I do have some place to go in a little bit," she lied.

Carrie slid into one of the outdoor chairs on the porch, "So, what's up?"

Morgan turned, a broad grin crossing his lips. "I was trying to tell you yesterday when I saw you leaving the store. I found something you might like."

Cocking her head to the side, Carrie wondered just what he could be referring to.

"You know that Easy Storage, the place up the road? Well, I went to one of their auctions the other day and I bought one of the units they were selling off." Rubbing his hands together, Morgan fidgeted as he continued to explain.

"Well, lo and behold, the one I bought – only cost me fifty dollars—was stuffed full of all kinds of things and when I was looking through the boxes I came upon these." He leaned into the car and pulled out a carrying case.

"You and that dead lady, Sarah Chambers were talking about these a while back, weren't you?"

Morgan held open the case and lifted a glass figurine from one of the smaller boxes inside

He held out *Apple Tree Boy*, thrusting it toward Carrie.

"Didn't you tell me your mother had some Hummels? Didn't you say you were supposed to get them one day but you never did?" He looked quizzically at Carrie. "You said you'd like to have even one, but you couldn't afford to buy any."

Carrie nodded a yes as she lit a cigarette, took a drag and placed it in a sea shell ashtray. "Yes, Momma was going to give me one, but it never worked out." Carrie leaned forward, curious about the statuette he held.

"I guess who ever owned the storage unit didn't know what they had, probably just thought they were some five-and-dime crap. Anyway, I thought you might like them." Morgan walked toward Carrie, now standing on the porch.

She moved down the few steps to the yard and met him halfway. "That was nice of you, Morgan. I'll be glad to pay you for them." Still holding the figurine, he urged Carrie to take it.

Cupping it in her hands, she turned it upside down to view the stamp. "This is the real thing, Morgan. How can I ever repay you for this?"

"Ah hell, Carrie. I got more than enough other stuff from the storage unit to make up for anything I'd get for these things." Lowering his head, Morgan glanced back to try to meet Carrie's eyes. He could not.

Backing up to sit on the porch stairs, Carrie anxiously pulled the boxes from the case. All but the one was taped shut. Carefully she tore the tape away from each box and withdrew a figurine.

Her eyes lit up as she held the Hummels, rubbing her fingers against the smooth muted colors. This was most definitely a surprise. She never thought she would ever possess so many.

"Wow Morgan! These are really great." She stood and rushed to throw her arms around his neck. "Thank you, thank you, thank you. Daggone, I just . . ."

"It's no big deal, Carrie. Like I said they cost me hardly anything and I don't really want them."

"But what about your wife? What about Roz? Doesn't she like them? Doesn't she want them?"

Stunned by her questions, Morgan searched his thoughts to come up with another excuse, another lie.

"Naw, she's not into stuff like this. She likes collecting Beanie Babies."

"Oh, well they're nice too." Carrie tiptoed to reach her arms around Morgan's neck and kissed his cheek. "Thank you so much, Morgan. You're really are a nice guy. Your wife sure is a lucky woman."

******

Carrie watched as Morgan pulled from her driveway; she waved and called out an earnest 'thank you'.

Holding the case of Hummels close to her chest she drew in a deep breath. "Jeez, he is such a nice guy and he didn't make any moves or anything. I guess he's okay–I guess taking it's okay to take them." She looked at the case, took a shallow breath and walked back through the front door to her living room.

Wiping a tear from her cheek as she placed the *Apple Tree Boy* in the center of the small corner cabinet of her living room, Carrie recalled her mother's cabinet and how she had arranged her own Hummels to make them the centerpiece.

Her father had brought them back from Germany after being stationed there in the 1950's. Her mother adored them. So did Carrie.

They had been fixtures in her childhood home and she'd grown to love them, expecting that one day they would grace her own living room cabinet.

She shook her head, recalling the day Rufus, her father's hunting dog, crashed through the front door and bounded through the living room, knocking things about with his tail.

By the time her father caught up with the dog he had tipped over her mother's cabinet— everything inside was broken.

The bittersweet memory of her father consoling her mother was something Carrie would never forget. He was always loving and tender with his wife, attentive and giving to his children.

The thought of her family warmed Carrie and as she held the figurines, she stroked each one lovingly. "They never placed the blame on one another and they always could look to the other for comfort." She thought of her parents and their love and strength.

That was what she wanted in a relationship.

"I guess if it's meant to be, it will be," she said as she stood back to consider how to arrange the new contents of her curio.

"You're going to look a little out of place among all the nautical knickknacks I have," she spoke aloud, as she arranged and rearranged the various items.

A few framed photos sat on the shelves amidst inexpensive trinkets and assorted bits and pieces she had found while walking on the beach.

A couple of whelks, shark's eye shells, olive shells and a seahorse had been placed among the other objects.

Clearing the bottom shelf, Carrie dusted the glass and placed all five Hummels inside, pushing one here then another there.

As she moved the *Apple Tree Boy* about she noticed a nick in its base; it was tiny and it certainly didn't matter, so she turned the little statuette so that the notch could not be seen.

Carrie spent the next several hours arranging and rearranging her curio cabinet, making the contents look as attractive as they could amid the shells, glass pelicans, sea turtles and tiny ships in bottles.

Standing back to look at them, Carrie thought once again of Morgan. He sure had seemed nervous—but maybe that was because he had a crush on her.

Carrie knew that, and she certainly didn't want to encourage him in any way. She shook her head, "No, I don't need that. And even if he wasn't married . . . no."

Drawing her fingers to her chin, she looked again at the Hummels. "They sure are nice, but maybe I shouldn't have taken them."

As she spoke the words aloud, an immediate feeling of loss fell upon her. Drawing her hand to her chest she moaned low, "But I didn't ask for them. I didn't do anything wrong, did I?" She lifted her chin upward. "Did I?"

"I bet Roz doesn't even know he had them." Carrie pondered the gifts and how Morgan had behaved. Something just didn't feel right. Still, it was nice to have something she always wanted. The ambivalent feelings lingered, gnawing at her.

She sat down on a low back chair near the cabinet; Joey and Bella sat at her feet sympathetically looking up at her. Her hands folded across her lap, she sighed loudly, "I need to think about this one," she cooed to the animals, petting them as they wriggled and wagged their tails.

"I need to take a long walk and figure this out," she said, gazing intently at the figurines. Carrie slipped from her thong sandals slowly and stepped into her clogs, locked the door behind her and made her way toward the road that led to the sound.

It was a good mile or so there and she drank in the sunshine and warmth as she walked, smiling gently to herself as she thought of her new knickknacks, curious of why she felt such ambivalence about accepting them.

Nearing the bridge to the island, Carrie veered to her right and found the small footpath that led to one of the many creeks just off the sound and Intracoastal Waterway.

There, away from the throng of tourists, she would find solitude—a place she visited on occasion where driftwood logs provided seating and where she could watch the hermit crabs scuttle about in the marshy soil.

"Ah, this is the life." Carrie leaned back against a limb and propped her legs on the trunk of a fallen tree. It seemed to cradle her body just right and she relaxed, her eyes wandering from the blue and pillowed sky to along the shore line.

Several hermit crabs were sidling across the spongy marsh earth; it amazed her as they balanced oversized shells on their crustacean bodies, all the while manipulating the one giant claw.

She tittered, watching as they fought for territory, moving this way and that, sidling to and fro.

Bubbles rose from the ground; she always wondered what that meant and why that occurred and she studied the small holes in the ground where she supposed other marsh life lived.

An egret paraded slowly by, its crest blowing softly in the breeze; suddenly its long neck jerked downward as its pointy bill pierced the silent waters to stab a passing fish.

A gull glided by, squawking as it headed southward; Carrie watched as it soared and dipped to the land somewhere deeper into the marsh. Another came by and appeared to land in the same site; before long Carrie had watched nearly a dozen birds alight in the same area.

Two buzzards circled overhead at the same place and slowly descended. A loud squawking and flapping of wings followed as the gulls angrily took flight; one had a fuzzy mass in its beak, two other gulls fought in midair trying to make it theirs.

"Something's dead." She rose to her feet, watching another buzzard circle and land.

Tiptoeing for a better look, Carrie climbed out onto the limb of a fallen tree for a better view.

Something, she wasn't sure what it was, but something bright was clinging to a reed, flapping about on the breeze. She inched her way a bit farther on the fallen tree and peered even more toward where the buzzards and flapping bright cloth were.

Carrie wanted to move closer, to see just what all the bother was about. Stepping down from the tree, she moved carefully among the reeds and spongy ground toward what appeared to be the landing site of the buzzards, she could hear squishy sounds and the flapping of wings.

Pushing the tall marsh grasses aside, Carrie saw what all the commotion was about. The birds were busy tearing at a mass mired in the marshy goo.

She took a step closer, disturbing the buzzards. They flapped their wings angrily and squealed, but they did not move away from the mass—the body— that they were tearing flesh from.

Grabbing a few large shells from the shore, Carrie lobbed them at the buzzards, "Get the hell out of here, scat."

They flew off reluctantly and settled on a nearby scrub oak limb, arching their wings and squawking.

"Good googamooga!" Carrie backed away at first, but then moved closer to the corpse. The body was twisted like a rag, arms and legs askew; the head was turned to the side, partially mired in the marsh. Crabs were working diligently on the eyes and other soft tissue of the body while pogy nibbled at his shoeless feet lying lifeless in the water.

She recognized the man as the one with the British accent—the one who always bought sparkling juice. That was all he ever bought, never any food.

She hadn't realized he was bald. "That must have been a pretty good rug you wore, I never noticed it," she spoke nervously as she gently made her way around the twisted body.

Stepping closer, she felt her feet slip in the mire and caught herself quickly on a nearby clump of tall grass.

She eyed the tattoo of a nude woman on the man's chest. On his abdomen was a tattoo of an Asian woman with a snake wielding its way through her enormous breasts. "Not likely," she snorted. "I knew there was something weird about you the first time you came through my line. Bet you were some frigging wacko."

Chapter Sixteen

"Oh darn, here he comes." From the comfort of the divan, Carrie watched as the faded black Dodge Charger approached the turn to her home.

Damn, he looks so good, I'm going to have to be mean to him again. I'm not going to get my panties in a twist over this one. She rose and padded her way to the front door awaiting his knock.

"Detective Belkin. So I guess you want to question me again?"

"Yes ma'am," He replied coolly, his eyes staring into hers. "You ran off so fast—I have a few more questions I need to ask you."

"Well, come on in." She opened the screened door wide and watched as her small dogs scampered wildly to the detective's ankles. The hair on Joey's back was raised and his teeth bared. Intermittent shrill yaps escaped Bella's shaking body.

"Just don't make any sudden moves. Okay?" Carrie warned.

Don Belkin moved slowly to the nearest chair, pulled a notebook from his rear pants pocket and seated himself.

Sliding his eyes to meet Carrie's he asked, "You wouldn't mind putting them in another room would you?"

The dogs continued barking and growling. Carrie smiled, "Afraid?"

Leaning back, the chair jerked suddenly into reclining position, the foot rest raised his feet far above the ground and out of the reach of the snarling dogs. Don assessed his new position, "This will work, I guess."

Walking to the adjacent chair, Carrie moved a decorative pillow from the seat and sat down, curling her legs beneath her.

She had felt his eyes on her as she moved; the butterflies in her stomach fluttered a bit as she lowered her eyes–*be mean, be mean,* she ordered herself.

With a forced scowl on her face, Carrie raised her eyes. "Well?" The dogs both jumped in her lap, standing staunchly, eying the man across from their mistress.

"Why did you leave the scene of the crime?"

"Officer Abbott said I could."

Don nodded, flipped to a blank page in his notebook and began writing. "Abbott said you could leave after you told him you were going to vomit."

"He knows me. He comes in the store all the time. And then I told him that h*e* could come by and question me anytime. I'd be glad to talk with *him*."

"Miss Adams. I notice the vehemence in your voice. For some reason it is there. I don't know why. Most people, when they take that tone with me, are hiding something. Are you hiding anything Miss Adams?"

Yes. I'm very attracted to you. That's why I'm acting this way. I don't want you to know that. Carrie felt her face redden. "I'm sorry. I've become accustomed to growling at people, especially in the summer during the tourist season—you know—it's all those damn Yankees."

Belkin smiled, his full lips laid gently across his white teeth, his blue eyes sparking a little as he let out a short laugh. "I'm one of those *damn Yankees* you're referring to."

Don pulled the recliner back to a sitting position. "I know what you mean about rude and arrogant people, Miss Adams. I deal with them all the time and they're not all Yankees, some are very, very southern." He half smiled, "And usually they dislike me even more when they realize I'm a police officer."

Feeling the color drain from her face, Carrie whispered, "Sorry." She began gently stroking Joey as she lifted her chin, "What all do you want to know?"

"Why did you want to leave the scene of the crime so soon? And don't tell me you had to up-chuck." He leaned forward, settling his elbows on the arm rests of the recliner.

"You're going to think I'm nuts."

"Try me."

Carrie cradled Bella in her arms. "I couldn't stand those people." She looked meekly into Belkin's eyes. "No, really. That first one you found, Sarah Chambers. Lordy, I couldn't stand that woman. Out of all the customers that come in the store, she was the one I couldn't wait to have leave. She was the one I despised the most."

"From what I understand, not many who knew her could tolerate her either."

"And the other guy, the Bourne man. Well, he irked the hell out of me." A quick "ugh" escaped her lips as she rolled her eyes.

"I couldn't stand him—there was something about him, I don't know—I just know he made me feel uncomfortable."

Carrie lowered her eyes, "And he wore shorts all year long—that bugs the heck out of me, especially when it's thirty degrees."

Carrie noticed the grin Belkin was trying to fight and realized how petty she must have sounded.

"I know," Don nodded, "but he had a right to be as stupid as he wanted to be."

"You're right about that, and I guess I shouldn't let it get to me," Carrie allowed a shallow smile to escape her lips. "But, I guess I feel defensive when I get that *attitude*."

Belkin rested the pen against the notebook and looked into her eyes gently, knowingly, then smiled. "It all sounds familiar. You work a stressful job and have to put up with demeaning people—most of them do not have a southern accent. So it's easy to bunch them all together."

"You make me sound so judgmental."

Shrugging, Don picked the ink pen up again to write, "It's an easy thing to do, and we all do it to some degree."

Carrie nodded, feeling embarrassed of how she had let her feelings get the best of her.

"Back to the body you found," the detective leaned back in the chair, he seemed relaxed.

Suddenly Carrie felt at ease too; her tension and worry disappeared as she became aware of the detective's physical presence. It was calming—even his voice was soothing as he asked questions about the murder site—what time she had left her house—how well she knew the man. Detective Belkin asked many questions, but he never appeared accusatory—never assumed an attitude.

There was something about him that made her feel comfortable—she leaned forward responding, willing to be forthcoming.

"What prompted you to go out into the marsh? It can be a dangerous place; you know, snakes and other wild creatures hide in the grasses."

The ease she had been feeling suddenly disappeared as she remembered Morgan coming to her house with the Hummels—and how she had accepted them.

She recalled the uncertainty she had felt when she placed them in the cabinet; she stammered, "I—this, uh, man gave me . . ." she glanced at the curio cabinet and the Hummels inside.

"Yes," Don's brow crinkled. "Gave you . . .?"

215

"Some man, a customer at the store, came over here this morning and brought me a gift."

"Yes?" Don continued sitting calmly; he showed no emotion at all.

"I accepted the gift and then I felt so confused about it. I was having second thoughts about accepting gifts from a married man." Embarrassed at her admission, Carrie slumped down in the chair.

"And . . ." Detective Belkin waited for her to continue.

The two dogs watched Carrie as they sat on the floor studying their master's movements.

"I was upset about him coming here, he's married and I know he has a big crush on me."

Don nodded as he listened.

"I should have refused the gift, but I didn't . . . I felt confused so to clear my head, I went for a walk–walking always helps me clear my head."

"Me too," Catching her gaze, the detective nodded. "I walk when I need an answer to something."

"The marsh is always quiet."

"That's why you went to the marsh, to think–right?"

"Yes, to think."

Lifting his head as if to ask another question, Don paused as he eyed the contours of her face, *She really is a pretty woman*, he thought. He'd noticed her at Grocery World, but hadn't she been seeing Hank?

Carrie waited for the detective to speak; he did not.

Finally after a silence that felt too long, Carrie spoke, "Wish I wouldn't have taken that walk now."

Don grinned, "I bet. It must have been shocking."

"You have no idea."

"Okay, I guess that'll wrap things up for me for now." Standing, Don slipped the notebook back into his pocket.

As he rose, Joey quickly walked to the man, sniffed his pant's leg, and then wagged his tail.

Bella sat quietly observing, and then curled her body into a soft ball to sleep.

"It's really a hot one out there today. Can I get you a glass of iced tea?" Carrie asked.

"Well . . ."

"I have disposable cups—I can put the tea in one and you can carry it with you." She turned to smile back at Belkin.

"Sounds good to me."

As Carrie busied herself preparing the tea, Belkin looked around the living area of Carrie's small home.

He noticed how neatly the woman had things organized. He liked the furniture—older pieces, obviously refurbished. The décor was simple, not busy or ornate. It felt cozy and welcoming in her home.

The corner cabinet caught his eye and he moved closer to look at the objects inside.

The top shelf held pictures—old pictures. He thought they must be her parents.

There were also pictures of young children, a boy and girl. Next to them were pictures of what looked like the same boy and girl only older.

His eyes lingered on a couple of the photos as he recognized the resemblance of the eyes, nose and other facial features—finding Carrie in them.

Looking down to the second shelf he noticed the nautical items—a coral piece with a gold dolphin, a sand dollar painted with fish and sea horses, glass sea turtles in various sizes.

On the bottom shelf, arranged so that the *Apple Tree Boy* was in the middle, were five Hummels. He looked curiously at them, paying special attention to the boy statuette in the center. Moving to capture the sides and back, Don examined the figurine. At the base was a small chip, just like the one that was on the figurine at Sarah's.

"So, just what sort of gifts did this married man give you?"

Carrie ignored the question.

"So, you collect Hummels?" he called out again.

"Um hum." She handed the plastic cup of iced tea to Belkin.

"I've been looking at yours, they're very nice. May I open the case and look at them more closely?" he asked, taking a sip from the plastic cup as he squatted down nearer to the bottom shelf of the curio. "Are these the gifts you were given by that married man you were talking about?"

Feeling the color leave her face, Carrie stopped for a moment.

"You don't mind if I take a look at them do you?"

"Do I have to let you?" Her tone turned icy.

"Do I need a search warrant?"

"What the hell is going on? One minute I think you actually may be human and then all of a sudden I feel like I'm being interrogated by the Nazis. Just what is going on, Detective Belkin?"

His eyes searched her face. He knew she was either a very good actress or was truly in the dark about the Hummels. Or maybe it was a coincidence that the Boy in the Apple Tree figurine had a chip in the exact spot as the one that had been in Sarah Chambers' étagère.

"Ma'am-Carrie—let's sit back down for a minute, okay?"

Nodding, Carrie sat once again in the chair facing the recliner. "So what's the problem with my Hummels? I just got them."

Don nodded, "So they were the gifts you mentioned earlier?"

He took another sip from the cup and set it on the table next to the recliner. "I can't really go into it. But I would like to know exactly from whom you got the figurines and how long you have had them. You mentioned that the gifts were given to you this morning."

Carrie nodded, and then told the story of Morgan bringing the Hummels earlier that day, how she had felt confused after taking them and her subsequent walk to figure things out.

"I saw the birds—the sea gulls and then all the buzzards—and I knew something was dead." She shook her head. "I don't know why I had to walk over there, but I did and that's when I saw this twisted mess that looked like the British guy that comes in Grocery World."

Detective Belkin wrote in his notebook. He asked no further questions. Finally when she was through, he looked at her apologetically.

"I'm sorry, Carrie, but I'm going to have to take the Hummels in."

"I knew it was too good to be true, Detective Belkin." She breathed an exaggerated sigh and grinned, shaking her head.

"And call me Don, please." He held out the empty cup of tea, rattling the remaining ice, "One for the road?"

"Sure." Taking the plastic cup to the kitchen, she filled it once again with ice and tea, then handed it back to Don. "I'll go get the case."

Returning from her bedroom, case in hand, Carrie leaned down and gently picked each Hummel from the cabinet. Wrapping them all carefully, she situated them in the case Morgan had given her.

"Thanks." Don opened the screened door and then turned back to face her; the regret in his voice was unmistakable. Holding her gaze for a moment, he then reached a hand to touch her on the shoulder. "I'm sorry, Carrie—you seem like a nice person—well, I'll let you know—hopefully I can get them back to you at some point."

As he walked slowly to the Charger, Carrie held the screened door open and called, "You can keep the cup." *Jeez, what a dumb thing to say.* She shook her head as she watched him walk away—he had a nice walk, slow, deliberate—it was definitely a turn on. She wondered if he could feel her eyes on him as she ogled the long slender curve of his legs. Her eyes moved upward to the slight sway of his back and the broadness of his shoulders, to the back of his neck and thick blond hair, cut short against it.

✳✳✳✳✳✳✳✳

Don sat on the edge of Sarah's king size bed and studied the contents of the cabinet where he had first seen the Hummels. He eyed the cheap ceramic pieces on the glass shelf.

Holding *Apple Tree Boy* in his hand, he pondered the connection of the theft and the murders. Could meek, ever-nervous Morgan Simpers be a murderer?

As he closed the cabinet door, he ran his fingers over the delicate statuette, examining it. *What is so special about you?*

Chapter Seventeen

"It is done," Hank spoke aloud, "and I'm glad Don Belkin didn't have to die. I like him. We could be friends."

Running his fingers through his hair, he pondered his last statement. "After all, he really didn't want to be involved with all the drugs. But friends? It's been a long time since I've had a friend. I don't think he'd approve." Hank shrugged, "too bad."

Opening the glass door to let his cat, Tango, back inside, Hank thought of the first time he'd seen the detective.

He'd been there the night Belkin was dragged into it all.

Hidden high up in a tree stand, he was there among the yaupons, pines and oaks—camouflaged, on Butler property.

The men's voices had carried in the still night air; he listened as Milton instructed Don on how things were going to be.

He caught the surprise and the rejection in Don's voice as he argued with Milton and the man in the skiff with the thick New York accent.

As he listened, it became clear to Hank that Belkin wanted no part of the selling and distributing drugs.

He saw the package in Reggie's hand—saw him hand it over to Milton. And he heard Belkin refuse, and argue with the two other men.

"What else was Don supposed to do?" Hank said aloud. "They had him between a rock and a hard place."

As he shuffled his bare feet to one of the overstuffed chairs of his living room, Hank scooped up Tango and cradled the cat in his arms. It purred loudly as it reclined comfortably against the man's body.

"Bastards." He leaned back into the chair and stroked the belly of the big black and white cat.

As he observed the three men that night, he decided right then to make it a point to get to know them—to do everything in his power to stop them. He wanted to expose these people—but he couldn't—no, *wouldn't* go to the police. He'd seen too many people get off with a slap of the wrist—he would take care of this in his own way.

Hank gently held Tango's head in the palm of his hand.

She kneaded her claws into his arm; his eyes teared.

The pain of watching people he had grown up with destroy their own lives with drugs was overwhelming—he didn't understand the weakness, the addiction.

It was easy for him to put down a drink, easy to turn down coke. Even cigarettes had been easy to quit. Marijuana had done nothing for him the few times he'd tried it.

Hank did not like the feeling of something controlling him, rather, he felt that he must always be in control of himself.

"Why?" Hank slowly shook his head. "How can people allow something to control them—that's what drugs do."

He'd seen personalities change—and dreams fade away and lives lost with no hope—and lives destroyed.

Drugs were like a thief; they stole your soul, and replaced it with wanton emptiness. They had taken his beautiful Emma from him and he would never forget that.

A teardrop fell onto the furry belly of Tango; Hank clenched his jaw tightly, then breathed softly through his mouth. As he gazed into the expanse of ocean before him, he pictured Emma; her head tilted back as she laughed, her eyes twinkling as they narrowed in laughter. She was beautiful, with her long blonde hair and freckles.

She was always laughing when her image came to Hank's mind.

Continuing to stroke the cat, his thoughts moved from those of his deceased wife back to his hatred for controlling substances and the low life scum who sold them.

"They, those scumbags who are too lazy to work for a living don't care who they hurt. They're part of all the *change* around here."

Since the hurricanes of '96 there had been a lot of changes on the island in surrounding communities. The place was growing by leaps and bounds.

Huge buildings hulked where sand dunes once stood. Soundfront property, where the most fragile link in the chain of aquatic life existed, was being destroyed, so someone could have a waterfront view. It made no sense to Hank and it angered him that dunes and land had been destroyed to satisfy someone's greed.

The price of land had gone sky high too. Even his land—his parent's land—had become priceless. It had gone from being worth cents an acre to thousands an acre. In fact, he'd been offered millions for the estate.

The little beach house and the fifty acres of mainland property facing Surf City would never be sold as long as he walked the earth. Here on his land, on the Butler family land, is what life had been like forty years ago—a hundred years, for that matter. He was not about to sell the last remaining stretch of land those generations of Butlers had farmed, hunted and fished; he loved it, its beauty and the peace it held.

In younger days, Hank crabbed and shrimped the sloughs and creeks there with his friends. He explored the marshes and tiny islands that dotted the sound waters.

Now, huge apartment complexes and upscale communities stood there; the sloughs and creeks had been dredged. In their place docks and piers moored forty-foot cabin cruisers, and sports fisherman boats used by weekend sailors.

So many local people were not even allowed the luxury of a simple walk in the marsh where they had spent their childhood. There were now regulations prohibiting casting a net to catch shrimp or gigging flounder. Not many locals did that anymore and Hank knew It was only a matter of time before it disappeared all together.

Taxes had shot up and those local residents, who had lived on the water for generations, were forced to sell their land. Some moved out of the area, many lived in rented trailers eking out a living—trying to abide by the new laws that restricted their fishing. Others tried learning a new trade—abandoning a generational lifestyle. Yes and a few did sell out.

Had his parents not been so frugal and not invested wisely, he would have been one of those who were forced to sell the land and move on. He was lucky to have the waterfront acreage and the beach house.

As the town grew, Hank saw the simple natural pleasures of slow southern living gradually disappear.

It ached his heart to watch as the landscape changed and as the history of the island became distorted and taken for granted. It was as if the past had never been at all.

Hank equated the changes with the loss of his wife, Emma. All the change, all the so-called *progress* seemed to coincide with the accident—with the loss of his darling wife.

It all tied together—this string of transformation from a sleepy island town to a tourist trap. It felt dirty to him, unnatural, and there was no way he could stop it. Hank felt like someone had put a curse on him and all that he loved and cherished.

So on that night, nearly five years ago, as he sat there in his tree stand, staring out across the water remembering his wife Emma—aching still and searching for someone other than himself to blame for her death—it came to him as he listened to the police officers conduct their drug exchange.

He may not be able to turn back the clock—he may not be able to wipe away all the hideous changes that had befallen Surf City and Topsail Island—but he may be able to put a dent in it. Retribution—that was the word.

Someone must pay. But who? He would wait. The right time would come. In the meantime he would find out all he could, make friends with as many of the police officers he could, become friendly with everyone who was new to the island. And then he would act.

Stroking Tango gently, Hank's chest rose and fell as he breathed heavily. "I hate them all."

He closed his eyes and smiled. "Except Don, I'm glad Don didn't have to die, he and I have become sort of . . . *friends* . . . he talks to me about his ex and the kid."

The cat meowed up to him, and purred loudly.

"And you missy, it's a good thing you can't talk. You've seen it all, since a kitten when Emma brought you home." He released the cat from his cradled arm; it sat facing him in his lap.

Stroking her back as she settled there, Hank's fingers scratched her favorite spot behind the ears. "Don's not a bad fella—he's been through hell with his family. Then his son, jeez—I can only imagine the hypocrisy he's been feeling since getting involved with Reggie and that bitch Sarah. We'll have to wait and see if he continues on the path or if he'll seize this opportunity to get out."

Hank stood, releasing the cat to the floor, he stretched widely and yawned then padded into the kitchen to open the refrigerator.

"Ah, fishy, fishy, fish." His eyes settled on a platter of cold filets. "You know," he spoke to Tango as she wound her body between his legs, "doing Mick was fun—I enjoyed getting rid of that womanizer. He had no respect for women, no idea how to treat them. You need to be tender . . ." The words caught in his throat as he closed the door of the refrigerator-the small framed photo of his deceased wife stared back at him. "My dearest Emma, oh how I miss you."

Chapter Eighteen

Phil skidded the bicycle to a stop, dust and gravel flew about.

Buck Butler lifted his head from beneath the hood of his Chevy pickup. Wiping the grease from his hands on the front of his faded overalls, he stood and gazed at the boy walking toward him.

"Ah shit," he mumbled to himself. "I don't need this kind of trouble."

As he neared the man, Phil called out, "Hey, bro. How's business?"

Buck's lips tightened. He didn't like being called *bro*, especially from this California know-it- all, "Um. Business? Speakin' of business, why don't you help me with some shrimping? I'm going out this evening–could use some help."

"Ha! don't know a thing about shrimping."

"It's never too late to learn, *bro*." Buck retorted.

The sarcastic tone in the older man's reply burned the teenager.

Phil slid his eyes toward the pickup. "That old hunk of junk broke down again?"

"Just changing a spark plug." Buck leaned and rested an elbow on the side of the Chevy. "Nah, really, why don't you come on out with me this evening? If you're going to live here, why not learn something useful? And besides, it's fun."

"Fun? I need another dime—that's fun."

"I've been thinking about that. You know, your father's a cop. He's been checking out all those murders. And that one, the last one—the English guy—he was the one who was supplying you with weed.

"Now the cops are all wound up looking for drug dealers. It won't be long before they start asking *questions* and I ain't getting myself thrown in the slammer for selling to you. I'm just gonna take care of me and mine from now on."

"Ah, come on now Buck. It's just a little old dime. That's not going to hurt you any. You could use the money, huh?"

"I'm going shrimping this evening to make money. I decided I ain't selling no more to nobody."

Phil could feel the anger rise inside of him, but he curtailed it quickly, "Whoa, man. This will be the last time, promise."

"I tell you what. You come out with me tonight and help me shrimp and I'll pay you your dime bag."

"Deal." Phil stuck his hand out to shake Buck's. Reluctantly Buck reached for the boy's.

"Now, you gotta work—I mean *work* for this. The shrimp don't just jump in the boat, you know."

"How hard can it be?" Smiling, Phil suppressed his eagerness to try something new. His dad would be pleased to hear that he was actually going to learn a little about one of the local businesses.

Ambivalent feelings stirred him as he pondered the possibility of pleasing his father for once. Did he really want to do that?

Buck threw out the tail bag and let the rest of the net feed out into the water. "Help me with the tickle chain," he called to Phil.

The boy glanced quizzically at Buck, "The what?"

"The tickle chain." His eyes slid to the chain that ran along the bottom of the net.

"Then help me throw these doors out."

"What do they do?" The poor boy peered curiously at the large flat pieces of wood.

"They hold the net open, dummy. Now, don't ask so many questions, just do what I tell ya to do and it'll all make sense later."

Phil threw the chained netting into the still waters and followed Buck's lead as he reached for the doors.

"This is more work than I thought it would be," Phil felt beads of sweat dampen his forehead.

"Hey, this is just the sound, you try doing this out there." He nodded eastward toward the Atlantic. "Now, that's what you call working."

"Why don't you go shrimping out in the ocean?" Phil asked.

"I get seasick."

The boy guffawed, "Seasick? a big tough southern boy like you?"

"Don't make fun, brat. If you've ever been seasick you'd know what I'm talking about. It hits you and you don't quit heaving, even after all the food's gone you're puking green bile. I'm telling you, you're begging God to let you die."

"Ha!" Laughing aloud, Phil kept his eye on the net as they slowly trawled. "I'd like to try it sometime."

"I got a friend in Sneads Ferry might let you go with him sometime. Now, he's got a big boat, near 'bout forty foot."

Relaxing as they moved slowly through the water, Phil studied the outline of the nighttime shore.

"This part's easy," Buck chuckled.

"Yeah ... how about letting me have a little grass while we're taking it easy?"

"Nope, that's something I don't do while I'm on the water, I don't get high and I don't drink."

"I'm not asking for a beer, *bro,* I'm asking you to forward a little of that dime bag to me," Phil shot back.

Reaching into a cooler near the starboard bulkhead, Buck pulled out a can of soda. "Here, have one of these. They're chock full of caffeine-that ought to keep you going."

Phil grabbed the soda and popped the top, leaned his head and swilled it to nearly empty.

They trawled mostly in silence. Occasionally one of them would comment on a house or boat they saw moored at private dock.

After a bit, Buck instructed the boy to help pull in the doors and the netting. It was a good night and their catch was well over one hundred pounds.

"So, it ain't such a hard job. Is it Phil?" Buck asked, turning to the teenager.

"No, not bad at all. I could get to like this."

"Well, how 'bout you help me out through the season."

"How long is that?"

"Through the summer . . . you'd be done early August."

"Sounds good to me, partner." Slapping the older man on the shoulder, Phil grinned then asked. "How about a joint to celebrate?"

Pausing, Buck considered the question as he looked about their surroundings. "I think it'll be okay. I don't see nobody else out here."

As the two relaxed on the transom, they passed a large hand rolled joint back and forth. Unaware that the anchor had not set, the boat slowly drifted close to a vacant pier house.

Suddenly, a swarm of policemen descended from the darkened structure.

Several bright lights glared in their faces; Phil and Buck lifted their hands high in the air.

******

With his arms folded across his chest, and his head hung low near his chest, Don sat rigidly in the chair waiting for Phil to be released into his custody.

He raised his head slightly as he heard the door to the holding cell open. Immediately he recognized the scuffed tennis shoes of his son.

Phil walked into the room slowly; he knew his father was aware of his presence but would not lift his head to meet his eyes. Don simply stood up and started moving toward the exit.

"Sorry sir, I didn't know he was your son–gave the last name of Cummings," said Officer Abbott.

Don acknowledged the officer's comment with a nod of his head.

As he waited for his son's presence beside him, he walked to the door and held it open, never looking at Phil.

Where is the lecture? Where's the red faced know-it-all?" Phil thought, the anticipation of condemnation from his father had him building the wall he was so familiar with.

The short drive to their home seemed hours long as his father slowly drove in silence. Phil wanted to speak–wanted to explain why he had used his mother's name–wanted to say he was sorry again, or at least offer an excuse, but the words wouldn't come and his father never opened the door for conversation.

He glanced at his father's profile, stern-unyielding. Still, he noticed the slump in the man's shoulders and the way his head was cocked to the side.

Surprised by the feeling of shame that swept over him, Phil could feel the sweat pop out on his brow and the clamminess of his hands, "Gee Dad, I didn't know Buck . . ."

He stopped abruptly when his father turned to him, the flashing yellow light of the stop signal illuminating Don's face. It was not anger there, nor sadness, but a look Phil hadn't seen before. His father's lips seemed to begin the formation of words, but none came.

Don paused and turned left toward their home.

******

Lying on his back; his arms resting behind his head, Phil stared at the bedroom ceiling. He felt rotten. "I'm a liar," he said aloud. Admitting it was not easy. Admitting anything to himself was not easy. Certainly, admitting anything to his father would be impossible.

"Besides, there's nothing wrong with smoking a little weed. Mom does it." He thought of his mother, how she'd sometimes buy for him. But then she hadn't worked in years, and she rarely bathed except when a *friend* came over to the house.

Those visits rarely lasted longer than an hour or so.

It's the law that needs to be changed—I did nothing wrong. The old man is an idiot. As he thought the words, Phil immediately felt guilty. He pictured his mother again toking on a roach, laughing, and then he saw her snort a line of coke.

"I'm not going to do that." Rolling to his left side, Phil closed his eyes to sleep.

Don didn't know how to approach his son. He didn't know what to say, anger rose too quickly when he considered confronting the boy.

He'd have to wait a while and cool off. Then they'd talk. But what about? *The kid doesn't listen*.

The energy seemed to drain out of his body as he contemplated the path of Phil's life. Don grimaced, *They let him off with community service— a misdemeanor. Is that going to be enough to scare him straight?*

Since the arrest Don had been distant to his son. Sure, he had gotten the lawyer for him and paid the fine, but the attitude. That was the real problem.

He wasn't condoning smoking pot, there were worse things. Lots of teens tried it. But Don had the feeling that Phil was beyond the *trying* stage. That worried him-and the attitude-that same condescending, arrogant attitude that Maggie had.

According to her, there was nothing wrong with doing drugs—any drugs. He didn't want to see Phil end up like Maggie.

That Sunday, Phil pulled on a pair of clean jeans and a polo shirt; he'd decided to go to church with his father without even being asked.

As he entered the kitchen, Don was seated at the table, his hands wrapped around a steaming coffee mug.

He looked up, "Thought you didn't believe any of that religious crap."

"I don't," the boy shrugged.

Don eyed his son; his hair was neatly combed. He wore a pair of docksider shoes on his feet; they looked clean enough. And there was a look on his son's face. Was it contrition?

He dare not say a word in fear of hearing an excuse or a half-hearted *I'm sorry*.

He'd heard enough *I'm sorrys* in his life to fill a thousand semi trucks. And he didn't want to hear another one.

Don would offer no more lectures on how to behave, or who to hang out with, regardless of how hard it was going to be. He knew it was up to the boy to accept his love—he couldn't make him want it.

There had been days when he had thought about giving up on Phil, just shipping him back to his mother. Lord knows it would have saved him a lot of money.

But he wasn't going to do that. He wasn't going to give up on his son like he had on his wife.

Had he tried hard enough with her? Don didn't know, but he did know that he would try again with his son, at least one more time—maybe a thousand times.

"This is my payback," Don said aloud. Having been lost in such deep thought he'd forgotten the boy was standing right in front of him.

"Huh?" Digging his hands in his jeans' pocket, Phil stared blankly at his father.

"Oh, nothing," Don grinned, "let me get another shirt on and we'll go."

Father and son sat quietly in the pew as the minister instructed the congregation to open their hymnals to page two seventy-five.

Don mouthed the words to the song; Phil looked at the page but said nothing.

As the minister spoke earnestly, Don watched the man's expressions, his gestures. He seemed so rapt in the words he spoke. But Don only heard bits and pieces as his thoughts wandered to scenarios of crime, loss, addiction and failure for his son's future—and the fear that he would end up like his ex-wife.

Phil sat tensely next to his father. His thoughts too, wandered to his own past-the way things were when he was a young child and the images of his mother drooling and vomiting—being with men, many men—these things filled his head.

"I'm sorry." Phil's head snapped quickly to the left as his father spoke. The two looked at each other, pausing as they heard the minister say, "The sins of the father are visited upon the son."

With trembling lips Phil brushed away a tear, *I won't cry,* he thought, covering his face with his hands.

The boy slumped in the pew and whispered, "I'm so sorry Dad, I'm not like Mom. I promise."

Don felt his son's body quake with sobs, he reached his arm around him and pulled him closer, "We'll talk. Okay?"

Chapter Nineteen

"That's the kid," Mindy nudged Carrie as she walked past her register, "the one that caught Sarah Chambers' ear on the pier."

Nodding, Carrie studied the slender boy walking beside Detective Belkin. He was nearly as tall and had the same blond hair. She watched as the boy grabbed a cart and as father and son walked toward the produce department.

"Looks just like his daddy." Mindy raised an eyebrow. "Wouldn't I like -?"

"Mindy!" Carrie's admonishing tone surprised the young cashier. "That boy can't be more than fifteen or sixteen. What are you thinking?"

"Not the boy, dummy, the father." Her hands on her hips, Mindy exaggerated a sneer, "I'm not that desperate."

"Well, I don't know about that," Carrie teased and grinned broadly. "You know, he was over at my house the other day."

"The boy?" Mindy smirked.

"Stupid . . . the father." Shaking her head, Carrie leaned forward as a customer approached her station.

Mindy nodded as she too welcomed a customer and began checking items. Shooting a glance to Carrie, Mindy raised her eyebrows and mouthed the word, *later*.

The woman at Carrie's register began unloading her groceries, placing all cold items together and boxed and canned items together, as well.

"Hello, how are you today? Welcome to Grocery World." Carrie quickly glanced at the woman as she slid the first item across the scanner.

Without lifting her head, the woman barked, "I want my cold items bagged in paper and I have environmental bags for the others."

She threw three cloth bags on top of the groceries and glared angrily at Carrie.

Setting the bags aside, Carrie grinned politely, "No problem."

"And don't break my eggs. The last time I was in here, all my eggs got broken."

"I'm sorry about that ma'am. I'll take special care to make sure that doesn't happen."

Smiling to herself, Carrie thought—*that had to be Joel. He had to be the one to check her groceries last. He loves breaking eggs—especially if the customer is a butthead.*

******

As Mindy and Carrie strode from the rear entrance of the store, Paula waved as she crossed from the parking lot, "Busy today?"

"Off and on, it comes in spurts," Mindy called back.

"Are you on break or leaving?" Nearing the picnic table where the two cashiers sat, Paula reached into a pocket and withdrew a long hair clip.

"Mindy's leaving—lucky dog," Carrie answered as she leaned against the table. "I've got three more hours."

"I'm heading to the beach as soon as I get my bathing suit on." Flipping her limp hair to the side, Mindy giggled as she pulled a yellow and blue bikini from her bag.

"Why do you always get scheduled so you get off before the sun goes down?" asked Carrie.

"Because I'm young and Fern understands that I need to have fun." Swinging her hips, Mindy laughed sarcastically. "Hell, I don't know why, but I'm not going to complain."

Carrie uncrossed her legs and patted her thighs, "It's all for the best, I guess. I look like a sack of potatoes in a bathing suit."

"You do not," Mindy chimed, "I hope when I'm your age I look as good."

"Thanks." Carrie rolled her eyes. "I guess." She paused for a moment and shared an understanding look with Paula as she approached the table.

"Tired? Back hurt? Or did a customer stick it to you again?" Paula pulled her hair back, twisting it, and then clipped it against her head.

"All of the above, but I'm numb now," Carrie sighed. "That old bat Chambers getting killed kind of took the hate out of me." Reaching into her pocket she withdrew a pack of cigarettes. "Or I've gotten to the point where it's all *sticks and stones*."

"But you *are* still squeezing bread," Paula chided.

"Yeah, but not with as much enthusiasm," Carrie winked.

"Give it a while and you'll be back to your old self." Taking a long drag from her electronic cigarette, Mindy settled herself on the bench.

Carrie and Paula both watched as the young girl exhaled vapor; releasing a pleasing cherry aroma.

"You need to try this sometime. These things will help you cut down on your smoking and maybe even quit," Mindy spoke authoritatively.

"And since I only smoke during *terrorist* season, well . . ." she paused, "You know, smoking causes those ugly deep lines around your lips and the older you get the worse it's going to be." She looked apologetically at Carrie.

"Anyway, that's what my momma says and she smoked for twenty years." Taking another long pull on the e-cig, Mindy continued, "And you sure were checking out *Blondie* this morning when he came in."

"Look at her," Paula pointed to Carrie.

A smile had settled on Carrie's lips.

"She's blushing!" Leaning in, Paula's eyes grew wide. "Okay, what's up?"

"He's been to my house." Smashing the butt of her cigarette in the sand bucket, Carrie sighed.

Paula positioned her elbows on the table, "So, you've been a busy little bee. You didn't tell us about—"

"Hunka, hunka, burning love," Mindy interrupted.

Carrie could feel her cheeks burning; she tried to wipe the smile from her face, but recalling the last moments of Don's visit and the tender look in his eyes, made it impossible.

"It was only official business." The color left her cheeks as she related events leading up to her finding Mick's body and the arrival of Detective Belkin. "I've been trying not to think too much about the dead guy." She shivered and raised a hand to her brow.

"So *you're* the one who found his body?" Mindy pulled again on the e-cig. "Why didn't you tell me? You've been here since lunch time."

"I didn't—don't like talking about it. It was really nasty, ugly . . . the body was so twisted and—"

"That's enough, honey. You just sit there and relax—don't think about it." Paula stretched her arm around Carrie's shoulder, patting her arm.

"Wow, I'm sorry Carrie." Mindy pushed the bikini back in its bag, "It's like, I can't believe you found a dead body."

Paula shot the girl an angry look. "I don't think she wants to discuss this, Mindy. Maybe your boyfriend Robby can fill you in on the gory details, he's a cop."

"I didn't mean to upset you, I'm sorry." Rising from her seat, Mindy leaned to hug Carrie. "It must have been horrible."

Nodding, Carrie gently pushed the two women away, "I'm okay. It's okay."

She looked at her cell phone and read the time, "I better get back to my register before I get fired."

"Yeah, I need to get my bikini on if I'm going to the beach," Mindy cooed, her eyes begging forgiveness. "I'm so sorry, Carrie," the girl repeated as she walked toward the parking lot.

******

"It was horrible, Paula," Carrie looked intently at her friend as she crossed legged on the divan; Bella jumped to her lap while Joey sat beneath the sofa eying Paula.

"I saw my granddaddy at his funeral and one of my aunts died when I was about ten, but I haven't ever seen anything like this and I don't ever want to again."

Nodding, Paula drew her lips in tightly, "I saw some guy who'd been chewed up by a propeller - years ago. It was gruesome."

"And all these dead people showing up around here—it's scary, I wish I knew who was killing everybody. I wish they'd catch who ever it is and throw them in jail."

"Yeah, it is scary. But I'll bet you ten dollars it all has to do with drugs."

"Really? You think all these dead people showing up has to do with drugs?"

Paula nodded as she pursed her lips.

"Even dumpy old Sarah Chambers?"

"You'd be surprised at some of the things that go on around here-and who does what. It sure is a lot different on the island than from when I was growing up. It used to be just a sleepy little town, the worst offense was when somebody got stuck in the sand. It's different now . . . drugs are everywhere and I'm not just talking about a little pot."

"That's sad."

"Yeah, it is. But one good thing about living here—the problems aren't nearly as bad as bigger towns and cities. It's still pretty low key."

Paula unclipped her hair and gathered it into a ponytail. Her eyes lit up as she changed the subject.

"So . . . Detective Belkin came to question you about the dead body you found, huh?"

"Yeah, and he found the Hummels."

"What?"

"The Hummels, little glass figurines—I had them in my curio cabinet."

"That one?" Paula pointed to the wooden cabinet in the corner. "I never saw them."

"Oh." Carrie paused for a moment considering whether or not she should mention Morgan Simpers. She searched her friend's face, "You have to promise."

"Promise what?"

"What I'm about to tell you. You can't say a word about it. Okay?"

Paula extended a finger and pressed it to her

chest. "Cross my heart. But who in the heck am I going to tell anyway?"

Taking a deep breath and settling her feet on the floor, Carrie began, "Morgan Simpers, it was him."

"He's the one who's been killing everybody?"

"No!" Carrie's brow furrowed. "It was Morgan Simpers who gave me the Hummels. He came over here a few days ago with a satchel—said he bought one of those storage units at an auction and that he found them inside one of the boxes."

"Why would he give them to you?"

"I don't know . . . he said he heard me talking about them with Sarah Chambers . . . uh-oh," Gasping, Carrie brought her hand to her mouth. "Maybe he *did* kill Sarah for the figurines, so he could give them to me."

Walking into the kitchen, Carrie opened the refrigerator door and pulled two cans of Pepsi Cola from the shelf. Bella and Joey followed behind, looking up as they waited for a treat.

Reaching into the pretzel bag, Carrie handed one to each dog, then held the bag out, "Want any?" she asked Paula.

"No thanks."

"He is kind of weird, isn't he?" Carrie spoke.

"Yep, if there's one thing Morgan is, it is weird. But I don't think he's a murderer."

Cupping her chin in her hand Paula continued, "You know, he used to bring me shrimp all the time." She tittered, "I knew he had a crush on me, but honey, there is just no way I'd mess around with poor old Morgan. He's just a lonely little guy."

"He probably *bought* the Hummels from Sarah." Carrie reached for two glasses from an over head cabinet and filled them with cola.

Paula nodded a thank you as Carrie handed her a glass, "I will tell you, if he was going to murder anyone it would be that wife of his."

"Really?" Carrie queried.

"Yep," Paula nodded. "Poor old Morgan is married to the witch of Topsail–the meanest, most condescending person, I've ever met. She even puts Yankees to shame."

"She must be something then," Carrie laughed, "poor guy."

"Hey, don't feel sorry for him. That guy's got it made in the shade. He doesn't even have a job– doesn't need to work."

"Well, how does he-?"

"His wife is loaded, sweetie. Miss Roz–her folks are loaded to the gills–used to have a lot of land around here, and some up around Raleigh."

"So he just kind of does *whatever*?"

"Hunts and fishes, and keeps that little mansion he and his wife live in looking like a magazine cover."

Carrie leaned back in the divan, pulling her legs around her. "I keep learning more and more about the people here, thought I knew everything by now."

"She keeps him on a leash–gives him an allowance." Paula chuckled, "Yep, and you still haven't told me about that gorgeous detective and his visit."

"Well, he was over here asking questions about that body I found out in the marsh—how I came upon it, what I was doing out there—and I offered him some tea and while I was getting it for him he saw the Hummels in my curio cabinet."

"So he was nosing around your living room?"

Carrie shrugged, "I guess. But he was very nice."

"Of course he's going to be nice, Carrie. He wants you to trust him so he can get all the information he needs."

Carrie thought of how he had looked at her—tenderly, with concern. *Don*, he had asked her to call him Don. She surely was not going to tell Paula that.

Searching her friend's face, Carrie shook her head, "Maybe you're right. He did, after all, take them and I haven't seen him since. Earlier this morning he was in the store with his son and he didn't even come to my station."

"You need to be less trusting, Carrie. Usually when people are nice it means they want something." Paula turned the glass of Pepsi up and drank the remaining bit. "As for Morgan, I really don't think he would kill anyone at all—I think he's harmless, just lonely for someone to be kind to him."

"But what about the Hummels? Why would Detective Belkin take them?"

"Beats me." As she stood to leave, Paula bent to pet the dogs; they sniffed politely at her hand.

Setting the empty glass on the end table, Paula shrugged, "I'm sure he had his reasons."

Chapter Twenty

Don held the small figurine in his hand; his fingers moved lightly over the chip at its base.

The statuette didn't look that special, it wasn't really—just a very ordinary statue of a boy swinging in an apple tree.

He'd researched Hummels; they'd become popular in the 1930s in Germany and even more so in American during World War II, as soldiers sent them to loved ones at home.

But they weren't even that valuable—maybe priced between two and four hundred dollars each. He figured the value lay in sentiment more than anything.

As Detective Belkin set the small porcelain piece on his desk, he aligned it with the four others he had recovered from Carrie's house.

He liked her and had been attracted to her ever since she'd moved to the island. But Hank had expressed an interest in the woman and Don wasn't about to move in on his territory.

They had, after all, become friends, sort of. He'd been out fishing on Hank's Robalo a couple of times, and a few times met at Batts' Grill for breakfast. That was about the extent of the friendship.

The last time he's seen him, Hank had been having breakfast with another girl. Don assumed the relationship was over.

Don's first impulse was sympathy for Carrie. And though he liked Hank, he was well aware of his reputation for dumping women.

His second impulse was to figure out the right approach—just how to ask her out for a date.

Yes, he liked Carrie, but just how much did she know and why had Morgan given the figurines to her?

Sarah Chambers' fingerprints were all over them. Only Sarah's, but then Morgan would have worn gloves. He wasn't stupid; he was just a good old boy who happened to be henpecked and maybe a little lazy.

He was sure Carrie hadn't taken them, at least he wanted to believe that; he pictured her reaching into Sarah's curio cabinet to steal the statuettes.

Shaking his head, Don curled his upper lip, he just could not see her taking the figurines. And, yes, he *did* believe the story that Morgan had given them to her. He was positive that the statuettes that had been in Sarah's house and the ones in Carrie's curio were the same.

Right now, Officer Abbott was placing Simpers under arrest. But it was hard for Don to imagine Simpers as a murderer.

He searched his memory for any interaction with the laid-back man. There'd never been any problems with him or his family . . . but what about that time during the winter–off season, when Morgan had been walking near the Welcome Center with his dog?

They'd exchanged some words about whether or not the animal should be on a leash. Morgan called the dog to him and immediately fastened a leash to its collar. He was apologetic.

Don remembered commenting on how much he liked the chocolate lab. Morgan had guffawed, and said something about him preferring the company of his dog to that of his wife.

Just the man's body language and manner suggested to Don that Morgan was a milquetoast and he'd heard enough from the other officers to know that he was not a trouble maker.

Still tapping his fingers on the desk, Don drew his lips into a tight line and shook his head. He knew he'd have to tell Carrie that he'd be holding on to the Hummels for evidence.

Should I call her? Don picked up the telephone, dialed a few numbers then set it back down.

All but one had been locked away in the evidence room. But he'd kept one, *Apple Tree Boy* out. He studied it, rubbing his thumb across the small chip at the base. *This is all I need . . . it's the very same one.* Don quickly recalled the first night he'd seen the piece. Gently he wrapped it and set it in the bottom drawer of his desk.

Rising, he grabbed his cap, settled it firmly on his head and walked out the door.

"I figured you'd be here," Don spoke as he peered through the screen.

His shadowy image nearly covered the entrance.

Joey stood in front of Carrie, barking at the voice beyond the door.

Stooping to scoop him into her arms, Carrie scolded the dog, "Shh, Joe." She stroked him gently, though he continued to growl.

Standing at the doorway, Carrie felt her muscles tense as she recalled Paula's warning about the detective being nice only to get information from her.

Still petting the dog, she faced Don through the screen door. She still wore the khaki pants and yellow shirt uniform of Grocery World. "I just got home a few minutes ago." She looked curiously at him, skeptical of his motives for coming to her home.

"May I come in, Carrie?" Don asked, a slight grin crossing his lips.

Nodding, Carrie stepped aside, "Sure, come on in Detective Belkin."

"Don, you can call me Don, remember?" He smiled broadened as he searched to meet her eyes. He found them for a split second before she turned away.

"Well?" Carrie posed the question as she leaned against her kitchen counter, Joey still in her arms.

Don suddenly felt uncomfortable. A surprise, he thought there had been a connection the last time he had spoken to her. *Why hasn't she asked me to sit down?* he thought.

His eyes rested on the chair near one of the windows.

"Well?" She repeated.

Don nodded as his back stiffened, "There were prints, Sarah Chambers'. The Hummels belonged to Sarah."

Carrie's face paled, and weakness streamed throughout her body. She released the dog, settling her hands across her stomach.

The detective reached an arm around her, "Slt down for a minute." He guided her slowly to the sun porch and helped her to the divan.

"That is so . . ." Carrie closed her eyes and swallowed. "It's just so . . . creepy."

Searching Don's face, she caught her breath, "So Morgan stole them. He stole them for me." Carrie released the breath, "Damn, this is just way too weird."

Watching the woman's shoulders slump, Don, reached a hand to gently push the loose hairs away from Carrie's face."I'm sorry."

She met his eyes, and then pulled away, releasing a nervous chuckle, "I knew those Hummels were too good to be true."

Don heard the words in his head, *Sarah won't need them anymore*.

He pulled his fingers away from Carrie's hair, startled at his thoughts.

"I'll need you to tell me everything you know about Morgan Simpers–how long you've known him–if he's ever been to your house."

Again Don's eyes searched Carrie's face, "If you have ever been intimate with him."

Don could feel Carrie's breath as she scooted away from him. "What?" She released another heavy breath, "Me? *Him*? You've got to be kidding."

"Then why did he give you the Hummels?"As soon as the words left his lips, Don regretted them.

"He's a nice guy! Maybe he wants me to like him. I hear his wife is a bitch–he's nice to other women too–I guess he likes the attention–hell, I don't know."

Don watched as the confused look in Carrie's eyes turned to anger.

"It's just odd that he would bring you–"

"He used to bring shrimp to Paula." Carrie glared. "I guess he's just a needy sort of guy, likes women to be nice to him–and yeah, he is a bit weird. But–"

"There's a saying I often repeat to myself–helps me put things in perspective." Pausing before he continued, Don grinned, "Everybody is weird but me."

Carrie raised an eyebrow, "Really. Everybody is weird but you?" She leaned back a bit. "Do you really believe that?"

"I say that to remind myself that *everyone* is weird, *me* included. We don't know other people as well as we think we do. That doesn't mean they are bad, but it just means that you really don't know what motivates someone to do things."

Relaxing, Carrie chuckled, "Hmm, I think you have something there." She nodded, "But you have to believe me, I didn't have Morgan steal those Hummels for me—and I sure as hell didn't take them."

"I believe you." As Don searched Carrie's eyes, he felt an overwhelming urge to comfort her.

His chest tightened as he lingered on her words—her lips, how they formed them. "Do you think he's the one who killed Sarah?"

Don continued studying her face—he wasn't thinking at all.

"Did you hear what I said?" Carrie's brow furrowed as she touched Detective Belkin's arm. "I said, do you think he killed her?"

"Yes."

"So you think he murdered Sarah, but what about the other men—the one I found?"

"No." Embarrassed that he had lost his concentration, Don endeavored to hide his confusion; he cleared his throat. "Yes, I was listening to you. No I don't think Morgan murdered Sarah or Reggie, or Mick Boles."

"Why?"

"He had no reason to."

"But what about the Hummels?" Carrie cocked her head to the side.

"He didn't steal them for himself, he stole them for you—to please *you*. I don't think he would kill anyone for those trinkets."

Feeling the detective's eyes on her, Carrie lifted her chin teasingly, "So I'm not worth killing for? Is that what you are trying to say?"

Don lowered his eyes, a grin held to his lips, "You're pretty enough . . ." catching himself before he completed the sentence, he shook his head. *What am I doing? I can't believe I said that.* The thoughts echoed in his head as he once again searched Carrie's face.

Biting her bottom lip, Carrie felt her cheeks burning, W*as this really happening? Was this beautiful man coming on to her again?*

Standing abruptly, the detective cleared his throat, "Ma'am . . . Carrie." He smiled, and then slid his eyes to the door.

"I need to be going—just wanted to let you know how things were progressing."

Carrie rose from the divan as well, "Thank you, Detective Belkin, I mean, Don." She smiled back at the man as they both moved toward the doorway.

Don reached to push the screen door open then turned to Carrie abruptly, "How would you feel about grabbing a bite, I'm starved." A tender smile crossed his lips.

Biting her bottom lip, Carrie returned the gaze, "You think you're funny, huh?"

"Well?"

"Okay, give me a minute or two and I'll be right out." She held onto the door handle as the screen door shut. For a moment she watched the man walk down the steps to his car.

"Why am I doing this?" A huge smile burst upon her face. A feeling of lightness filled her as she rushed to her bedroom to change.

******

"Nothing fancy," Don began.

"I'm not in to fancy," Carrie interrupted. "This place is just fine."

Each ordered the special, whole fried flounder, cole slaw, French fries and hush puppies.

Within minutes, before they had even begun a conversation, the waitress had already brought the hush puppies and iced tea.

They smiled at one another and just as Don opened his mouth to speak, a hand fell on his shoulder.

"I see you have finally decided to ask this beautiful woman out." Hank cast a gleeful look towards Carrie and winked.

It felt odd that he should look at her that way, Carrie felt her face redden. She felt bare, as if totally exposed.

Carrie felt uneasy; she glanced at Don, then dropped her eyes to the plate before her, *Are they going to compare notes now?* she thought.

Don caught the look in her eyes, he responded with an apologetic gaze of his own.

As he turned to Hank, he nodded, "She is beautiful, isn't she?" He smiled reassuringly at Carrie.

As if a switch had been turned off, Hank's demeanor became almost sullen, his smile disappeared and his shoulders fell from their regular stance.

Pursing his lips, he patted Don on the shoulder once again. "Well, old man, I better get myself home. Hope you two are getting the flounder, it's great as usual."

Turning suddenly, he walked briskly toward the door.

Carrie didn't have to say the words, obviously Don shared her sentiments.

"That was odd," he shrugged.

"Yeah."

Their meal arrived, and the couple, now both feeling awkward, ate in silence.

Pushing his plate a distance from him, Don placed the crumpled napkin atop it; he drew a deep breath. "This place has the best flounder around."

Carrie pulled a fork full of meat from the boney fish. "I can't argue with that." She brought the fork to her mouth and chewed the soft meat.

Don watched and folded his arms across his chest. "Going out locally can have its distractions."

Carrie tittered, "Really?"

"I think you and I deserve some time to get to know one another—and not over murder, and not here on the island. How about having dinner with me tomorrow . . . we'll go to Wilmington. I know a great restaurant that I think you'll really enjoy."

Carrie nodded, "Maybe . . ."

"Come on, I'm not such a bad guy, even if I am a damn Yankee."

Laughing, Carrie pushed her plate and settled the fork and napkin to its side. "I get off around four thirty."

"I'll pick you up at six. Will that give you enough time?"

Carrie nodded again, "That'll work."

"Hope you're okay with this place?"

Carrie nodded as she pulled her chair a bit closer to the table. "This is fine."

She had wanted to respond, *twice in one week? Wow!* it had been so long since she had enjoyed a meal from a restaurant other than fast food places.

The waiter greeted the couple and they both perused the menus for several minutes.

"Order anything you like, price is no object," Don joked.

"Really?" Carrie sniggered, "I guess . . . let me see. What costs the most?"

"Like I said, price is no object, I'm just going to sell a couple of those Hummels and—"

Carrie's stare stopped Don immediately.

"Never did know when to keep my trap shut," he sighed heavily. "Sorry, just joking."

"I'm sure, but it's a rotten joke."

Nodding in agreement, Don continued, "Really—have anything you like. The pot roast is great and so is the veal." He continued studying the menu, "The fish is good here too, salmon, flounder, mahi mahi, blowfish."

"Had flounder last night, hmm . . . " Carrie scanned both sides of the menu. "Ah, there it is, blowfish. That looks good."

"You know, that's how they died. The lab found blowfish in their systems."

"Really, blowfish? I didn't know the ones around here were poisonous."

"They're not. The lab says the ones they found were the kind from the Far East and are referred to as fugu."

Carrie rested her menu on the table and tilted her head a bit to the side, "So, what does that mean? Did somebody have it shipped here?"

Shaking his head no, Don explained how in the past few years the deadly fish had been sighted several times by local divers.

"What's the difference between the fish? How do you tell them apart?"

"The meat is the same color—almost white." Don studied Carrie's finger tips as they wound around the water glass before her. Her long fingers were smooth and tanned; her nails trimmed short and unpainted.

As the waiter approached, he placed a basket of warm corn muffins in the center of the table, "Are you ready to order?" he asked politely.

Handing the menus to the young waiter, Don replied, "I'll have the cabbage rolls."

He looked questioningly at Carrie, "And you? What have you selected *ma'am?*"

She smiled back at him, crinkling her nose.

Don followed her movements as she lifted her head to speak to the waiter.

What was this tingle he was feeling? Don asked himself as he lingered on Carrie's profile. He hadn't been this excited about being with a woman in years.

Yes, he'd had his share of dates and affairs, but this girl, this woman with the freckles brought out a youthful playfulness he wasn't even sure he was comfortable with.

Carrie leaned her head to the side; a puzzled look quickly passed as she spoke her selection, "The blowfish please, with the broccoli and potatoes."

The waiter thanked them both and refilled their glasses with water.

"What was that?" Carrie cocked an eyebrow and teased, *"Ma'am*—you're not still going to be calling me ma'am, are you?"

Don shook his head, paused and studied Carrie as he fumbled with his napkin. "It's habIt."

"That's alright, I kind of like it."

"You didn't have to get the fish, you know."

"I know, but I wanted to try it."

Silence held for a few moments before Don spoke, "I'm glad you came out with me tonight. And I hope you enjoy the food, they have a little different selection here than most of the restaurants."

"You bring all your dates here?" Carrie asked teasingly as she relaxed against the back of her chair.

"Sometimes," Don raised an eyebrow and leaned forward, "not really, most of the women— and believe me, there have not been many since my divorce, wouldn't appreciate a place like this. They'd expect something more *chic*, more expensive."

"I like it." She paused and held his gaze, I'm glad we came here."

"It's a mom and pop place that serves regular food. Nothing fancy, but it's all good."

As he pushed his chair from the table, Don's expression turned solemn, "Look, I like you. But I thought you were having a thing with Hank Butler or I would have tried to get to know you earlier—I'm not just seeing you because of the case."

Fidgeting with the napkin in her lap, Carrie raised her eyes to meet Don's. "Hank was a just a passing phase." She looked down at the place setting before her. "Nothing to worry about there, just another of the many mistakes in my life."

Carrie felt awkward, as if her private life was strewn everywhere. What did Don know? Had Hank told him about their night together?

She felt the color leave her face.

"It's a small town, Carrie. Everyone knows who goes out with whom, who is involved with whom and when they aren't together any longer . . . it's no big deal."

Nodding her head, Carrie recalled Paula mentioning that *she* had gone out with Don one time.

"You're right, it is a small town. I guess I should have known better."

"I've been here for several years now and sometimes it feels like everyone is either your brother or sister—you get to know everyone so well—sometimes *too* well, especially in my line of work."

Raising the glass of water, Don swallowed a few sips. "Sometimes I know too much."

"I can imagine," Carrie nodded. "I guess there are pros and cons to living in a small town."

"And a tourist town," Don chuckled. "I've seen some of those looks you've given a few of your customers."

"Yankees."

"I'm a Yankee," Don's eyes twinkled as the corners of his lips curled.

"Oh, you know what I mean." Carrie struggled to justify her remark. "You aren't *all* bad," She teased. "I mean, it's more of a city thing than a Yankee thing . . . and it's more New York, New Jersey, and . . ."

"Be careful now, I think you're digging yourself into a hole–trying to explain when I know perfectly well about how the locals feel."

She felt her defenses sharpen and she tightened her fingers around the napkin in her lap. "Look, I've had money thrown at me, credit cards thrown, and the attitudes–that condescending attitude–that because I'm from the south I have to be stupid and backward."

"Don't get so upset, Carrie. I know what you mean. I get the same thing, but I get it because I'm a cop. When someone finds out I'm a cop, their whole demeanor changes."

Drawing a deep breath, Carrie calmed herself, "Sorry, I guess . . ."

"Nobody has a monopoly on stupid or arrogant, you'll find it in all classes of people from all over the world."

"You're right," Carrie bit the side of her bottom lip. "It just seems that the summer months are so hectic and it's easier to blame other people than practice my own patience."

"We all do it. I find myself checking license plates and even though I'm from the north, I seem to pull over more folks from up there than from here. I figure they drive crazy because they're on vacation and feel like they don't have to abide by the rules." He paused for a moment, watching a couple next to them place their young child in a booster seat.

"And I try to get out every morning before I go on duty and walk the beach for an hour or so—really calms me."

"During the summer months I just sort of get in a rut, you know, get up—go to work, come home, eat, go to bed—and then the whole thing starts all over the next day."

"You have to make up your mind to not let negative people get to you. Focus on the good. There's lots of it out there—that's what that walk on the beach every morning does for me—makes me appreciate all the good."

What was there about this man that relaxed her? Carrie studied Don's face as he continued.

"That's what I brought my son out here for."

"I saw you two the other day when you and he came in the grocery store."

Don nodded, "He's a good kid . . . or wants to be." He shrugged. Continuing, he began sharing the history of his relationship with his son and ex-wife.

266

For some reason the words spilled from his mouth; he found it easy to share his thoughts with Carrie.

"Sometimes it gets to be too much and I don't take my own advice, but for the most part and with any stressful job, you have to find a way to tap into some sort of peace." He looked earnestly into Carrie's eyes. "Or you just won't make it."

"I know, I let my job get to me." She laughed, "I let my marriage get to me—or rather my ex-husband."

Don listened as the woman shared her life too—the story of her marriage and two children and how proud she was of them.

"And I did something about my stress—I moved here," she laughed again, "—except for those few months of *terror*, I am in such a good place." She patted the spot over her heart.

Their conversation paused for a moment as the waiter brought their meals. Immediately after, they continued talking, enjoying their food as the evening progressed.

"This place kind of grows on you." Don dabbed the corner of his mouth with the napkin.

"And the food smells . . . so good." Carrie slid a glance toward Don's plate.

"I know exactly what you are thinking, Miss Adams." Don lifted an eyebrow.

"Really," Carrie's eyelashes fluttered as a coy grin settled on her lips.

"The blowfish, I bet it's good. And it doesn't smell half as bad as my cabbage rolls."

"I love fish, any kind and I eat it as often as I can." Lifting her fork to spear a broccoli floret,

Carrie teased, "I've never been a fan of cabbage unless it's made into cole slaw."

"Yes, I should have gotten the fish, maybe the mahi mahi."

Nodding, Carrie agreed, "I like it too, it's a mild fish."

"A few weeks ago, our friend Hank gave me some, must have been around seven or eight filets in the bag."

Stopping to place a forkful of cabbage roll in his mouth, Don chewed and then continued, "He said he had so much he didn't have any more room in his freezer. So I appreciated it . . . mahi is my favorite fish."

The couple ate in silence for a few minutes, catching each other's gaze once or twice.

As Carrie ate, she thought of Don's last comment. She wasn't sure how to take it. Why had he brought Hank up again? Was he prying?

The thought angered her, but as she pondered the words her thoughts drifted and she found herself thinking how odd it was that only a few weeks ago she had eaten dinner at Hank's home. She would never forget that night; she felt the color rise in her checks and tried to brush the thoughts away.

Hadn't she put a bag of fish in the freezer for Hank that night? She paused for a moment, endeavoring to focus on that evening and the meal she and Hank had prepared together. Hadn't the freezer been empty?

"You look so deep in thought," Don chided. "Is everything okay?"

Brushing the thoughts of her "date" with Hank from her mind, Carrie grinned, "Oh, it's great."

Again they ate in silence, Carrie's thoughts wandering back to the meal she and Hank had made—something just didn't feel right. *Why would Hank lie about how much fish he had?*

Her brow furrowed a bit as she pierced a piece of the blowfish and brought it to her mouth.

Don studied her expression for a few moments. "I know there is something on your mind," he began.

Carrie lifted her chin and brought the napkin to her lips, "No."

As he squared his shoulders, Don set his napkin next to the plate. He paused again, "I know, I mentioned Hank. That must be a sore spot for you. I wish I would have known you well enough to warn you about him."

"Warn me?"

A soft grin swept his mouth; Don relaxed his shoulders, "He's not . . ."

"I know," Carrie interrupted. "He's footloose and fancy free," she added sarcastically.

"Sorry."

"Everybody warned me, Don. I'm a big girl, all grown and able to make my own mistakes." Carrie closed her eyes briefly and shook her head.

"We all make mistakes."

"I know," Pausing for a moment, Carrie brought a finger to her lips, her eyes shifted downward, "But that . . . as embarrassing as it might be, is not what I've been thinking about."

"Oh . . . well, if I may ask."

"You said something earlier about the fish—the mahi and how Hank gave you some a few weeks ago. Well, I don't know why it bothers me, but that was about the time I was seeing him and we had mahi for dinner."

"I don't understand." Don leaned back a bit in his chair.

"Well, Hank told me that he didn't like keeping fish in the freezer—his was totally empty except for the ice maker and a bottle of vodka."

Don folded his arms across his chest and listened.

"And he told *you* he had a freezer full of fish. I know there was nothing in his freezer and he also said he hated frozen fish."

"I've been out on his boat with him—he's the nicest guy you'll ever meet." Don caught himself, "Except with women—he is a womanizer."

"He didn't make me do anything I didn't want to do, Don. And I think he's a nice guy too, but there is something about this that is odd."

"Look, I don't want this to sound the way it's going to . . . but . . . sometimes when women are *dumped*, they get a little angry."

Settling her fork next to her plate, Carrie pursed her lips. "So that's it. I'm mad because the man didn't want a long term relationship with me and so I make up a *fish story* about him? Is that it?"

Don placed his hands In his lap, rubbed his thighs and felt the tension building in his neck. "All I know is since I've been on the island I've never had any trouble out of him, nor has anyone else. And I find it hard to believe—" A flash from a conversation he'd had with Hank, burst upon him. Pausing, Don gathered his thoughts. "But then again—maybe you're right."

"And . . ."

"I really don't know him that well, I guess. But I don't think anyone knows Hank *really* well."

"You know about his wife?" Carrie asked.

"That's what I was thinking. I know she died several years ago and that she had problems."

"Wasn't she pregnant?"

Nodding, Don searched his memory. *Hadn't Hank's wife Emma been an addict? Hadn't he heard that she had become addicted to cocaine?*

"She was pretty, a local girl. No one would have ever thought . . ." Don scowled as he recalled the conversation between he and Hank several months back-right before he went to California to pick up Phil. *I mentioned Maggie to him, how sorry a mother she was, what a coke head she was. How she needed to be thrown in jail. What was it that Hank had said?*

"Thought what?" Carrie paused, studying the expression on his face. "Finish your sentence—you said no one would have ever thought—what did you mean?"

"She, Emma Butler, was married to Hank for only a couple of years. I'd heard she was a down to earth, real sweet kind of gal. And then she slipped one day when they were out on their boat and cracked a few vertebrae in her back."

"That boat sounds like it was bad luck."

Don shrugged. "Anyway, the story goes that she got on pain pills then. And later after her death, the autopsy showed cocaine in her system."

"And she was pregnant. That couldn't have been good for the baby." Carrie sighed. "Hmm, was there any speculation that Hank pushed her? Were thy having marital trouble?"

"I wasn't living here at the time, but from what I saw in the report, no—there was no evidence of that, in fact, it was the opposite. He was so in love with her; for Hank, who never had any problem finding women, Emma was elusive—really made him work for it. He bought her all kinds of jewelry and a car—anything she wanted.

"When she got hurt, he waited on her hand and foot. And afterward, after the boat accident when she died, he blamed himself. Somebody told me he spent a few weeks in a psych unit trying to come to grips with it all—attempted suicide. But he was never charged with anything. Everyone knew how much they loved one another and he treated her like a princess."

"It's a sad story."

"Yes, it is." The words Hank had spoken the day they had been talking about Maggie suddenly came to Don's mind. *'She'll never stop. She'll be better off dead.'* Those were his words; emphatically he had added, *'I know how you could make it happen and no one would ever know.'*

Folding the napkin, Carrie placed it next to her empty plate. "The meal was fabulous, Detective Belkin. And I apologize if I was a bit obnoxious earlier—you know, talking about Hank and that *thing* we had. Maybe the fish and Hank are just silly. Maybe I'm just being silly about the whole thing."

As Don lifted his head he caught Carrie's look of diffidence. "No, don't be sorry." Don chuckled, "Everybody's a suspect and it just goes to prove that you have an inquisitive mind."

Shrugging, Carrie relaxed and reached for the glass of water. "It just seems odd."

"Yes, it does." As he pierced the last bit of cabbage roll with his fork, the detective considered the drugs, and the possibility that Hank could be a suspect.

"I wonder if that fish you put in his freezer is still there."

"What?" The word slid slowly and softly from Carrie's lips.

Chapter Twenty-One

Carrie slid her feet into a pair of brown Crocs and stood to examine herself in the floor length mirror hung on the back of her bedroom door. She ran a brush once again through her shoulder length hair and smiled.

That was nice, last night, she thought, looking at her reflection. "Hope he calls me up or comes by, I'd really like to see him again."

Leaning down to pat the two dogs wiggling at her feet, Carrie grabbed a pack of cigarettes and headed out the door. "See you later, puppies, DO NOT get in the trash can and DO NOT pee on my floor." She glared at them sternly.

It had been ages since the dogs had done either but she warned them anyway. Snickering, she closed the door behind her.

The walk to Grocery World was pleasant, she felt cheerful, assured that no one was going to spoil her day at work.

There was barely a cloud in the sky, yet there was a nice breeze that kept the heat from pounding on her face and body.

Her walk today seem perfect as she relaxed into a comfortable feeling, one that left her satisfied as she recalled the previous evening.

No, Carrie wasn't thinking she had met *the one*, or worrying whether or not she had said or done the right things, she simply felt good; it felt right—her evening with Don had opened a door and she liked it.

As she approached the Grocery World shopping center, Carrie noticed Paula pulling into the parking lot. The stern expression on her friend's face puzzled her.

Rolling down the window of her red Camaro, Paula motioned for Carrie to meet her at the picnic table.

"Did you hear? They arrested Morgan Simpers for the murder of Sarah and those two men." Paula scowled and sat abruptly on the picnic table bench. "I bet it has something to do with those little glass knickknacks he gave you."

Nodding, Carrie pulled a cigarette from the pack and rolled it between her fingers. "Yes, I heard . . . and the Hummels . . . the whole thing is creepy."

"You never know about people." Checking her watch, Paula crossed her arms, "Poor ol' Morgan, can't win for losing."

"I feel badly that he stole the Hummels for me, but I don't think he would ever hurt anyone."

"And you know that it was poison that killed them?" Paula questioned. "It was the fish, right?

"How did you know it was poison?"

"Mindy, remember–her boyfriend is Robby and he never could keep his mouth shut."

"Have you ever seen any of them–those blowfish–around here?" Carrie asked. "I've heard there have been a few sightings of them."

"Never in an inshore catch, or for that matter, I've never seen any at all. When I go commercial fishing, I always use traps, and nope . . . never seen any at all."

"Hmm," Carrie brought a finger to her mouth and bit the nail.

"But a friend of mine," Paula folded a stick of gum into her mouth, "caught a couple–showed them to me. He says they just started showing up here recently–they're really rare."

"You can't eat them, right?"

"People in Japan do. They have to cut the meat in a certain way. Certain organs and the skin are poison, from what I hear."

"Wonder how they got into our waters?" Carrie asked.

Shrugging, Paula added, "These little blows around here are smaller, really tasty and you don't have to mess with any bones."

"I know," Carrie threw her butt into the sand bucket.

"You do?"

"Yes, I've eaten blowfish, it's really tasty."

"Well then, the Oriental blowfish is just like it, except larger."

An image of her meal the previous night came to mind; a chill followed. *Why didn't I notice it last night*, she thought. *That's the same kind of fish I put in Hank's freezer.*

Turning her back, Carrie walked a few paces away from Paula and pulled the cell phone from her pocket, *I have to tell Don,* she thought as she dialed the number to the police station.

"Detective Belkin, please," she whispered into the phone.

"Okay, thank you . . . no thanks."

"Why are you calling Belkin?" Paula asked.

Annoyed by her friend's question, Carrie scowled and turned her back.

"Hey, don't get all bent out of shape. I know you and him have a *thing*."

"What?" Carrie pulled another lung full of nicotine through her lips.

"I heard you were at the Galley the other night having dinner and guess who walks in and up to your table?'

"Yeah, that was *really* uncomfortable," Carrie shook her head, "but how—?"

"Mindy's cousin is a waitress there and—"

"It's a small town."

"Yep." Tittering, Paula seated herself on the picnic bench. "Can't sneeze around here without someone saying bless you."

Carrie inhaled from her cigarette again, and nodded as Paula spoke.

"You know, he doesn't smoke." Paula cocked her head to the side and tapped her fingers on the table.

"I know," Carrie held the cigarette between her fingers. "I should quit, but I'd weigh five hundred pounds within a year."

"Get one of those things like Mindy has—one of those e-cigs."

"You know, you're not supposed to quit for someone else, you're supposed to quit for yourself." A snide glare lifted from Carrie's eyes.

"Hey-whatever works. Use whatever you can to motivate you."

Chapter Twenty-Two

The last time she'd called, Carrie left a message for Don to call her. But that had been two hours ago.

She stood, her eyes drawn to the huge sliding glass doors as she scanned and welcomed customers. Rude comments and arrogant attitudes seemed trivial and she ignored them as images and questions filled her thoughts.

Reflecting on the men—Morgan and Hank—Carrie wondered what made her think she knew them well enough to judge them. She'd been living at Topsail for less than two years, that wasn't really enough time to get to know anyone.

"Lady, are you going to check my groceries or are you going to daydream all day?" The man appeared to be in his mid-forties; he scowled deeply and muttered a few words.

"Well, I don't know. What do you suggest I do, Sweetie?" Carrie smiled and looked sternly into the man's eyes; she batted her lashes.

The man chuckled.

Pulling one item at a time across the scanner, Carrie relaxed, "Yes sir, it is such a lovely day today. I hope you and your family enjoy your stay here." Again she looked directly into the man's face and smiled.

"You too," The man returned the gesture.

As she watched him exit the doors, Carrie beamed, *That was easy–it **is** all about my attitude– how I let others affect me.*

She looked over to where Paula stood, still checking a customer, and gave a thumbs up sign. *She's right; just don't let them get to you.*

From her peripheral vision, Carrie saw Don enter through the glass doors; he walked toward her and glanced at his watch.

"You get off soon don't you?"

"One hour."

"I want to talk more with you about what you mentioned last night-the freezer, the fish."

"Okay. I'll be home. Just come by."

Nodding, Don stood before her, his hands resting on the counter, all seriousness having left his face, "You look nice today." The words slid earnestly from his lips, their corners slowly curled. "How about I fix you dinner at my place?"

Carrie contemplated the question as she recalled the last time she'd been asked to have dinner at a man's house.

"My boy, Phil is going to be there. Relax–no hanky panky, just a nice dinner."

Blushing, Carrie nodded, "Okay,"

"All right then, I'll pick you up in a couple of hours."

Carrie watched as he turned and exited the sliding glass doorway.

Checking the time once again, Don pulled his Dodge Charger onto the gravel parking lot of Thomas Seafood.

As he walked through the open doorway, the strong aroma of fish slapped him in the face.

He walked up to the man behind the counter and nodded, "Hi, how's it going today?"

"Not bad." The older man grinned. "What can I help you with today, Don?"

"I'm not sure." Browsing the large containers of assorted fish and shellfish, Don nodded toward the grouper. "Give me three nice filets."

"Just got them in this morning." The man wrapped the fish in plastic bags and walked toward the cash register.

"I got a couple of questions for you, if you don't mind." Don pulled his wallet from his back pocket and laid the cash on the counter.

"Shoot." The man leaned against the counter and grinned.

"Have you seen any of that oriental blowfish around?"

"It's poisonous—fugu, that's what it's called. I've seen a couple, but that was a while back—just started showing up this past year but the guys out on the boats kill it if they get any and throw it back."

"Can you tell me what it looks like?"

"Just like the local stuff, same color, similar markings-just bigger-and when it's skinned, you can't tell the difference—except like I said, it's larger."

"Thanks," Don called as he turned to leave.

"See you around."

As Don drove home, his thoughts bounced from Hank and the fugu to Carrie, preparing dinner for her, and having her meet his son.

He'd ask her about the fish in the freezer at Hank's—have her describe it. And maybe they'd talk a little bit about the case. But mostly he wanted to get to know her better.

As he imagined the woman relaxing in his home while he cooked, his eyes lit up. He nodded, *sure would be nice*.

Right now he wasn't even sure if or how Hank was involved, but he was curious, the fish thing—the freezer—it bothered him. *Maybe I'll just cruise on over to his house and have a chat.*

He looked down at the fish resting in the passenger floor board of the Charger. "Better drop this off first."

The small cottage was in sight, and he slowed the vehicle a bit, thinking—feeling optimistic. Right now he didn't give a damn who killed Sarah and Reggie. He shrugged, "They're dead—gone, I'm out of the loop—I'm free. I can live my life now—I hope."

He looked in the rearview mirror as he parked and stared into his own eyes, *If it wasn't for that last body, Mick Boles, I wouldn't give a damn about any of it.*

From the car he could see his son Phil inside, slouched on the couch playing video games.

At least he's not out getting high, Don thought as he leaned out of the car window. "Hey," he called, "How about putting this in the fridge for me?" Don held the bag of fish from the window.

"What's this?" Phil asked as he approached the car.

"I'm fixing grouper tonight, bringing a guest over for you to meet." He smiled shyly at his son.

"Yeah?" Phil grinned broadly. "You got a lady friend, Pop?"

"Just someone I know. Thought you might entertain her while I fix us a great seafood dinner."

Phil grasped the bag, "Where are you going?"

"Just want to talk with someone before I pick up our guest." He looked up at the boy, "Would you mind opening up a can of baked beans and," Don raised an eyebrow, "Do you know how to make a salad?"

"No problem, I got it—you just go do your stuff and I'll take care of things."

"Thanks." Don slid the gear shift into reverse and called, "I'll be back in about forty-five minutes, okay?"

The boy waved and walked back into the cottage.

As he headed toward Hank's house on Ocean Front Drive, Don considered the traffic and how it had increased in the last couple of weeks. Now there was a steady stream of cars. He waited impatiently for several to pass. Finally a space opened up and he pressed his foot sharply on the accelerator and slid into second gear. He thought about

Carrie, *She's only been home a few minutes. I won't be at Hank's that long—-just a few questions to clear things up, then I'll swing by and pick her up. I hope Phil likes her.*

Hank's Red Volvo XC90 was parked in the driveway; Don pulled next to it and turned the ignition off. He paused for a moment before exiting the Dodge.

I'll see if I can get a look in the freezer. His hands still gripping the steering wheel, he breathed a sigh, "Don't really like doing this, he's a nice guy."

"Hello Don," Hank called from the patio. He held a glass of wine in his hand as he walked to the side door where Don stood waiting.

"Just by for a friendly visit? Or do you have something on your mind? Maybe about that lovely cashier—Carrie?"

"All of the above." Suddenly the pit of Don's stomach rolled, he felt uneasy as he walked into the living area of his friend's house.

An ominous aura fell upon him as his eyes scanned the living room. "Just had a few questions about Sarah Chambers. Seems nobody liked her." A weak chuckle escaped his lips.

"Have a seat, Don." Motioning toward a chair, Hank held out his wine glass. "Care for some?"

"Not now," he shook his head. "I won't be here long, just wanted to clear up something."

"It's the fish, isn't it?"

Don's head rose immediately to face Hank. "What?"

"I saw your car parked at Thomas Seafood earlier. If you were there . . . I'm guessing that you were asking about blowfish and fugu."

Stiffening his back into the chair, Don focused his eyes firmly on Hank and listened as the man continued.

"So I knew that Carrie and you must have been talking." Leaning against a chair Hank swirled the wine in the goblet. "And the other night I saw you two, as a couple . . . yes . . . *a couple*. I saw the way you looked at her and the way she blushed." Hank took a sip from the wine glass; a knowing smirk settled on his face. "I knew sooner or later you two would get all mushy and lovey and spill your guts to one another." He sneered and rolled his eyes. "Sooner or later the subject of the fish in my freezer was bound to come up."

Hank's demeanor changed swiftly, his eyes darkened and his body tensed. Releasing a heavy moan, Hank growled loudly, "Damn, I should have put that damn fish in the freezer myself!" He spat the words angrily and slammed the wine glass to the end table, spilling the contents onto the floor.

"It was so easy-getting rid of Sarah." Hank laughed aloud. "And you're right, nobody liked her —especially me. And *Reginald*—Reggie. I didn't like him either. You should be glad they are gone—now you have a way out."

Stunned, Don began, "You knew ?"

"I was there that first night, I saw Milton—I saw what he and Reggie forced you into. I knew you didn't want to."

"Why didn't you tell me?"

"Curiosity mostly, just wanted to see if you'd go along with it and for how long."

"Hey, I thought we were friends. We've been fishing and . . ."

"Just wanted to get to know the enemy, you know—keep your friends close, but your enemies closer."

"And if I would have come to the meeting with Sarah and Reggie, I would have been murdered too."

"Yes," Hank nodded emphatically. "Yes, you would have died too. You have been helping distribute drugs all over this island. And you have an ex-wife who is a junkie and son that is dabbling."

"Were you going to kill me next? Maybe invite *me* to dinner?" Don barked the words sarcastically.

"No, I'm tired of death and this is your way out. I'm giving you your way out. You don't have to be involved anymore. Just let me go."

"I don't know if I can do that, Hank."

"This is your chance to get your son on the right path and never turn back; excuse me a moment—"I need to clean this up." Hank pulled a cloth from a kitchen drawer, threw it on the wine spill and returned to lean against the chair. "I'll even give you the girl."

His face muscles drawing tight, Don cast a puzzled look toward Hank. "What do you mean?"

As if he had not heard the question, Hank rose from the chair and walked toward the kitchen counter, "I was so excited about finally being with her . . . I thought that maybe . . . maybe she would be the one." He glanced sharply at Don.

"She's an *earthy* girl, like Emma was. You know, barely any make-up . . . she never needed it." Sorrow filled Hank's face as his eyes filled with tears. Blinking them away, he resumed talking, "She has the look, Carrie does, like my Emma . . . and that sweet, trusting way about her . . . she wears her heart on her sleeve." He moved closer to the detective.

"Go on." Don crossed his legs and let his hand fall to his side, closer to the holstered pistol he wore.

Hank grinned, "No need, Don." He smiled broadly this time, "Let me show you something," He leaned his head to the side and called to another room, "Okay, you can come out now."

Carrie walked slowly into the living room; her legs nearly dragged the floor. Hank reached out to keep her from stumbling.

She looked at him, a string of spittle drooled from her lips and she moaned.

Instinctively, Don gulped as he gently unsnapped the strap to his holster and wrapped his fingers around the gun.

"Now, I told you there was no need for that Detective Belkin."

Gently guiding Carrie toward the chair, Hank turned to Don again, "You can see how she is . . . she has drugs in her body. So you have a choice, shoot me and she dies, because I'm the only one who has the antidote." He chuckled, "Or listen to me . . . let me go . . . and save her."

The look he held, his entire face appeared evil, his breaths came fast and heavy, "Don't try to be a hero."

As if a switch had been turned off, Hank's demeanor changed; he was calm, almost pleasant. "Have a seat, Darling." He leaned close to Carrie and pressed a long thin filleting knife against her neck.

"Now, I told you there was no need for a weapon, Don. Shooting me will not solve things and besides, I know you like me and I know you're glad Sarah and Reggie are dead."

He leaned in, "I did you a favor."

"You should have come to me. We could have gone to the Chief, they'd be behind bars, not dead."

"Drug dealers don't change."

"What about the English guy? Why'd you kill him?"

"That jerk was no more English than my cat is. And for your information he was providing your son with pot, amphetamines, and from what I have learned, spice."

Don clenched his teeth, his eyes narrowed.

"See? I did you a favor. That crap will mess you up—next, Mick was going to introduce him to a little coke. Now, how about that? Would you have liked that?"

"It doesn't matter now."

"But it does, you mentioned one time when we were out fishing that you did not believe in capital punishment." Lifting his brows, Hank winked.

"So what's next?" Don spoke sternly, "You don't want to kill this girl." His jaws tightened as he glanced at Carrie sitting slumped next to Hank.

She was lethargic, unaware of where she was and with whom. He called to her again, "Carrie? Talk to me." He said the words tenderly, then looked to Hank.

"What have you done? What have you given her?"

"Oh, just a little something to keep her from causing any trouble."

"Bastard."

"No, I had a momma and a daddy who were married, I'm not a bastard," Hank chuckled.

Don leaned forward, "Honey, tell me—"

"She's not going to tell you anything Detective Belkin—and if you don't get her to the hospital she's not going to say anything ever again," Hank casually stroked Carrie's hair. "So, what will it be Detective?"

"The same stuff?" Glaring, Don struggled to keep calm. "The poison from the fish?"

"Tetrodotoxin, it's deadly, no antidote. But that's not what I shared with little miss Carrie. I didn't give her anything quite so lethal." Hank stroked Carrie's hair again, pushing a loose strand from her face.

"I really don't want her to die. She a nice girl, uh woman—I guess. She is starting to get a few crow's feet."

Hank ran a finger along her cheek bone, "But I wouldn't kick her out of bed." He chuckled, "I didn't kick her out of bed-and I might have gone on seeing her, but I could tell—so much like other women that I've met—that she wanted *love*—to fall in love. I don't think I will ever love anyone again."

Sliding the filet knife along the contours of Carrie's neck, Hank turned the blade sharply and nicked her skin. Immediately a bright red line of blood trickled the length to her collar bone.

"I'll have your gun, Don." He raised his chin; the penetrating gaze of his eyes bore into the detective's.

Slowly Don pulled the gun from the holster and laid it on the end table.

"On the floor, please and then kick it toward the kitchen." He watched as Belkin obeyed.

"Then walk into the bathroom, first door on your left," Hank nodded, "leave your phone on the table, please."

Again, Don obeyed, setting his cell phone on the end table by the chair. "Anything else?" he asked sarcastically.

Pointing toward the hallway, Hank answered, "Just walk to the bathroom, okay?"

Hank helped Carrie to her feet; she leaned against him for support. As they followed Don down the hallway, Hank kicked the gun farther into the kitchen.

"Notice the wooden rests, I built them last week." Nodding at the two by four resting against the wall as they approached the restroom, Hank chuckled. "And don't try to grab *that* either. It won't take a second to push this into her carotid artery."

Once inside the room, Don turned to face Hank, instantly he found Carrie being thrust into his arms. The bathroom door was pulled shut before he could think.

Don's mind raced as he heard the thud of the two by four falling into the rests and the subsequent slamming of the entrance door.

Chapter Twenty-Three

Resting against his shoulder, Carrie lifted her eyes to study the man's profile.

She recognized it and closed her eyes again. Was he responsible for the condition she was in? Everything was a blur.

"Take another sip," Don ordered, gently pushing a coffee mug to her mouth.

It was hot against her lips and tongue; she sipped sparingly.

"You've been out for hours," the detective pushed Carrie's hair from her brow. "I need you to clear your head and tell me what happened."

A puzzled Carrie searched the man's face. She wondered what he was referring to and then Hank's face flashed before her eyes.

"Ooh." She rubbed her forehead, "I'm not sure." Pulling the mug to her lips again, Carrie took a longer sip of coffee.

"I don't know . . . "Her voice trailed off to muttering sounds.

"Come on now," Don pressed the mug against her lips again.

"He . . . he . . . Hank . . . was in the parking lot when I got off work." Carrie grasped the mug with both hands and sucked the coffee through her lips.

"What did he say to you?"

"He said he saw my dog laying in the road . . . Bella, my little Yorkie . . . " Carrie winced and lowered the cup. "Do you know . . .?"

"I don't think—it was probably a ruse to get you inside his car."

Carrie shook her head, "Poor little Bella."

"We'll check that out later, now tell me what else Hank said to you."

"He said she'd been hit by a car . . . that he'd stopped and pulled her to the side of the road . . . Then he opened the door for me . . . held it open for me and said he'd give me a ride to my house."

"Then?" Don asked.

"I got in his car, I was so worried . . . I was crying . . . then that was it."

"You don't remember anything else?"

"No," Confused, Carrie shook her head. "Things . . . vaguely . . . dreamlike . . . I remember Hank leaning over me saying he was sorry and then you too. I think you were sitting in a chair talking to me."

Carrie touched her hand to her neck, feeling the gauze bandage. "This, what's this?" She squinted and recoiled from the pain.

"Hank had a knife to your neck."

"Oh."

"He threatened to kill you."

She rubbed her brow and moaned, "Why? Why would he do that?" Slowly taking another sip, Carrie continued rubbing her forehead. "What in the world did he give me? I feel I've been hit by a train."

"Hank gave you some heavy duty pain meds—I thought he'd given you the fish poison but when we were in the bathroom I found a note he had taped to the mirror saying he'd only give you a few tizanidine."

"He's nuts . . . " Carrie closed her eyes and groaned. "What were we doing in the bathroom?"

"That's were he threw us when he got my gun. We were in there for a few hours, I bandaged your neck and then Phil came and found us."

"Phil? Your son?"

Don nodded, "Yeah, remember we were all going to have dinner tonight."

"Umm," Carrie sighed, "I was going to meet him."

"After a couple of hours went by and we didn't show up, Phil decided to go looking for me—saw my car at Hank's and pounded on the door."

Suddenly Carrie pulled herself erect; her eyes flew open, "Where is he now?"

"Right here." Sitting slumped against the back of an overstuffed chair, Phil waved to Carrie. His fingers clicking swiftly on the pads of the video controller.

She smiled over to him, "Nice to meet you. I've seen you a few times in the grocery store but we've never spoken."

"That's okay." The boy nodded.

Carrie turned to Don, "Where's Hank?"

Chuckling softly, Don answered, "Who knows."

Carrie was puzzled.

"He had almost three hours to get away. Abbott and Rosell checked his dock on the mainland—the Robalo was gone—he's gone. We've got a B O L O out. They've been searching for him all along the coast."

Carrie nodded, "He might come back, you know."

Her eyes begged for comfort, her voice said fear; Don pulled Carrie close to him and kissed her forehead.

"We'll find him." He spoke the words softly as he stroked the woman's hair. *I hope not, I hope he gets away and is never found. Now I'm free.*

Made in the USA
Columbia, SC
12 August 2017